READ
ME
LIKE A
BOOK

READ

ME

LIKE

A

BOOK

LIZ
KESSLER

CANDLEWICK PRESS

Copyright © 2015 by Liz Kessler

Excerpt from "This Be The Verse" from *The Complete Poems of Philip Larkin* by Philip Larkin, edited by Archie Burnett. Copyright © 2012 by The Estate of Philip Larkin. Reprinted by permission of Farrar, Straus and Giroux, LLC.

Published by an arrangement with Orion Children's Books

First U.S. edition 2016

Library of Congress Catalog Card Number 2015937226
ISBN 978-0-7636-8131-9

16 17 18 19 20 21 BVG 10 9 8 7 6 5 4 3 2 1

Printed in Berryville, VA, U.S.A.

This book was typeset in Dante

Candlewick Press
99 Dover Street
Somerville, Massachusetts 02144

visit us at www.candlewick.com

*For Jenny — because who else would it
ever have been dedicated to?*

*And for Laura — because who else would I
ever have wanted to share this moment with?*

PART
1

1

Where's your best friend when you need her?

I mean, seriously.

It's Saturday night, and here I am in Luke's front room with his sister, Zoe, and a bunch of his mates, listening to a rock band blaring about how we're all going to die and watching a couple of lads do something that I think is meant to be dancing but looks more like they're being slowly electrocuted.

Oh, and did I mention? It's my birthday. Mum said I could have a few friends over if I wanted to, but it turned out Luke's parents were going away for the weekend, so he offered to throw me a party at his house.

I keep glancing at a couple in the corner who seem to be the only ones having a good time. Their arms and legs are wrapped around each other as tight as rope. They haven't come up for air once since I've been here. Not that I'm jealous. Not that I'm wondering how nice it might be to have someone desperate for that much of *my* attention.

My phone beeps in my pocket, and I pull it out. It's a Snapchat notification. I open the link. It's a selfie of Cat and her mum, both holding up bottles of San Miguel and grinning at the camera. The text across the photo reads, *Happy birthday, mate—wish I was with you!*

Two seconds later, my phone beeps again. Another Snapchat. This one's a picture of a tall, dark, handsome, presumably Spanish waiter carrying a tray of drinks. The text across the picture reads, *On second thought, quite glad we're here!*

I can't help smiling. Cat always manages to do that. It's why she's my best friend, I guess. Even when she's not here, she knows I'm going to need cheering up—and she knows how to do it. At least, she knows one way. Try to sit her down and discuss feelings with her, and she'll run for the hills, but give her any crappy situation and she'll find a way to get you to laugh your way out of it.

And she wouldn't thank me for saying this, as it might cramp her style, but she's not here so I'll say it anyway: she's one of the most caring, thoughtful people I know.

Take this weekend. Yeah, it's my birthday and everything, but it's also the anniversary of her mum and dad's divorce. He left years ago, and Cat is cool with it, but her mum, Jean, always needs cheering up, and Cat remembers that kind of thing without having to be told. So you know what she did? She worked extra shifts at her Saturday job for months, then bought tickets for a weekend break in Magaluf for the pair of them—her and Jean. That's the kind of thing she does.

And I love her for that. I do, really. But it does leave me standing on my own, fiddling with the top of a can of Diet Coke and wondering if it's rude to be the first person to leave your own birthday party.

I'm on the verge of sinking back into some self-indulgent wallowing when this boy strolls out of the kitchen. . . .

Super-skinny jeans with white Calvin Kleins sticking out the top, black sneakers, a kind of surfy-type T-shirt, messy dark hair that might have taken an hour to fix or could have been like that since he rolled out of bed, deep, intense brown eyes that scan the room as though he's searching for someone. Then he spots me and comes over.

"Is that Corsa yours?" he says. "It's blocking me in, and I need to nip to the grocery store for some supplies."

OK, so, no, it's not the most romantic chat-up line in the world. But given the standard of the evening's highlights so far, it's good enough for me.

"It's my mum's, actually." I smile up at him. "She's lent it to me for the night."

For a second, I bask in the idea of myself as a mature, responsible person. Someone who can drive herself to a party. I mean, sure, we only live two blocks away. And, yeah, Mum had to sit in the passenger seat when I drove. And, OK, Luke had to promise to sit with me when I drive home. But, still. It's the principle. The fact that I can.

The boy is kind of nodding slowly, then there's this long pause. Is he shy? I'm about to ask what kind of car he's got, just to keep the conversation going, when I suddenly realize what he's said. It wasn't a chat-up line at all.

"Oh! Wait! You want me to move it! I'll get my keys."

My cheeks burning up, I go in search of Luke and move the car.

Let me tell you a bit about Luke. He's one of the good guys. You know the type. Wears nice clothes—not the trendiest ever, but not geeky or scruffy. Helps old ladies across roads. Does his homework on time. Gets along with people's parents. Has lovely blue eyes that crinkle and shine when he smiles—which he does a lot—and light brown hair, parted neatly.

He's what my nan used to call well groomed, but not so much that he comes across as vain. I'd probably fancy him if I hadn't grown up thinking of him practically as a brother. I've known him forever. We were at nursery school together and have hung out together pretty much ever since.

For the past year or so, he's been extra nice to me because he fancies Cat and he figures if he keeps in with me, then one day she'll realize what a good guy he is and go out with him. Unfortunately, Cat only likes boys who are unavailable or who treat her badly. Luke thinks he can save her from all that. He's always asking me to put in a good word for him. He hasn't realized that she doesn't like good words. Maybe if I tell her he's an absolute bastard, then she'll notice him.

Who knows? Even I can't figure Cat out sometimes.

So, a bit more about Cat. Her real name is Catherine, but the only people who call her that are teachers, doctors, and me, occasionally, if I'm trying to annoy her, since she *hates* it. She's small, mischievous, somewhat feisty, and fiercely independent. She's like, well, a cat.

I guess she's what someone in a shop might call petite, except that sounds a bit too prissy for her. Plus she never shops in the kind of places that have a petite section. She buys *all* her clothes from thrift shops, and the wackier the better. Her favorite outfit at the moment is a pair of jeans that are so ripped you can see more skin than denim, a pair of yellow Doc Martens, and pretty much anything on top as long as it's tight enough to show off her figure and bright enough to make sure she gets noticed. She has crazy blond curly hair, bright-green cat eyes, a tattoo on her butt, amongst others, and piercings in her ears (four on each), nose (just one), mouth (two at the side), and left eyebrow.

Luke is not Cat's type.

So that's Luke and Cat. Now back to me.

I've moved the car and am scanning through Luke's playlist looking for something to lift the party mood before we all sink into clinical depression. I pick out Zoe's One Direction album. Luke's mates won't like it, but it's better than their music-to-slit-your-wrists-to, and I think I have the right not to end up in a room full of dead people on my birthday.

"I got you a drink." Calvin Klein is tapping me on the shoulder.

I give some careful thought to his words before replying. I know they're not very complicated, but there's no way I'm going to make the same mistake again.

"Here." He smiles as he hands me a can of Coke.

I take the can without removing my eyes from his face: (a) to check that he's not messing with me, and (b) because he's totally gorgeous and I'm not sure how to get my eyes to move away of their own accord.

"I owed you one. It was a bit mean, making you move your car like that. On your birthday and everything."

"It's fine. Nothing. It's OK." Smooth, Ashleigh. Turn into a tongue-tied idiot the minute a half-decent boy talks to you.

Actually, wait a second. I'd better get something straight here, just in case I'm giving the wrong impression. I'm not one of those brain-dead bimbos who talks about boys and makeup all the time. For one thing, I hardly ever wear makeup, and for another, boys are, well, they're OK, but they're not everything. As soon as I start going out with someone, I seem to lose interest in them. Most of the boys at school are losers of one variety or another. I think they all take secret lessons in how to become utter morons when they turn fifteen or sixteen. Sometimes I think we'd be better off without them.

Sometimes, but not right now.

We get talking. His name's Dylan, and he's in a band. He works at a clothes shop in town ("just till the band takes off"). He's come with some friends, but they're all getting drunk in the next room and he's bored because he's the driver.

We're getting on really well when Luke comes over, looking flustered.

"Ash, you've got to talk to Zoe. Nick's just broken up with her, and she's locked herself in the bathroom. She said she won't speak to anyone except you."

"Why me? You're her brother!"

Yes, I know it's selfish, and I'm sorry, OK? But, come on. It's my birthday and I'm talking to the only decent guy in the place.

Luke gives me his sad, pleading eyes. "Will you go up?"

I glare at Luke while simultaneously trying to smile seductively at Dylan (not easy — try it sometime), and head for the bathroom.

Zoe opens the door a crack to check that there's no one with me. Then she pulls me inside and plonks herself down on a wicker laundry hamper in the corner of the room. I perch on the edge of the tub, waiting for her to say something.

She's heartbroken. Kind of. She's been seeing Nick for three weeks and thought he was The One. But let's be honest here. Zoe does tend to have slightly unrealistic ideas of what might constitute The One. And, to be fair, after a few days of utter despair, another One generally comes along quite quickly.

Zoe is a year younger than us. She has long blond hair (which she swears doesn't come out of a bottle, but which was totally mousy brown for at least the first fourteen years of her life), enormous blue eyes, and pretty much her pick of all Luke's friends.

It seems her rebound rate is speeding up, as it turns out the only reason she wants me is to find out if Dylan's here on his own.

"It's just that, if I met someone else, it would help me get over Nick," she whimpers between sobs.

"He's just asked me out, actually," I reply quickly.

And yes, OK, hands up, I admit it isn't *technically* one hundred percent true. But I've learned that you don't take chances with Zoe.

She makes this kind of choking noise as she stares at me, as if I've just said the most unlikely thing in the entire world. Thanks, Zoe. Then she recovers and hides her shock with a cough. "Oh. Right. Great." She yanks a towel off the radiator, wipes her nose on it, and chucks it into the hamper. "Go for it, then."

I feel a pang of guilt. "Are you sure?"

Zoe's leaning over the sink to squint at herself in the mirror, already over it. "Of course," she says, getting out her lipstick. As I generally don't have quite the same pickings as her, I decide to accept her blessing and give it a shot with Dylan.

I check myself out in the full-length mirror on the wall. My hair looks OK. It's sort of blond, thanks to highlights, and sort of straight, thanks to straighteners. Not short, not long, it peters out somewhere around my shoulders. It's got one obstinate kink down the left side, which I try to flatten with my hand, but fail. I look at myself sideways and hold my tummy in, even though I'm not fat. I'm kind of average, I guess. Average clothes, too. I suddenly wish I'd gone for thicker mascara, brighter eyeshadow, and something a bit more interesting than jeans and a T-shirt. But I haven't. I don't; it's not me.

"You're positive you're all right?" I say as I turn to leave.

Zoe looks at me from the mirror. "'Course I am. I'm

fine, honest." She smiles. "Go on. Go. I'll be down in a minute. Good luck!"

I give Zoe a quick hug from behind and charge back downstairs.

Dylan's nowhere to be seen.

After I've sauntered casually into every downstairs room twice, and all the upstairs rooms that aren't locked and/or don't have any noises coming from inside, I give up and go in search of Luke instead. He's in the kitchen. There's a long wooden table with about twenty cans of Stella and two boxes of wine at one end and five plastic bowls of nibbles at the other. I slide onto the bench next to him and grab a handful of cashews.

"So. Where's that what's-his-name?" I ask in my best indifferent voice.

"Who's what's-his-name?"

"Umm, what was it, now . . . ? Dylan, I think." Dead casual.

"Oh, him." Luke's hand hovers briefly over the pretzels before plunging into the tortilla chips. "Had to go. One of his friends threw up, and Dylan offered to take him home."

My heart sinks under the table. "Is he coming back?"

"Don't think so."

My head drops. And so do my hopes. The perfect ending to a perfect birthday.

Then Luke mumbles through a mouthful of peanuts, "He asked for your phone number, actually."

"*What?* Did you give it to him?"

"I couldn't remember it—sorry."

11

"*Sorry?* That's *it?*"

Luke looks crestfallen, like he's only just this second realized that he's messed up. "Ash, I'm really sorry, mate. I'll make it up to you. I'll get his number and tell him you like him. . . ."

I can't stay angry at Luke. "It's OK," I say, trying to smile. "It's not your fault. I wasn't that keen on him, anyway."

Luke gives me a "Yeah, whatever" look, and I turn to my Coke, ready to sink back into my birthday blues.

Then I notice something. A piece of paper stuck in the top of my can of Coke—like in the old days when they used to put a note out for the milkman saying, "Two pints tomorrow." Except, obviously, better than that.

Ash,
I liked talking to you. Get in touch if you want.
Dylan

Under his name, he's written his phone number.

I read the note three times.

After that, I no longer care about the music or the dancing or the couple in the corner who are, by the way, still so intent on snogging each other's brains out that I'm surprised they haven't died from lack of oxygen.

Dylan liked talking to me. He gave me his phone number!

I sit smiling to myself as I finish my Coke. After a bit, I decide it's time to call it a night. I fold the note, put it carefully in my pocket, grab my coat—and Luke—and drive the two blocks home.

2

The teachers used to tell us we'd be treated differently when we got to high school. "Like adults," they said. But high school hadn't been invented a hundred years ago, when they were young. No wonder they were so wrong.

It had crossed my mind that this year might be different. Wrong again. So a few days after my birthday party, it's back to school with a thud.

We've hardly been back five minutes when the headmaster, Mrs. Banks, has Cat and me in her office for a Verbal Warning. She says she wants to start the term on a positive note, make things clear before we get into any bad habits. We have to sign this contract she's drawn up.

I will attend all my lessons and complete all my homework on time. I will not watch YouTube videos, update my Facebook status, tweet, tumbl, tinder, or text my friends while my teachers are talking.

How am I expected to get through the lessons, then?

I sign it when I see Cat scribble her name on hers,

although when she tells me later that she'd signed it Lady Gaga I could kick myself. I wouldn't exactly call it a positive start to the term, unless Banks means she wants to make us positive we hate everything about this place.

Mr. Kenworthy's gone. Which is kind of good as we never learned anything in his English lessons—other than to avoid sitting in the front row unless you wanted to be poisoned by alcohol fumes. But kind of bad in case we get a new teacher who insists on us actually doing any work.

Turns out we've got a temporary replacement: Miss Murray. She's all right, I suppose. Fresh out of teachers' college, I reckon, so she's brought the average age of the staff down by about fifty years.

We've got English after lunch. She makes us play this game where you have to pick someone in the room and describe them by saying what they'd be if they were a flower or a car or an animal. Then everyone has to guess who it is. I normally hate that kind of thing, but she makes it OK somehow. She smiles a lot and laughs at the same kinds of things we laugh at, not like the rest of the teachers, who just glare at you the minute you look as if you might actually be enjoying the lesson. Not that that happens often, but if it did, they'd probably think they were doing something wrong.

Robyn describes me. I don't really know her that well. She sat on the other side of the class last year, but they've moved the desks around and we've ended up next to each other. She's OK, I guess. She's kind of mousy-looking: brown bob, brown eyes, glasses. Quite pretty when she smiles. Gets along with teachers. You know the kind. Harmless enough, just not really my kind of person.

Anyway, she has me down as a cactus, a lion cub, and a Mini Cooper. I've no idea what she's going on about, but Miss Murray works out that it's me after a few others make wrong guesses.

It's beginning to feel like we're goofing off when Miss Murray glances at her watch. "Right, enough of the fun and games," she says. "We'd better get down to some work." A muffled grumble spreads through the room.

She goes to the front of her desk and half sits, half leans back against it, as if she wants to show us she's totally cool and laid-back but can't bring herself to go all the way and sit on the thing.

"So." She clasps her hands together, brings them up to her mouth. It reminds me of morning prayers at primary school.

"Hands together, eyes closed," Mr. Jackson, the headmaster, would say, and we'd deliver the Lord's Prayer in three hundred synchronized monotones.

"Our father, who art in heaven, Harold be thy name," I intoned earnestly every morning. It was years before I realized God wasn't actually called Harold.

I look up at Miss Murray. She's propping her lips on her fingertips, eyes almost closed, and, for a second, I wonder if she's praying too.

"So," she repeats. "Can anyone tell me a poem they've read and enjoyed recently?"

No one says anything. A *poem*? That we've *enjoyed*? I stifle a laugh and look down at my desk like everyone else.

"Oh, no!" she suddenly exclaims and goes back behind her desk. She picks up a piece of paper and frowns at it. "I must have written down the wrong room. I thought this was an English A-level class."

Why do teachers *always* have to be sarcastic?

But then I notice her cheeks have gone red. Just a bit, just enough to make me feel sorry for her, and I don't care about the silent agreement. So I do something I haven't done for as long as I can remember. I put my hand up.

"Does it have to be an actual poem, miss?" I raise my eyes to look up at her without lifting my head.

"What did you have in mind? Ashleigh, isn't it?"

"Ash, yeah."

"What did you have in mind, Ash?"

"Well, there's this song I wrote the words out to; I think it's kind of like a poem." *What am I doing?*

"That's great," she says with a smile that feels like it reaches right into me and looks around inside. Can a smile even *do* that?

"Can you remember it?" She's leaning forward, looking at me so intently I'm afraid she's wading through all my hidden secrets.

I can feel a room full of gobsmacked eyes zoning in on me. So I pull myself together and give the only answer that'll save me. "No. Sorry."

Miss Murray purses her lips, still looking at me.

16

"But I know it's good," I add feebly. She's going to think I'm an idiot now. Not that I care what a teacher thinks of me. At least, I never have before now.

"Maybe you could bring it in sometime," she says as she turns away and picks up a book from her desk. I feel dismissed, and I'm not sure I like it—although it does mean I've gotten away with not looking like a total weirdo in front of my peers.

"I'd like to see it." Her head, slightly tilted, turns her smile into a question, and I shrug in reply.

"Good." She opens the book. "Now, here's one of my favorites."

Then she says, "They fuck you up, your mum and dad."

I look around the class. Everyone has stopped doodling and passing notes to one another; the air's tightened.

"They may not mean to, but they do."

Is it a poem?

She holds our attention all the way to the last line, when she puts the book down and says, "Philip Larkin." Into the silence, she adds, "He's a poet."

As she passes photocopies around the room, we study them with suspicion.

"Any thoughts?" Miss Murray asks.

I find myself nodding as I read the poem, as I relate to every word. It's as if the poet knows exactly what's going on in my head. I want to say so, but I've already done my bit, so I do the looking-down-at-my-desk thing again and wait for someone else to speak. The tension spreads awkwardly around the room, seeping into every little space.

Finally, Luke breaks the silence. "Is that really a poem, miss, or did you make it up for a laugh?"

But before she has time to answer, the bell rings. Bags are instantly on top of tables, chairs scraped back.

"Excuse me!" she shouts over the racket. "I didn't tell anyone to go anywhere."

She's standing in front of her desk, arms folded, and frowning as she looks around at us. We eventually stop moving while we wait for her to speak. Weird. We never did that for Mr. Kenworthy.

There's something about her. It's as if she's not on the opposite side of a high wall, like most teachers. She makes the wall seem like a thin line — as though she can reach across to our side of it. Maybe it's because she's probably only about five years older than us. Maybe it's because she smiles more than most teachers. Maybe it's because she shared a poem with swear words in it. I don't know what it is — I just know that, yeah, OK, she's cool. For a teacher.

Outside the room, people are already running past the door, chasing each other to the bus queue.

"As we've been getting to know each other today, we've not had time to study this poem," Miss Murray goes on. "We'll continue with it tomorrow. In the meantime, I'd like you to read it again at home and jot down your initial responses to it. Any questions?"

In reply, we grab our bags and squeeze out to join the corridor rush hour.

• • •

I catch up with Cat at the bus stop. She draws on a cigarette while I tell her about the party. We've hardly had a chance to talk all day.

"D'you think I should call him?" I ask. "Or text?"

Cat grins. "Send him a topless selfie?"

I laugh as Cat finishes her cigarette and chucks it on the pavement. I wish she wouldn't do that. Wish she wouldn't smoke at all, to be honest. Not out of being a goody-goody. Mainly because it makes her stink, and hanging out with her makes *me* stink and makes Mum and Dad accuse me of smoking—which I don't. Dad's never convinced, no matter how much I promise I don't smoke. Tried it. Didn't like it. But I don't have any intention of telling Cat what to do; it would only make her do the opposite.

"So, tell me about Magaluf," I say, happy to change the subject. "Did Jean score?"

Cat bursts out laughing. "Actually, nearly. She and I had a contest to see who could get the most smiles out of the waiter I sent you the pic of. She got the most, so I told her she'd won."

"Hadn't she?"

Cat smiles her cheeky Cat-smile. "Depends if you count making out with him behind the recycling bins as a winning move!"

"You didn't!"

"'Course I did. Anyway. Come on. Back to the party," she says as the bus rounds the corner. "What're you going to do about message-in-a-bottle boy?"

We get on the double-decker bus and go upstairs, where we carry on sorting out the minutiae of each other's love lives till we part company at my bus stop. "FaceTime me later," Cat calls as I get off the bus.

"Will do," I call back as I brace myself for an evening at home.

Mum and Dad are driving me mad. They've had a row and haven't spoken a word to each other for three days.

Dinner is a nightmare. A silent nightmare.

Mum perches martyr-like on a stool at the other end of the kitchen while Dad and I sit at the table. He's reading the paper while he eats, and she's staring pointedly out the window.

It's been like this for months. Things will be OK for a bit, then it all blows up over something tiny and the atmosphere makes the North Pole feel like a Caribbean cruise.

It upset me when it started happening. I tried to make them sort it out. I'd be crying and I'd beg them to make up. And they would, kind of. At least, they'd be civil to each other in front of me. Then they stopped doing even that.

I guess I've kind of cut off from it now. It's horrible. I hate myself for it, but it's better than crying my eyes out in my room because I can't make them stop.

Dad is slurping his soup. It's making me want to scream.

Has he always done that?

I've got a vague memory of very different mealtimes: Mum cooking while Dad would open a bottle of wine and pour them both a glass. They'd talk about their day, smiling, interrupting each other, refilling their glasses. Then we'd play word games while we ate, and afterward Dad and I would clear up. He'd wash, I'd dry, racing each other. He'd flick bubbles in my face to try to distract me. He'd make me laugh.

Mum interrupts my nostalgia trip. "Ashleigh, please could you ask your father to remember to put the trash bins out?" she says as she gets up and takes her plate to the sink. "And it's recycling this week too."

A while ago, I might have said to ask him herself — but it's easier to give in and do what she says.

"Dad, remember to take the trash bins out tonight," I say.

Dad doesn't raise his head from his newspaper.

"Dad. It's trash night. And recycling."

Nothing.

This is what it's like. Arctic, I'm telling you.

I try a new tack. "Dad, by the way, I've dropped out of school, become a drug addict, and committed a string of violent acts."

Dad turns the page and looks up briefly as Mum leaves the kitchen and closes the door behind her. "What, dear? Sorry. Oh, good, that's nice," he replies before going back to his paper.

I get up with a sigh and decide to sort the trash out myself.

That Philip Larkin knows what he's talking about.

Later, as I scribble down a few thoughts on the poem, I get this weird feeling about the next English class. As if for the first time in forever, the lesson might be remotely relevant to my life. As if I'm looking forward to it or something.

What the hell is *that* about?

3

It's a week later and I have to say, my parents are not the number-one thing on my mind. Nor is my English homework.

I'm on a date. With Dylan.

I sneak a glance at him as we drive to the cinema. He's got his window open, his elbow leaning on the frame as he drives. His other hand is resting on his knee, fiddling absentmindedly with the fraying rip curling into a smile in his jeans. Kiss FM on the radio. Does it get better than this?

It's easy to get away with looking at him. He's doing most of the talking, so it's only polite. It would probably be polite to listen more carefully as well—and then I might not come across as a complete moron. Example:

Him: There's a chick flick, a French film, or the new James Bond at the Odeon. Which d'you fancy?

Long pause while I stare at him (out of politeness).

Me (suddenly realizing it's my turn to speak): Oh, the Odeon, definitely.

Or:

Him: What did you think of the party?

Long pause, etc.

Me: Oh, I just borrowed it off my mum for the night.

What? Why?

We pick the James Bond film in the end, and he's engrossed from the first trailer onward. I wait for his arm to creep around my shoulder. It doesn't. Why not? I study my options while he glares at the screen.

A. He's a perfect gentleman. *(Good option. Bodes well for future. Unlike Cat, I actually like this in a boy.)*
B. He's shy. *(Could go either way. Might be sweet at first, but would lose appeal if it goes on too long.)*
C. He's totally engrossed in the film. *(He'd rather watch grown men with big guns and little gadgets chase each other around than get with me? Not good.)*
D. He doesn't fancy me. *(Clearly the worst option; I refuse to consider it a possibility at this stage.)*

Still, it's a good film, and we have a laugh on the way home. Dylan feels easy to be with. Plus I keep getting wafts of what smells like honey and almonds, which makes me think he must have washed his hair before he came out—or at least had a shower or something. Either way, he's made an effort, which has to be a good sign.

When we get home, the living room lights are on. Dad's a complete fascist about wasting electricity, so they must be up. There's no way I'm going to run the risk of ruining everything by inviting Dylan in, so we talk in the car.

After about ten minutes, I know curtains will be twitching. Mrs. Langdale across the road doesn't like to miss anything. I can just imagine the conversation the next day:

"Ooh, who's got herself a new boyfriend, then?"

"He's not my boyfriend, actually, he's just—"

"I mean, fancy courting at your age!"

"I am seventeen now, you know."

"Seventeen! In my day, it wouldn't do to be on your own with a man until you were almost married. Sitting there in a car with him for all the world to see, it would have caused a scandal."

"But we weren't doing anyth—"

"Yes, yes, dear, I know. Got to rush; I'm late for my wash and set."

No, a grilling from Mrs. Langdale is to be avoided at all costs. So we say good night, and that's that. There's an awkward moment when we don't know whether to kiss or not. He's fiddling with the rip in his jeans so much I'm worried he's going to tear them off from the knee down.

In the end I get out and say, "See you around, then,"

in my flippant voice (which I've been practicing lately, along with complete indifference and total spontaneity).

He mumbles something that sounds like, "Yeah, see you," but I'm halfway up the drive by then. I've ended the evening in control, and that's good. Then, just as I get to the front door, I suddenly remember I haven't given him my phone number. Without thinking, I turn and run back to the car.

"My number," I pant. A sprint down the drive is more exercise than I'm used to.

He smiles and says, "I've already got it."

"You have?"

He waves his mobile at me. "It's in my phone. You texted me, remember? I texted you back."

Oh, God. I'm an idiot! But he saved my number! He's got me in his phone. "Oh, yeah," I say nonchalantly. "I'd forgotten."

I try to regain a bit of the cool and hard-to-get ground as I let myself into the house without turning around to wave.

When I get in, no one's up. Damn. I could have invited Dylan in after all.

Dad skips breakfast, and it's only when I go into the living room to look for my bag that I notice the sofa bed's out. This is a first. My heart flips into as much of a tumble as the disheveled sheets. I'm torn between wanting to know what it might mean and wishing I'd never seen it.

Mum's at the kitchen sink, scrubbing hard at the grill pan.

"Mum, why's the—"

"Late for work, darling." She doesn't turn around. "I'll speak to you later." Then she whips off her rubber gloves and flounces out of the room.

You can see where I get my *If I pretend to myself it's not happening, maybe it'll go away* strategy.

I grab a bowl of cereal and occupy my mind by reading the list of ingredients. Any second now, Mum'll shout, "Don't be late for school." A simple "good-bye" doesn't happen around here. Then she'll go off to work, and I'll be left alone with nothing to distract me from wondering what the hell is going on.

But Mum doesn't shout anything. A minute later, she's back in the doorway, rattling her keys, rain tapping on the window behind me.

I look up. "What?" I don't mean to snap at her, but I can't help it. If neither of them can manage to treat me like a grown-up, why should I act like one?

"When do you have to be in this morning?"

"Half past ten."

"Right," she says. "How about a nice cup of tea?"

I look up. "What about work?"

She slaps on her secretary smile and says, "I'll phone them. You're my daughter and that's more important." Then she's gone.

Oh, no. I don't like this. She's never late for work. And we've never had a "nice cup of tea" together. I don't even drink tea. Shows how much notice she's taken of me lately. She could tell you more about the town's biggest criminals than her own daughter. She works at a law firm. Started as a temp five years ago, and she practically runs the place now.

"Right, that's settled." She's back at the door, fastening her briefcase. "We're going out. My treat."

"What about school?"

"You can be a little late."

I guess she's got it all sorted. Whatever it is Mum wants to tell me, I'm going to have to listen—even if I really, really don't think I want to hear it.

We small-talk about the weather all the way. I'm telling you, we're professionals at this avoidance stuff.

I squeeze into a table at the back of the Starbucks around the corner from school. Mum slides in opposite me while mellow music and the smell of bacon and burnt toast waft over the counter in equal measures.

"This is nice, isn't it?" That slap-on secretary smile again.

I pour milk in my coffee and force myself not to reply with the angry sarcasm that's building up inside me. As I stir in some sugar, I try a different tack. "Mum, I don't know—"

Mum interrupts me. "Ashleigh, I need to talk to you."

I stop stirring and look at her. *Detach, detach, don't get drawn in.*

"I don't want you to be upset," she goes on. "None

of this is your fault, but your father and I . . ." She stops, picks up her tea, sips it.

"Look, it doesn't matter," I say quickly. I'm suddenly positive about one thing: whatever she wants to tell me, I don't want to hear it. I'd prefer to keep lying to myself and pretending everything's fine than have her actually confirm out loud that it isn't. "What you do is your business."

She looks out the window. "I just don't understand what—I mean, everything was all right before . . ." Her voice trails away, and her eyes mist over. She blinks at me. What does she see? Hardness? Fear? The strongest desire in the world for her to please just STOP?

"*We're* all right though, aren't we, Ash, you and me?"

I can't speak. "Mmm-hmm."

She closes her eyes while she wipes her mouth with a paper napkin, leaving a bit of lipstick behind. "Just because your father and I can't seem to get on with each other at the moment doesn't change how I—how both of us—feel about you." She pauses, then says, more quietly, "I do love you very much, you know."

I stare at the swirls in my coffee and the grains of sugar stuck on the rim of the mug. What am I meant to say? I've got absolutely no idea. So I say nothing.

"I do, Ashleigh." Mum reaches out for my hand, and I quickly pick up my coffee.

"I know, Mum." I look around the café. Look at the tables. The counter, the ceiling—anywhere but her face. "Can I go now?"

As soon as I've said it, I feel awful. I glance at her.

29

She's clenching her teeth, and a tic is beating in her cheek. Her eyes are dark. I want to take the words back, but I've got nowhere else to put them, so I leave them hanging there.

"Is it so awful to spend a few minutes with your mother?" she whispers. "Am I that much of a terrible person?" She dabs at the corners of her eyes with the edge of her napkin, then tilts her head away and looks up at the ceiling. The strip light buzzes and flashes sadly like at the end of a school dance.

"Mum, you're not a terrible person at all," I say. "And, for what it's worth, I don't think Dad is either. I just wish you'd sort things out."

Mum nods. "Thank you, darling. That means a lot."

"And I'm sorry if I was a bit sharp," I add. "I don't mean to be. I've just got stuff on my mind too." Like the fact that Dylan hasn't been in touch since our date, and wondering whether I should text him first, and if Cat'll be at school so I can ask her advice. All of which, frankly, is a welcome distraction from having to think about any of this.

"I know," she says, "and I'm sorry. All this nonsense between your father and me, it's not fair to you. I don't even know what's gotten into us. We used to be so . . ." She makes a strange noise, like a cross between a choke and a gulp. "Well, things have changed," she says finally. "He barely looks at me nowadays. We don't speak to each other. Don't even know what to say or where to start."

Makes three of us.

"I'm sorry, Ashleigh. I just want us to be a family again, and I'll try my best to make that happen. Will you give me a chance?"

"Yeah, of course," I say. I look up quickly and she catches my eyes. For a second, a tiny window opens between us and I remember when I was little and she was my idol. She used to tell me about the first time she took me swimming. I was two and I had a turquoise swimsuit with a white frill around the bottom. "I held you against me and heard your little heart beating against mine," she used to say, and I'd make her tell me again and again. I never knew if I actually remembered it myself or if I'd just heard the story so often I could picture us there. My little arms around her neck, hot cheek against her ear, her safe arms holding me tight.

When did she stop being my best friend?

I smile back and we sit in silence for a second before she picks up her bag. "Just nipping to the loo."

"Look, I need to get moving. I'm going to be late."

As I edge out of my seat, she studies my face, brushing my cheek with her thumb as though she's looking for something. Then the moment has passed and we go our separate ways.

Leaving the café, I force the conversation out of my mind. They'll sort it out. I'm sure they will. They've got to, because the alternative is, frankly, unthinkable.

By the time I reach the school gates, my thoughts are safely off Mum and Dad and back onto the other pressing issue: When is Dylan going to ring?

4

Cat and I get our lunch and take a seat in the cafeteria. For about a millisecond, I toy with the idea of talking to her about my parents. I decide against it. Saying the words out loud to Cat would make them all too real. Instead we discuss what might be going on with Dylan.

We don't come up with much.

"Perhaps it's like that film," Cat ventures through a mouthful of chips.

"What film?"

"You know. What's it called?"

"*He's Just Not That Into You?*" I offer.

"No, I meant the one where the guy loses his short-term memory. So, like, he meets someone one day, or even knows them really well, but by the next day, he's completely forgotten who they are."

"How does it end?"

"Um. He finds out that he's murdered his wife."

I laugh. "I think I prefer my suggestion."

"OK, moving on." Cat bends down and rolls up one leg of her jeans. "I'm thinking of getting a new tattoo." She points at her ankle. "Dragonfly, just here. Or a butterfly. Or maybe a ladybug. What d'you think?"

We leave Dylan behind and discuss the relative merits of various winged insects instead. Cat shows me pictures of each of them on her phone. She already has five tattoos. I think she's addicted. Personally, I'm not keen on pain so I don't think I could do it myself — but they always look great on her.

But as this is the sixth time I've been through this process with her, I can't help a bit of me switching off. Sorry if it makes me a rubbish friend and a terrible person, but while I'm saying, "Yeah, that'd be lovely," and "Ooh, that's pretty" and "Mmm, maybe that one," there's a bit of me inside that's thinking, "Maybe Dylan's *not* that into me."

By the time I get home, I've decided I've had enough of thinking about Dylan. He clearly isn't interested, so it's time to get on with my life and stop wasting any more time on him.

Only trouble is, there's not a lot to distract me. Nothing nice anyway. Mum and Dad still aren't talking, and I don't fancy sitting in silence in front of some boring documentary that none of us wants to watch but no one will offer to change because that might involve having a conversation. So I shut myself in my room and consider my options. I'm even on the verge of doing some homework.

And then Dylan turns up. Just like that. Come to save me from an evening of potentially studying the history of the Corn Laws, like a knight in shining armor. Well,

OK, more like a shop assistant in a battered Fiesta, but it'll do just fine.

I see him pull up from my bedroom window, and I'm suddenly faced with a major conflict. In about one minute, he'll ring the bell. Not that our drive's so long it takes a whole minute to walk up it; it's just that Dad recently installed a new gate that you can only figure out how to open if you happen to be a genius who's won *Eggheads, The Weakest Link,* and possibly *Wipeout,* too. By the time a normal person's worked it all out, the burglar-detector light has flashed on and our latest first-time visitor is rooted to the spot by a glare that a trained interrogator would be proud of. He likes his gadgets, Dad does. And his security.

Anyway, the question is,

The boy of your dreams turns up unexpectedly at your house late at night. You have one minute to get to the door. Do you:

A. *Frantically brush your teeth, sort out your hair, spray perfume over your body, and apply makeup; or*
B. *Get to the door before he rings the bell, thus avoiding any chance of your parents meeting the boy before he's even kissed you?*

Under normal circumstances it would be "B."

Mostly Bs: You are impetuous and feisty, a crazy chick who enjoys life to the fullest, takes no prisoners, and is prepared for any situation.

That's me. Except for one thing. I'm halfway down

the stairs when I realize I've still got my pajamas on. Well, I wasn't expecting him to come around, was I? Which leaves:

C. *Change out of your PJs with the teddy bear pattern and piece of string holding up the bottoms because the elastic's gone?*

Mostly Cs: Oh, dear. You are the one who's always left behind as you haven't quite figured out how to keep up with the go-getters. Try to think ahead a little. Get in shape, get it together, but most of all, get a life.

Without thinking, I tear into my bedroom, fling a pair of sweatpants over my pajamas, and throw on a sweater I bought from New Look over the weekend. I glance at my feet: Mum's cast-off slippers with a hole in the big toe. I'll have to go barefoot. I hurl myself out of my room, down the stairs, and across the hall just in time to get to the door before Dylan rings the bell—and before Mum and Dad have noticed anything.

"Hi," he says with a grin.

"Oh, hi." Heart racing and totally breathless, I try to sound as if I just happened to be passing by the door.

Dylan keeps smiling and my knees start to buckle. So there I am, barefoot, out of breath, and holding on to the door knocker to keep myself upright, when he starts laughing.

"What?" I ask.

"Well, it's your top. What's . . ." He reaches forward. My heart stops. My eyes half close. This is it!

And then he says, ". . . this?"

My eyes snap open. He's holding a bit of cardboard, and it seems to be attached to me. No! I've only gone and put my new sweater on backward and left the bloody tag on! I might as well give up and go home. Except I am home. I can't even do that. Brilliant.

But then he does it anyway—looks at me for a second and puts his hand on my shoulder. I gaze back at him, and I'm just starting to feel awkward when he leans forward and kisses me.

I'm about to collapse, Hollywood-style, into his arms when I suddenly remember three things:

1) I haven't brushed my teeth.
2) We're on my front doorstep (and center stage as far as Mrs. Langdale's concerned).
3) My parents are still up and will soon notice a draft if we stand in the doorway much longer.

"Come on." I grab a pair of wellies from the porch and push him out the door.

"Where are we going?"

"Anywhere. You're driving." I softly close the door behind me.

So we're driving along, it's late in the evening, I'm wearing wellies and a backward sweater with my pajamas underneath, no socks, no money, no coat, no idea where we're heading. And I'm in heaven.

I keep sneaking little looks at Dylan. He does the same, and every time I meet his eyes, I get this back-flipping butterfly action in my stomach.

After about ten minutes, he pulls over, switches off the ignition, and turns to face me. He keeps opening his mouth, taking a deep breath, and then closing it again. "Goldfish" is what comes to mind, but I don't want to say it, so I look around while he gets it together. We're in the middle of one of those modern housing estates: the lawns all very neat and tidy with symmetrical borders and perfectly trimmed edges. The houses all look the same, except for the odd one where someone has made a stab at individuality with a bit of ivy creeping up the front wall or a bit of decking instead of a lawn.

"Ash, I need to talk to you," Dylan blurts, suddenly grabbing hold of my hand with both of his and looking at me intensely. "I don't think I've been completely honest with you," he says after a few more gulps of air.

I don't *think* I've been honest? Only a boy could say that.

"Look I wanted to tell you . . . I've got, had, I mean, you're, she's—"

"*She's?*" Out of the heap of words thrown together in no apparent order, that one gets my attention. "She, who? She, what?"

We gaze at each other in silence for a few seconds. His messy hair is falling into his eye, and he looks like a Labrador puppy with floppy ears. *I want him; can I have him? Please can I?*

He turns away. I sneak a look at him fiddling nervously with his fingers. His nails are bitten all the way down, and there's red, sore-looking skin around the sides of them. I take hold of his hands.

"Whatever it is, you can tell me," I say in my best reassuring voice. "I'm not going to run away."

I'm not a hundred percent sure about that last bit, actually. I mean, it could be anything.

"I've brought you here to tell you to leave me alone. I can't stand you."

"The thing is, I've got this nasty genital disease and I keep passing it on to others out of revenge against the woman who gave it to me."

"I've killed someone and I'm scared I might do it again."

"Look, this is the situation," Dylan says, breaking into my thoughts—thank goodness; I dread to think what the next one would have been.

He takes a deep breath and turns to face me. "I had a girlfriend," he says steadily, then lets out his breath in a big rush and falls silent again.

"Ye-e-s?" Does he think I've never been out with anyone? "I have had a few boyfriends in my time, you know," I tell him. "I don't mind if I'm not your first."

For a moment he squints at me, then he almost laughs. One look at my face and he stops, though. "No, I mean, I *just* had a girlfriend. Kind of recently."

I ease my hand away. *"How* recently?"

"Look, I wanted to tell you." He pushes his hair back and turns away from me. "We've been together about a year, but we've not been getting along lately. Last few months we'd more or less split up anyway."

I raise an eyebrow. Try to anyway. It's one of those things I just can't do, no matter how much I practice. I just know I look more like a rabbit about to sneeze than an assertive young woman who's totally in control of the situation. "More?" I ask. "Or less? Which?"

He glances at me, then turns back to the windshield. "We talked about splitting up, but . . ."

"But what?"

He stares straight ahead. "Well, we didn't actually, finally do it. But we have now. Once I met you. After we went to the cinema, well, that was it."

I can't stop my face from twitching into a smile. He looks at me again and half smiles back. "I waited for you to get in touch all week after Luke's party. I didn't think you were going to. But then you texted me. So I rang Em and we met up today—"

"Today? As in the same day that you snogged me on my doorstep?"

His cheeks are growing redder by the minute, and a frown creases up his forehead. I want to reach out and smooth it over but remember just in time that I'm too cross.

"Look, we went to the park, that's all, and I told her it was over. She was dead upset."

Ahh, my heart breaks.

"But we talked. And I think we can still be friends."

Er, not if I've got anything to do with it, dude.

39

"And then I just wanted to see you straightaway. Tell you I like you. And see if you want to, you know, go out with me."

He's biting his nails now and has nearly reached the skin. Then he looks up and gives me a shy smile—and he's done it. He's won me over.

"I like you too," I say with a shrug. "And, yeah, OK, I'll go out with you."

For a moment we look at each other and neither of us says anything. Then he leans over, takes my face in both hands, and kisses me again.

When it starts to get uncomfortable leaning over the hand brake, I pull away and straighten myself in my seat. "Where are we anyway?"

"Oh, just around the corner from my house. Do you, er, d'you want to come over?"

It's getting late. My parents will go mad if they notice I'm out. "I think you'd better take me home."

I get him to drop me at the end of the street. I don't want to attract attention to myself. And I want another of those kisses but daren't do it outside our house.

"See you later," I say, trying to sound casual as I get out of the car.

He rolls the window down and leans across the seat. "I'll text you soon."

"Yeah, whatever," I call back without turning around. Good thing he can't see how big my smile is.

I weave my way along the street and up the drive, avoiding the burglar-detector trigger spots like a professional.

The house is quiet. Mum and Dad must have gone to bed. I'm about to head up to my bedroom when I notice something: a sliver of soft lamplight under the living room door. Are they still up? I hover outside the door, then I hear Dad's voice and for a split second I feel a huge wave of relief. They've made up. They're talking again. Then I realize—he's not talking to Mum. It sounds like he's on the phone. I lean into the door and listen.

"No, not yet," he says in a low voice. "It's tearing me apart. I don't know what to do." Long pause. "Yeah, I know. I'm just glad I've got you to talk to or I'd be lost."

I'm glued to the floor. Who's he talking to? What's he talking about? Is he in there sleeping on the sofa bed again? What's going *on* around here?

I don't want to dwell on *any* of the questions suddenly filling up my mind and blocking out the whole of the last blissful hour with Dylan. I can't risk thinking about them, or I might have to think about the answers too.

I creep up to my bedroom, my happy bubble well and truly burst. I try my hardest to think about Dylan's kisses instead of Dad's whispers, and finally I drift off into an unsettled sleep.

5

Next morning, I doze through my alarm, ignore Mum's wake-up call ("Don't be late for school!"), and wait till she and Dad have left the house before I get up. I can't face them. Whatever's going on between them, I just want them to hurry up and sort it out so we can go back to normal. Whatever passes for normal. Not sure I can even remember.

I don't *want* to be late for school, for once. We've got English first. English has been the only decent thing in school lately. It's Miss Murray. She's like an oasis of fun among a wilderness of dinosaurs—if that's not mixing too many metaphors. Look, see, she's gotten to me already. When would I ever have used the word *metaphor* before?

She keeps going on about bringing in poems, which a couple of the others have done. I printed out the lyrics to the song I'd mentioned in our first lesson and keep meaning to show them to her. I haven't managed to get beyond thinking I'll look like a nerd if I do, so I haven't bothered up to now. I want to, though, and it's weird. She's the only teacher who's ever made me want to do something like that, in more than a decade of compulsory education.

Everyone seems to feel the same way about her. I've noticed the smile rate is a lot higher in her lessons than anywhere else in school. She makes everything into a game. It doesn't feel like learning. Or it didn't. It's changed a bit this week. We've started reading *Wuthering Heights* and, to be honest, I can't get into it.

We were supposed to read the first three chapters before this morning's lesson, but I could barely get to the end of the first page. It's all "capital fellow" and "soliloquised in an undertone of peevish displeasure." By the time I got to the "range of gaunt thorns . . . craving alms of the sun," I'd pretty much given up.

To be fair, between agonizing over Dylan and trying not to get drawn into my parents' marriage troubles, it's fair to say I've had other stuff on my mind too.

Thing is, though, once we get talking about it in class, the book doesn't seem so bad. Miss Murray says it's one of her favorite novels ever, and you can tell. She walks around the room, holding it in her hand all the time and breathlessly reading bits out loud. She seems to know half the book by heart. She asks questions about every little thing: How does the setting reflect the characters? Did Lockwood have a nightmare or was it real? What is Nelly Dean's role? What have we learned of Catherine and Heathcliff's relationship so far?

If anyone says anything good, it's as though she's just unwrapped her perfect Christmas present. "Yes, *exactly,* Tom. Brilliant!" Or "Fantastic, Robyn! That's just how I see it."

You can see how her compliments make people feel. It's like she switches a light on inside their eyes. There are great big smiles whenever someone gets a tiny compliment from her. It almost makes me wish I'd tried harder with the book. I've nothing to offer, so there's no smiley light switch for me.

I think about guessing at an answer or two, but decide not to bother. I'll only get it wrong and make a fool of myself. I don't want her to think I'm stupid. Not that it would matter if she did. She might be a good laugh at times, but she is a teacher, after all.

Still, when she tells us to read to page 65, I sneak my pen out and write it on my hand so I'll remember to do it tonight. Can't do any harm to give it another go.

At the end of the lesson, I take my time packing up so I'm the last to leave. I'm going to give her the song lyrics.

Miss Murray's shuffling papers together at her desk; she looks up and smiles as I approach. Does she smile at *everything?*

"Here." I shove the crumpled piece of paper across the table. "That song I told you about. Sorry I've not brought it in before. I kept forgetting."

She looks blank for a second. Now I feel like an idiot as well as a nerd. I'm about to grab it straight back when she says, "The song lyrics that you said were like a poem? Excellent. Let's have a look." She picks the paper up.

I stand in front of her desk, my face burning up while she reads. She's frowning at the piece of paper, and I suddenly realize what a fool I must look.

I'm miles behind in everything we did last year, I couldn't be bothered with even the first page of a book everyone else seems to love, and now I've given in some stupid song lyrics when she's expecting a poem. Right, that's it. I'm dropping English. I'll see my tutor next week.

"It's great, Ash," she says, breaking into my thoughts. "Generally, I think that a song needs all of its component parts in order to work. If you hear the music without the words, there's an emptiness to it. Do you know what I mean?"

"Yeah, I think so."

"And the words never seem to stand up to much scrutiny." She looks at me like she's waiting for me to say something. "Synergy," she adds.

I nod slowly. What's she on about?

She laughs. "It means when the whole of something is greater than the sum of its parts."

"Right."

"I don't know this song, but I agree with you — some of the lyrics have a real sense of poetry in them." She leans forward so we can both see the words. "Look, I like this verse:

'And they sing
At the end of the beach,
Out of reach.

And the rest of the world
Tightly curled
In its nest
Of content, happy dreams.'"

"Yeah, I know," I say. "It's like everyone thinks they know what it means to be happy, but they're not even awake—it's as if they're not really alive. But these others, they're the only ones who really understand how to be happy, and that sets them apart. It sets them free."

She looks at me as if she's only just noticed I'm there.

"What?" I ask.

"That's absolutely it. Brilliant!" She looks back at the song. "Yes. I like it."

"It's one of my favorites," I say, hoping she won't remember me saying I didn't know any of the words.

"Who's it by?"

"Just a small indie band. You won't have heard of them."

"Try me."

"Angel's Rock."

She laughs. "You're right, I haven't. But I'll look out for them from now on." She hands the sheet of paper back to me.

I look at my watch. I'm late for sociology. Maybe I'll skip it and have another go at *Wuthering Heights* while it's fresh in my mind.

"Ash," she says as I reach the door. "Page sixty-five. Don't forget this time."

46

How does she know I hadn't read it?

"I won't," I say and tramp down to the cafeteria, something new and unfamiliar lighting me up inside.

Mum's acting really weird with me when I get home, but she doesn't say anything till we sit down for dinner. Doesn't say anything then either, actually, but I know she wants to. You can always tell when my mum's in a bad mood. She doesn't speak, but her actions are like words with a megaphone. Her body gets really tense, and her face is all pinched up. If you ask if anything is wrong, she'll always deny it, but in a way that lets you know that there definitely is. You can almost feel her hedgehog spikes of anger.

And I don't know why, but I just haven't got the patience for it anymore. I'm getting pissed off now. I mean, I am their daughter. It might be nice if perhaps one of them could, at some point, consider me. Whatever's going on between them, it's not my fault. At least, I don't think it is. So keep me out of it. Put on a happy front for the kids and all that. But, no. Neither of them has considered doing that for a second. Which means that at this moment, I have zero inclination to make an effort with them either.

So we're eating in silence as usual, only this time, instead of doing everything she can to ignore Dad, Mum keeps trying to get his attention. Banging her cutlery on her plate, then looking at him pointedly and coughing. He's got the *Telegraph* open in front of him and doesn't notice any of it. I guess I learned most of my switching-off tricks from Dad. He's the master of deliberately not having a clue what's going on around him.

Which is how he manages to politely put his knife and fork together, fold up his paper, and say, "Right, that was smashing. I'll just be off to—"

Except he stops when he sees Mum's face. Even *he* can tell that this wasn't what he was meant to say.

"Gordon, we discussed this," Mum hisses.

He looks blank for a second, then he suddenly nods and says, "OK. Right you are, then." He turns to me. "Ash. We, ah, well, you didn't by any chance nip out last night, did you? It's just that when we got up this morning, the porch light was on, and we noticed a pair of your boots at the bottom of the stairs, and, well, it just seems a little odd, that's all."

I weigh up my options. Do I go for the casual approach: a quick "No, course not, Dad" or the emotional "How could you?" with lots of eye contact, an emphatic denial, and a tearful exit to my bedroom? Or the truth?

I can get away with almost anything with Dad, except lying. The one and only time I tried smoking, he caught me at it. He came home from work early and spotted me sitting on the wall around the corner, holding Cat's cigarette and trying to inhale without coughing.

"All those times you denied it," he said that evening, shaking his head sadly. "I don't like lies, Ashleigh.

Especially from those I love." He never mentioned it again. It crushed me more than if he'd screamed and yelled and grounded me for a month. It's probably why I never bothered smoking again. That and the sore throat I had for a week afterward.

So I decide on some form of the truth. But before I've opened my mouth, Mum squeaks from between tight lips, "Is that it, Gordon?"

"Hmm?" He looks at her, genuinely bemused.

"Is that *it*?" she repeats, growling the words like a pit bull on a bad day. "The Gordon Walker school of discipline. That's it, is it?"

Dad's face has gone slightly pink and seems even thinner than usual. "Give the girl a chance to answer, love," he says calmly, but with a bit more force than you usually get with Dad. Think "poodle," but with attitude.

"It's *obvious* she was out. I heard the *door*, Gordon! You *must* have heard the door."

Dad's pink deepens into mauve.

"The door?" I break in. "When?"

"You tell me, young lady," Mum replies without moving her eyes from Dad.

If there's one thing I can't *stand*, it's when Mum starts calling me "young lady." The only thing that annoys me more is when she uses my full name.

"Yes, Ashleigh, I'm talking to you." She turns to me. Face like a brick wall.

Seriously? This is what we're doing here? The pair of them give each other the silent treatment for days on end, and then, instead of sorting out their marriage problems, Mum decides to turn her anger on me?

Something's starting to bubble inside me, like the beginning of a pan coming to the boil. How many times have they been through this? How many times have I tried to block it all out, left them to fix it, convinced myself it'll get better if I don't say anything? How many things have I told myself I haven't seen, haven't heard, because if I admit I have, it means admitting how awful things really are around here? And while I'm doing all this, *nothing* gets better; it gets worse and worse. And then they turn the whole thing on *me*? Like that's fair?

"Steady, Julia," Dad says, trying to crack a smile. "Even criminals have a right to defend themselves before being hung, drawn, and quartered, you know."

I kind of appreciate Dad for trying to make a joke of it, but it's a bit sad too. His inability to stand up for himself and deal with what's going on is just as annoying as Mum taking out her frustration on me.

The bubbles boil more fiercely.

"What if I *did* go out?" I grumble.

They both turn to look at me.

"I mean, can you honestly blame me for not wanting to be in this house? Do you *know* what it's like living with you two, day in, day out?"

Mum's jaw drops open. Dad blinks at me.

"Let me tell you. It's horrible. When you're not scrapping like wild dogs, the atmosphere around here is cold enough to give us all hypothermia. You're so busy scoring points off each other, neither of you has noticed I *exist* for months. And then, when *do* you notice me? When I'm not bloody *here!*"

"Ash." Dad reaches a hand across the table toward me.

"No, Dad. Forget it. I'm sick of you both. You can't even tell me off without it turning into a sparring match between the pair of you."

Under normal circumstances I'd storm out at this point, but I'm sitting at the far end of the table with Mum and Dad on either side and I think it would take the lightning out of my storm if I had to squeeze past them saying "excuse me" along the way.

So I stay put and fold my arms.

Dad's looking hurt. Why does he always have to be *hurt*? Why can't he just get angry? Mum's glaring at me, then turns to him. "See?" she says.

"What?"

"This is what happens when you don't stand up to her. This is how she talks to us. What do you expect when she knows her father will never tell her off?"

"For God's sake, Julia," Dad says, quiet anger rising in his voice. "I told you I didn't want to bring it up. Why didn't *you* do it if you were so bothered?"

"Why do I always have to be the baddie?"

"I could ask the same thing," he says between his teeth.

"So it's all my fault, is it?" She slams his plate onto hers and takes them over to the sink, throwing them both in so hard I can't believe either will come out in one piece. "What a surprise!" she says without turning around. "Of course, none of this is your fault. You're so bloody perfect, aren't you? Never do anything wrong, I'm sure!"

"See?" I shout, pulling away from the table now that Mum's moved out of the way. "Even when you're supposed to be angry with *me*, you just turn it into an excuse to have another argument with each other. You don't care about anyone except yourselves! You're the most selfish pair of —"

Mum grabs my arm. "Ashleigh, don't you dare speak—"

"No, Mum." I shake her off. "I'm not having it. You're not telling me what to do anymore. And until you stop acting like five-year-olds, I don't want anything to do with either of you. Just get it sorted one way or another, and leave me out of it till then."

This time I do storm off, slamming the kitchen door behind me. And the hall door, and my bedroom door. And then, because there just aren't enough doors between the kitchen and my room, I open my closet door and slam that too.

6

Next morning, it crosses my mind to leave home, but I've done that once before and it wasn't much fun. It was last year. I'd gone into town. It had poured with rain and I was sheltering in a shop doorway, waiting for it to stop. I couldn't even afford a cup of coffee. All I had was two quid for my bus journey, God knows where to, but I knew I'd have to end up going somewhere.

So I was standing there minding my own business — well, feeling totally sorry for myself — when this woman came up to me and started yelling.

"Why don't you go and get a job, you lazy scrounger?"

"I'm a student," I replied, looking at her in amazement, too shocked to get angry.

"Yes, I'll bet. At the University of Life, is that?"

"No, St. Martin's."

"Don't get clever with me, young lady."

I switched off after that. I thought, if I'm going to get lectured by mad old bints who shout at me and call me "young lady," I might as well be at home. At least I can get a cup of coffee there.

So, no, I'm not going to run away.

Walking to school in a daze, I'm suddenly aware

someone is calling my name. I look around and see a load of people stumbling along in the rain, heads down, hoods dripping water in front of their faces, like miserable versions of those Mexican sombreros with little trinkets hanging on strings from the brim. Then I notice Cat, waving like a mad thing. I wait for her to catch up.

"Bloody hell, Ash, I've been yelling at you for the last half a mile," she gasps between wheezes as she gets out her cigarettes.

"Sorry."

"What's up, mate? You look like a zombie."

"Nothing. Just my parents."

"I know what you need," she says as she lights up.

"Let me guess, I need to ditch school and come into town with you."

"Oh, go on, Ash. It's been ages since we've gone out and had a laugh together. We can go to all the clothes shops and—"

"I haven't got any money."

"Who needs money? We'll just go window shopping."

I don't really want to miss school. We've got English this morning. The good thing about shutting myself in my bedroom for most of yesterday evening was that I managed to read a good chunk of *Wuthering Heights*. And, shock horror, it's actually pretty good once you get into it. Not that I'd tell Cat that; I'd never hear the end of it. Teachers and books and lessons are not on Cat's list of favorite things.

We go back a long way, me and Cat. We met when we were both eight. She'd hung a flier; she had a hamster who'd just given birth to seven babies, and I persuaded Mum to let me have one of them. Cat had sold all the rest and she missed them, so I said she could come and visit mine. It all took off from there.

A few years later, I had my first boyfriend, Scott Brown. I was twelve. I'd been going out with him for three weeks and he hadn't kissed me. Finally, we were dancing to the last song at the school dance and I practically *made* him snog me. I was nearly sick. He thought the idea was to stick his tongue as far down my throat as possible. I did actually retch when he did it, but I don't think he noticed because he didn't stop. The next day, Cat confessed she quite fancied Scott, and I told her she could have him. After all, she'd given me her hamster. So that was that. He was hers. About three weeks later, we both agreed I'd gotten the better deal.

I've lost count of the number of scams and deals we've hatched up since then. If it's her idea, it's usually a bit crazy, occasionally dangerous—and always a laugh.

So I agree.

Cat breaks into a grin, and I can feel my mood lift as we head into town.

Half an hour later, we're in Boots, experimenting with anything we can find that has the word "tester" on the side.

"What d'you think?" Cat holds up her wrist and I try to distinguish this latest aroma from the four I've been offered already. Her arm smells like a garden center.

I cough loudly.

"Yeah, maybe not." Cat withdraws her arm and moves on to the makeup.

I sniff a classy-looking bottle and try to find a bit of skin that I haven't already sprayed. I'm like a junkie looking for a virgin piece of arm for the next fix.

"Nice," Cat replies as I shove my wrist in her face.

"Yeah it is, isn't it? Sea Mist." I look at the bottle and nearly faint. "Thirty-eight quid! That's a rip-off! I could *get* to the bloody sea for that."

I put the bottle back reluctantly and join Cat. We find these mini bottles of hair dye testers that you comb into your hair. Cat combs a bit of purple into my bangs; I'm about to pick one up to try on her when I notice her slip one into her pocket.

"Cat!" I whisper in alarm.

She shoots me an angry look. "Keep it down, Ash! D'you want to get the store detectives on me?"

I'm terrified, but kind of excited too. I know Cat sometimes nicks stuff from shops, as she's told me, but I've never seen her do it before.

"Chill out," she says. "Anyway, it's your turn now."

"No way. I'm not going to prison over a crappy tube of hair dye."

"Don't be daft. No one's going to prison. What about that perfume?"

I breathe in the musky smell on my arm and imagine putting it on for a date with Dylan. I am tempted. But scared.

"Go on. It's your moral obligation."

"How d'you make that out?"

"You said yourself it was a rip-off. It's scandalous that they should charge that. They're the thieves." She pauses and lets a slow smile crawl up her face. "Come on, Ash. I dare you!"

She knows I can't resist the challenge of a dare. I wander back to the perfume counter and pretend I can't decide which one I want. I pick up Sea Mist and hold on to it as I look at the others. It's heavy and hot in my hand. I wander around the displays, pretending to look but not seeing anything. My heart is beating so hard it's hurting my chest. Then I casually put my hand in my pocket and carry on walking, both hands in my pockets now. I try to look relaxed, but I feel clumsy and heavy. I know my face is bright red, and the bottle in my pocket is slipping against my wet palm.

I walk around a bit more, telling myself to stay calm and look natural. I think of all the times I've wandered around this shop with no intention of stealing anything, and try to act in the same way. After a few minutes, I can feel my face cooling down. I take one last look around to make sure no one has seen me. Here goes.

I take my hands out of my pockets, hold my breath, and saunter out of the shop. Easy.

• • •

I am euphoric for a moment. Eight seconds, to be precise. That's how long it takes the store detective to catch up with me. When I feel the hand on my shoulder, I think it's Cat and I'm laughing as I turn around.

"Ha, ha. You can't fool—"

"No. You can't fool us either." A dodgy-looking bald geezer in a raincoat is staring down at me. For a second I stare back. My first thought: *Isn't it sad when men try to hide the fact that they're going bald?* He's a comb-the-remaining-three-strands-across-the-shiny-expanse-of-skull-and-no-one-will-notice type.

My second thought: *Oh, shit. I'm in trouble here.*

I don't like the look on his face. I saw him earlier, actually, and thought he was some kind of pervert. He kept looking across at me from behind the mascara stand, and at one point I'd thought he was going to open up his raincoat and give me a flash of the shop's biggest bargain. Then he disappeared and I didn't give him a second thought. Till now.

It slowly dawns on me that he isn't a pervert. Well, he might be in his spare time for all I know, but it's not his day job. His day job is much, much more terrifying for me right now.

He pulls a badge from an inside pocket and waves it at me. "Store detective," he announces.

I smile innocently. "Can I help you?" I ask. Sweet, misunderstood child.

Over his shoulder I notice Cat quickly walking

out of the shop like she doesn't have a care — or a conscience — in the world. *What?* She dragged me into this mess and now she's leaving me to fend for myself? Just wait till I —

"Come on, young lady."

Oh, God, not another one. *I'm not that young,* I want to shout, *and I'm not a bloody lady!* He takes hold of my elbow and starts walking me back into the shop.

Then, just as we're going in, Cat turns up.

"Ash, what's going on?" She looks outraged. *What the hell is she playing at?*

"I've been—"

"Sorry for dragging you away from your shopping, it's just—"

"Excuse me," Three Strands says, interrupting her. "Your friend has been caught shoplifting, and I am escorting her to the manager's office."

"Shoplifting? You've got your facts wrong there, mate." Cat looks appalled. Even *I'm* convinced. "It's all my fault."

I start to panic. Surely she doesn't think he's going to let me off just because she dared me?

"I was calling her from outside the shop. I was positive I saw that guy off *The X Factor* walking down the road. Ash came out to see what was going on, so it's my fault that she walked out of the shop. She'd never steal anything, would you, Ash?"

"Er, no." I try to play along, but I'm not sure what the game is.

"Well, we'll see about that, shall we?" Three Strands

is getting impatient. "Would you mind emptying your pockets, please?"

I don't budge. Now what? Cheers, Cat. He reaches for my jacket and helps himself. When he pulls out the perfume, I gawp at him. "Oh, my God, I don't know how that got there. Honestly," I say as convincingly as I can, innocent confusion plastered onto my bright red face.

"It was my fault. I called her," Cat breaks in. "She didn't have any *intention* of stealing anything, did you?"

And finally, I realize what Cat's up to. We've been doing the Theft Act in our law class and one of the things about stealing is that they've got to prove you "intended to permanently deprive" the shop of it or something. Luckily, it's the one law class Cat has been to this term, although I'm amazed she took it in. Mr. Cartwright would be proud. Somehow I doubt we'll be running to tell him about our field trip, though.

They're both looking at me.

"N-no," I stammer, finally getting into my role. "Of course not. I must have been dreaming, not thinking about what I was doing. I just heard Cat calling me and thought she was in trouble, so I went out to see what was up. That must have been when I *accidentally* put the—"

"All right, all right." Three Strands looks crushed. He doesn't believe us for a second but knows we've come up with something that would wash in a court. "On this occasion, I will not call the police to press charges, but you're both banned from this shop. That means don't come back, all right?"

The compromise hangs in the air between us. I catch Cat's eye and she gives me a quick nod. "OK," I agree.

"And you will, of course, pay for the perfume."

"But I haven't got thirty-eight pounds!" I protest.

Three Strands raises an eyebrow and I quickly shut up. This is the best offer I'm going to get, and I'd better take it or prepare for a bit of finger-painting on a police file.

Cat is getting her purse out. "I'll lend it to you," she offers. Yeah, too right. It's her fault I'm here in the first place.

Three Strands escorts us to the checkout, and we pay for the perfume.

"Can I have it gift-wrapped?" Cat flashes a winning smile at the checkout woman. I hold my breath. The store detective's face has gone kind of purple. One of his strands has fallen out of place and is sticking up in the air. For a moment I feel sorry for him. He's only doing his job, after all. And he has been quite generous to us, all things considered. If Cat has blown it now, I'll never forgive her.

When the checkout woman sees the look on his face, she just shoves the perfume into a plastic bag and gives us a dirty stare as she passes it across the counter.

"Nice doing business with you," Cat calls over her shoulder as we leave the shop.

I don't say anything till we're safely down the road, then I explode. "What the hell did you do that for?"

"What?"

"Ask to have it gift-wrapped. Hadn't you got me into enough trouble already?"

"It's a present," she says.

"What d'you mean it's a—"

Then she holds the perfume out to me. "It's for you. Sorry."

She can always steal the wind out of someone's sails, Cat can. There's a moment of silence as I take the perfume from her.

"Right. Thanks," I say, half of me touched, half still wanting to be angry. But I never can stay angry with Cat. I give her a hug. "I am *never* doing that again, OK? Never. Not even if you triple dare me."

"Fine." Cat shrugs, then mumbles, "Goody-goody."

"And I don't want you doing it either," I add. "You'll end up in prison, and what will I do without you?"

Cat laughs. "You should've seen your face when he tapped you on the shoulder, though. Priceless."

I half-smile, half-grimace. "Never! Just don't. OK?"

"Yeah, yeah, whatever." Cat waves a hand dismissively, then grins and nudges my arm before turning away. "Come on."

I follow her to the park at the end of town and we head for the swings. We push ourselves, higher and higher, daring each other on and on, laughing from the adrenaline, from the relief, and from the rush of air as we watch the world turn upside down and back again with every kick of our legs.

7

"You want to come to my house to plan for next lesson?" Robyn asks as we pack up at the end of English the following week.

I'm keen to get out of the classroom quickly. I gave Miss Murray a dumb excuse about having a stomachache for why I missed the last lesson, and I'm sure she knows I was lying. She's like that. Sees the truth behind your lies. She looks at you so intently it feels as if she can see right into all the little hiding places that no one else is bothered about.

Robyn and I have been paired up for a debate we have to do next lesson. We said we'd research it together. "Sure," I say.

Robyn smiles as if I've just given her my last Rolo. "Cool. I'll see if Mum will make us pizza and milkshakes."

"Whoo," I say with a touch of sarcasm. What are we, twelve? Then I feel bad. I mean, Robyn's OK—a bit keen, a bit well behaved, but she's nice enough. She hasn't done me any harm. Plus she'll probably be really good at the debate and I'll be rubbish. I don't want to muck up our pairing. I smile at her. "Sorry. I mean, that's great. Thank you."

We head out together. Miss Murray's busy shuffling papers around and doesn't look up as we pass. I should be glad I've gotten away without being grilled about last class. Instead, I suddenly feel flat. Is she ignoring me? Is she annoyed with me because I ditched the last lesson? Or am I flattering myself and she doesn't actually think about her students enough to care one way or the other?

Whatever it is, I realize I don't like it. I don't want to be ignored by Miss Murray; I want to be smiled at and praised.

Why I should give a toss either way, I have no idea — but I do.

I smile at Robyn. "Come on. Let's go to your house and get to work. We're gonna win this debate, right?"

Robyn grins back at me as we head out of school together. "Right!"

"The fact is, the death penalty saves lives."

Kirsty Peters pauses to add dramatic effect to her statement. "The threat of paying the ultimate penalty could halt many potential offenders before they commit horrific crimes such as murder and violent rape. Furthermore, it is also the fairest way to offer justice to victims of such crimes. Why should the state pay to keep someone alive, feed them, and entertain them for the rest of their lives, when it is better, fairer, and safer to rid our society of them altogether? As the Bible says, an eye for an eye . . ."

"That's complete bollocks, Kirsty!"

"Ash!"

I look up at Miss Murray.

"Language."

"OK. But how can she say that? Someone commits murder, so the state commits another murder to prove that the first murder is wrong. You can't call that fair. It's bollocks."

"Language!"

"Sorry! But she's wrong."

"Explain why, then. Argue your case. Remember, you are supposed to be honing your communication skills so you can develop an effective argument. This is a debate, not a break-time scrap in the gardener's shed."

How does she know about the gardener's shed? She's only been here five minutes and she already knows the top smoking hole. I'll have to warn Cat.

I take a deep breath. "Right. Thank you, Kirsty," I say super-politely. "Now I'd like to put forward our argument with some actual *facts*."

I pick up my notebook and read from the scrawl copied down the other night with Robyn. We had quite a laugh doing it, actually. Turns out she's good company. And her mum makes amazing pizza!

Robyn gives me an encouraging smile. I clear my throat. "OK, so firstly, there is no evidence at all for the idea that the death penalty acts as a deterrent. Scientific studies have consistently failed to show that executions deter people from crime any more than long prison sentences."

I take a breath and carry on. *"Furthermore,"* I say heavily as I glance at the opposing team, "executing the offender does not undo the damage that has been done. Much better to invest in programs to prevent similar crimes by potential offenders. Oh, and while we're on the subject of spending money, it is, in fact, more expensive to use the death penalty than it is to keep someone in prison for life."

I glance at Robyn. She gives me a quick thumbs-up and mouths "miscarriage of justice" at me. I nod at her and turn back to the others.

"And what about the wrongly convicted?" I carry on. "How would Kirsty and her cronies —"

"Ash!" Miss Murray warns.

"Sorry. How would Kirsty and her esteemed colleagues deal with this? The answer is, they wouldn't. They couldn't. Hundreds of people facing the death penalty have been released in their last days on death row, some only minutes away from execution. What if their lawyers hadn't worked so hard? Innocent people — dead. Is this the kind of society you want? Horrific violence matched by state-run barbarism and murder? The death penalty is a *symptom* of a culture of violence, not a *solution* to it. Vote for sense, vote for dignity, and vote for human rights. Vote against this motion."

Heat creeping around my cheeks and neck, I sit

down while some in the class clap and a few boo. Robyn cheers. My heart is racing.

"All right, all right." Miss Murray waves her arms at us. "We've heard lots of arguments on both sides this afternoon. Now it's time to vote. Those in favor of the motion to bring back the death penalty in the U.K., raise your hands."

I count the hands: six.

"Those against?"

Twelve hands go up, and so does a cheer from the back. Robyn and I slap hands as though we've just won a gold medal at the Olympics.

"Abstentions?" Miss Murray shouts over the noise, and the remaining two put their hands up — Christine and Helen, who sit at the front. They couldn't get off the fence if it was on fire.

Miss Murray looks up and smiles at me on my way out at the end of the class. Robyn's gone on ahead as she's got a guitar lesson.

"You know, we're starting a debating society. You should join us, Ash."

I laugh in her face. I don't mean to be rude, but I can't help it. Me? Join a school club? I don't think so.

Miss Murray frowns. "What's the joke?"

I stop laughing and prepare for a lecture. All my teachers must have said that to me at some time or another: "Would you mind telling us all what you find so funny, Ashleigh?" They know they've got you trapped when they say that. If you say, "nothing," you get a typical sarcastic-teacher put-down: "Well, if it's nothing, I suggest you stop laughing and get on with some work like the rest of the class."

But if you told them what you were really laughing at, they'd have a fit. You can just imagine it, can't you? Like in sociology last week. "Sorry, Mr. Foster, Janet was just telling me how the condom got lost while she was having sex with some lad she met at a club over the weekend, and how they tried to find it by —"

And then you'd get, "That's enough, thank you, we don't need the details. Just get on with your work." You can't win.

So I'm just about to go for the noncommittal old favorite "Dunno" when I glance up at Miss Murray. She has this expression on her face: sort of interested and kind, and looking right into me, her eyes soft and wide open. It's that thing she does that makes you want to tell her the truth. She should have been a lawyer or something, not a teacher.

"Well, I've never, I mean it's not my kind of, I don't . . ." What am I trying to say? What *is* the truth? That I don't think I'm good enough?

Then it's Miss Murray's turn to laugh. I can feel myself blushing. Forget honesty. "I just don't see the point in giving up precious time to go to some boring meeting with a load of pimply boffins," I snap.

As soon as the words are out of my mouth, I wish I could take them back. Why on earth did I go and say something so pathetic? I'm definitely in for a lecture now. I try the nonchalant slouch — hands deep in pockets, mouth stifling a yawn, eyes semiglazed over — and wait for it to come.

Nothing.

In the end I have to look up. She's still looking at me. And smiling. Not laughing. Not out loud anyway, but she must think I'm a right idiot.

"Sorry," I say eventually.

"Don't worry about it. But you should think about it. You'd enjoy it." She starts packing her grade book and pens into her bag. "We could do with someone like you."

I kick my feet against each other and hope she doesn't notice my ears have turned pink.

"Someone loudmouthed and opinionated," she adds with a gentle laugh.

I look up at her and can't help laughing too. She's teasing me, but not in a horrible way. Not like Mrs. Banks. *She* wouldn't know a sense of humor if it slapped her round her coiffured head.

What's the deal with Miss Murray? She isn't like a normal teacher. She's more like . . . I don't know. I *really* don't know. Something I can't place. It's unsettling.

"You are very articulate, Ash. And very persuasive."

I haven't got a clue how to reply. In the end, I manage to mumble "Thanks" and shuffle out of the room.

Cat's waiting for me at the gates.

"Where've you been?"

"Sorry, got held up, talking to Miss Murray."

Cat rolls her eyes.

"About some work," I lie quickly, brushing away a stupid feeling of guilt. "Don't even know what she was on about, really. I didn't take much notice." Why am I trying so hard to play down the fact that I enjoy talking to Miss Murray? For Cat's benefit, or my own?

Cat isn't even listening. Or looking at me.

"Cat?"

"So, how're you doing? How's your mum?" she asks.

"My mum?"

"And . . . and your dad."

I stare at her.

"Just I haven't seen them for ages. I mean, at home, at your house. Not been invited round for a while."

"I know. Sorry. I've been a bit busy with other things." I wink and wait for her to pick up her cue and ask how it's going with Dylan. She doesn't.

"So they're OK, then, your parents?"

I think about the past few weeks: the silences, the sofa bed. I've forced myself to not think about it so much that I've hardly even talked about it with Cat. Just mentioned it in passing. Too nervous to say too much — and too embarrassed. It feels like admitting a failure or something. On the other hand, this is Cat. My best friend. I can tell her anything. To be honest, it might even help to talk about it. "Well, actually, I'm not so sure," I begin. "My dad—"

Cat stops and looks at me. "What about your dad?"

I'm trying to work out how to put my unease into

words when I spot a familiar black Ford at the curb. Dylan! Suddenly thoughts about my parents are gone. "Cat, I can't talk now. I'll ring you later, OK?"

"I thought you were coming back to my house."

I'm about to answer when Dylan gets out of the car. He comes over and puts his arm around me.

"Hi. Fancy a lift?"

"Cat, this is Dylan. Dylan, Cat."

"Hi," Dylan says, smiling at Cat.

Cat looks him up and down. "The wonderful Dylan," she says.

Dylan laughs and pulls me closer.

I give Cat a half-pleading, half-guilty look. "Do you mind?"

She shakes her head. "I'm fine. Go on."

"Can I drop you off anywhere?" Dylan asks Cat.

"I'm all right with the bus. Ta."

I give Cat a hug.

"Call me when you get in, OK?" she says.

"I will."

Dylan opens the door for me and I can't help feeling a twinge of guilt as we drive past Cat, lighting up a cigarette and heading to the bus stop.

We drive down to the canal for a walk. Dylan holds my hand as we amble along, kicking leaves at each other. Dead romantic. Then we get to a bench and sit down to stare into the canal.

It's been ages since I've been down here; it's like a

secret world. It's just getting dark and there's a line of mist above the water. We're the only people around. A bit further down, there's a blue boat tied up, smoke drifting in a straight line from the chimney. It smells of autumn. And it's so quiet. We only parked about ten minutes' walk away, but it feels as though roads don't exist. I squeeze Dylan's hand while I look around, breathing in the stillness of the woody air.

When I turn to smile at him, he lets go of my hand and pulls me close. Then he starts kissing me, hard. He hasn't kissed me like this before. It doesn't feel right. Not here.

"Hey, chill." I pull away from him after a bit, my lips stinging from his teeth.

"There's no one around."

"I know. Doesn't mean I want to be eaten alive."

He smiles, like he thinks I'm teasing, and I suppose maybe I am. "Sorry," he says. "Let's try again."

So we do. He kisses me slowly, and I don't stop him this time. He runs his fingers through my hair, kind of holding my face next to his. A moment later, his hands are moving down my body. For a second, I wonder if I should protest. I don't want him to think I'm easy. But it feels good. When he puts his hand up my sweater, it makes me jump; his hand is icy on my skin. He stops to look at me, a question on his face.

"Just a bit cold," I say with a quick smile, and he kisses me again, pressing me up against him and fiddling with my bra. I shiver when he undoes the clasp.

A second later, I'm aware of something on my

72

ankle. I pull away and look down. A scruffy gray terrier with bracken in its fur is looking up at me and panting. Its owner isn't far behind. A thin woman wearing big headphones over black, straggly hair. She doesn't even look at us as she strides past.

The second she's gone, Dylan leans over to take up where we'd left off, but I push him away. "No. Don't." The moment's passed.

"What's up? You were into it, weren't you?"

"Yeah. It's just, let's take it slow, OK? What's the rush?"

"OK," he says with a smile, but I know he's disappointed.

I reach my hand out and he takes it as we sit quietly, watching a perfect line of ducks waddle past. I laugh and look at Dylan. He smiles weakly and squeezes my hand.

Later, when he drops me off at the end of the street, he starts fiddling with his nails. I know by now that this means trouble.

"What's up?"

"I want to ask you something."

Oh, God, here we go again. "Yeah?"

"It's just that, well, my parents are going away for the weekend . . ."

"Y-e-s?"

"Well, d'you want to, kind of, come round on Friday and, you know . . ." His voice trails off. It's obvious what he's asking, but we've only just gotten together and I'm not sure. I've had a few boyfriends. I've never gone all the way, though. It's just never happened. I don't know if I'm ready to do it with him.

"Can I let you know in a couple of days?"

"Yeah, course."

I give him one last kiss before going in.

"Hello, darling," Mum says, greeting me in the hall, wearing an apron and a smile that doesn't reach her eyes. "Did you have a nice day?"

When did she last express interest in my day? "Yeah, all right."

"Dinner's in half an hour. I've made lasagna for us all. Your dad should be home any minute. I rang work and he's just left."

"Right. I'll just do some homework." I go upstairs. Does this mean that they've made up? Will we be able to get through a meal without angry icicles forming around our plates?

It's at least forty-five minutes before I hear Dad's car roll into the drive. It reminds me of when I was little and they'd gone out. I'd sit on the window ledge and wait for the car to come back. If they were really late, I'd have gone to bed, but I could never sleep till they were home, the headlights fanning out across my ceiling as they turned into the drive. Sometimes I'd still be awake when they tiptoed into my bedroom together to kiss me good night. I'd have to force myself not to grin.

When did they last go out together?

I finish my chapter of *Wuthering Heights* and am about to close my book and head downstairs when I hear voices. Shouting. I close the book and lie back on my bed, looking up at the ceiling.

Ten minutes later, the front door slams. The car leaves again.

I lie on my bed, fuming. Can they not even get from the front door to dinner without arguing?

Eventually, Mum calls me and we eat together in silence. She doesn't pretend to smile anymore. I want to say something, but I don't know what, or how.

After a bit, Mum pushes her plate away.

"You've hardly touched it," I say.

She shrugs. "I'm not hungry."

There's a ball of something in my throat. It's getting in the way of my words. So, instead of trying to speak, I get up and take Mum's plate to the sink. I'm about to go back to my room when I turn and look at her, still sitting there. Upright. Tight.

I go back to her and put my hand on her arm.

She looks up and smiles weakly at me. Puts her hand on mine. "Thanks, love," she says sadly.

I smile back. I haven't really done anything. I don't know how to. I wish I did. I'm sure we used to talk, once. When? What about? How did we do it? It's as if we're on opposite sides of a crack in the earth, and it's growing wider every day.

I can't help wondering what it would be like to have a mum like Cat's, one you could talk to.

Cat! Oh, no—she's going to kill me. Somewhere

between Dylan's invitation and Mum and Dad's marriage breakdown, I forgot to call.

I text her on my way back up to my bedroom: *Soooooo sorry. Are you in now? Will call in a bit.*

She replies. *Cutting Mum's hair. She's got a work thing on Saturday.*

Cat's actually a pretty skilled hairdresser. It was what she wanted to study at school, but Jean thought she should take A-levels instead. Reckoned it would give her a better start in life—which might perhaps have been true if Cat actually paid attention to any of her subjects.

See you at school tomorrow? I text back.

Maybe. Not sure if I'm coming in. If not, I'll come to your place after.

Cool. I'll tell Mum. You can stay for dinner, I send back.

I pick up the book and open it where I'd left off earlier. A few minutes later, I'm thankful to be engrossed in someone else's chaotic life so I can forget about my own.

8

"Have you finished chapter sixteen?" I ask Robyn the next day as we head to the cafeteria.

"Read it last night. God, all that wild passion!"

"I know. I can't imagine ever feeling like that about anyone."

"Miss Murray said that's her favorite bit. I can't wait to discuss it this afternoon. She's brilliant, isn't she?"

I look at her sideways. So it's not just me who thinks she's cool. For a teacher. "Yeah, she's—"

"Excuse me, girls," Luke says, butting in as he joins us in the queue. "Less of the bad language, if you don't mind."

We look at him blankly as he holds his plate out for a helping of undercooked chips. "Books, lessons, 'brilliant' teachers. Isn't this all getting a bit freaky? Are you forgetting where we are? This is school! We're not here to work! There's plenty of that to come when we're too old to party. Which reminds me, are you coming on Friday, Robyn?"

"Coming where?"

"Party. Dylan's house."

"Party?" It's my turn to butt in. "What party?"

"Don't tell me you're not coming!"

What happened to the evening on our own that I've been worrying about? "Of course I'm going! I just didn't realize the whole world had been invited."

"Well, not the whole world. And I wouldn't exactly say 'invited,' as such. But that's what happens when your parents go away, isn't it? Remember your birthday? My house? Time to return the favor."

Before I can think of anything to say, Luke's paid for his lunch, scribbled something on a piece of paper, and shoved it at Robyn: Dylan's address! I don't believe it! Wait. Isn't Luke into Cat?

"See you Friday," he calls over his shoulder, and Robyn blushes. Uh-oh.

"OK, Dylan, I'll try to explain it one more time."

We're sitting in his car, in what seems to have become our spot. For some people that would be a little wooden bench in the middle of a park, surrounded by beautiful old oak trees and pale pink blossoms. For us, it's a knackered old Fiesta with no heating and nasty plastic orange seats, alongside a row of wheelie bins. The bin men dump them at the end of the road on Tuesdays, and you have to go around lifting the tops off them all to find your own. Ours has got "34," with a smiley face painted inside the lid. God knows why. It's no reflection of what anyone ever does in our house.

Dylan looks interested when he hears the word "party" but seems to have completely missed one crucial point.

"Dylan, you're the host!"

"But I don't know anything about—"

"Have you told anyone about your parents going away?"

"Well, I might have kind of mentioned it to the lads after band practice . . ." His voice trails off and he bites a piece of skin off his thumb.

Great. Not only am I freaking out about whatever I may or may not do on Friday, there's now going to be a whole load of people turning up for a party while I may or may not be doing it.

"We'll just tell them we can't let them in," he says.

Great thinking, Dylan. "Yeah, right. Ever heard of King Canute?"

He looks up, puzzled.

"The geezer who tried to stop the tide from coming in."

We're sitting in silence trying to work out what to do next when there's a loud knock on his window. It's bound to be Mrs. Langdale. I slide down in my seat.

"I don't want her to see me," I mouth at Dylan as he winds his window down.

"Huh? But it's—"

"Hi, Ash." Cat's face appears at the window.

I heave myself back up, snagging my top on a hardened cigarette burn on the back of the seat. "Hi, Cat. Sorry, I thought you were . . . I was just . . .

Oh, never mind." I open my door. "Thanks for the lift, Dylan."

"But what are we going to do about—"

"Look, just sort it out, OK? I'll see you Friday." I kiss him on his ear.

"You mean . . ." He smiles and raises his eyebrows.

"I just mean, whatever. See you Friday."

"He's quite cute, I suppose," Cat says as we walk up the road.

"Yeah, he's OK," I reply, holding my smile in. Cat doesn't give compliments very easily, so "quite cute" from her is more like "completely bloody gorgeous" in anyone else's book.

"What d'you want to do this evening?" I ask before she says anything to undercut her near-compliment.

Cat shrugs. "Just hang out. What d'you want to do?"

"Well, actually, I want to ask your advice about something," I say as we get to my front door. "But not a word to anyone, and don't mention it in front of my mum, right?"

Cat stops. "Ash, is it about your dad?" she asks in a whisper.

"My dad?" I stare at her. "Why would it be about my dad?"

"Sorry. I dunno," she answers without looking at me.

"Cat. What? What about my dad?"

She shakes her head. "I . . . Well . . . I thought I saw him the other day. He was . . . he . . ."

80

"He what?"

Cat clears her throat and looks straight at me. "Er, well . . . I just thought he looked troubled."

I think back to the sofa bed. The arguments. The silences. The way all of it is too painful to talk about—too raw to even think about. "Yeah. I guess he is a bit," I say. "But I don't want to talk about it. Not just now. Is that OK?"

Cat nods. "Sure. Whatever."

I smile a thank-you at her and unlock the door.

Mum wanders out of the kitchen as we let ourselves in. Her hair's falling over her face. "Hello, darling," she says to me. She turns a tired smile onto Cat. "Nice to see you, Cat. I'll call you both down when dinner's ready."

"Thanks, Mum. See you in a bit." I drag Cat upstairs.

Cat chucks her jacket over the chair and sits on the edge of my bed with a magazine. I scroll through my playlists, picking out some music while I work out what I want to say. I know I've probably talked about Dylan quite a lot over the past few weeks, and I don't want to drive Cat mad going on about him—but I need her help. This feels like a decision that's too big to make on my own.

I'm being stupid, I suppose. At least half the girls in our year have lost their virginity, some of them ages ago, but I've always done my best to avoid the when-did-you-lose-yours? conversations. They're like the when-did-you-start-your-period? ones from the changing-room gossip a few years earlier. I remember the feeling when I first told Miss Anderson I couldn't go swimming. I didn't explain why and she never asked.

Some of the girls used to go into detail on purpose because they knew it embarrassed her. Not me. I don't know which of us was more awkward about it, actually: me, stammering and blushing and taking about half an hour to get the words out, or her, fidgeting as she laughed nervously, clearly wanting me to go away and not say any more.

But there was a good side to it, too. Pride. Feeling like I was part of a club. I could complain with the others about PMS and about how badly my stomach hurt. I could smirk with the confidence of one who's in the gang when we asked the new girls if they'd met "Henry" yet. And I felt the smug glow of importance as we explained in hushed voices who Henry was: "He comes to visit you once a month, but if you're naughty, he doesn't visit for nine months."

It's always tempting to be part of a gang, but now that I'm teetering on the edge of this exclusive club, I don't know if I want to join — or if I'm prepared to pay the entrance fee.

Is that why I want to do this — to join the club? If I *do* want to. Surely that's a bit of a naff reason. Isn't it meant to be about love or something? Not because you want to be in with your mates.

I know Cat isn't a virgin because she told me. She lost it to this guy she went out with last year. An older dude with a motorbike and about three times as many piercings as her. He was the first boy her mum had ever disapproved of. Jean's hard to offend. Maybe that's why Cat did it. Or maybe it was just that she really, really liked him. She said she did—but she never talked about it all that much. She doesn't, really. It's weird. We're so close she feels almost like a second skin at times, but when it comes to talking about emotions, well, it's just not her thing. "Can't be doing with hearts and flowers," is what she says. Which suits me just fine, right now, when it comes to talking about life at home. But not about this.

I sit down next to her on the bed. "I want to ask you something."

Cat puts the magazine down. "OK. Shoot. What's it all about?"

"Dylan."

Cat groans. "Really? I never would have guessed," she says sarcastically.

I'm not sure if she's joking. There's a kind of edge in her voice. I open my mouth to ask, but she carries on. "I mean, I'm not being funny or anything, but have you noticed that you haven't talked about much else other than Boy Wonder since you got together? 'Dylan's in a band,' 'Dylan kissed me,' 'Dylan hasn't phoned for three minutes.'"

"Ha, ha," I say, trying to smile. "I get it."

But Cat hasn't finished. "'Dylan's broken up with his girlfriend for me,' 'Dylan turned up to see me out of the blue,' 'Dylan's got yellow undies, green socks and—'"

"OK, enough! I said I get it." I jump up from the bed

83

and turn the music off. Why can't she ever be serious about things that matter to me? "Why are you being like this?"

"Oh, come on, Ash, can't you take a bit of gentle teasing?"

Good question. Can't I? Maybe on this occasion I just wanted her to be serious. For once. Is that too much to ask of your best friend? "Since when is insulting me *and* my boyfriend 'gentle teasing'?" I ask.

Cat stares at me. "Since always, mate. That's me. You've known me long enough. You ought to know what I'm like by now."

She's right. I don't know why I'm getting so angry. Maybe because of the atmosphere in this house. Maybe because of all the stuff I'm *not* talking about. Maybe because I've worked myself up so much about Friday. Or maybe because it would just be nice if she could do something other than joke around for once. Either way, she's wound me up and my insides are coiled tight.

"You're right," I say before I can stop myself. "I *should* know you by now. And to be honest with you, I don't even know why I thought I could talk to you in the first place."

Cat pulls herself up from the bed, her voice harsher to match mine. "Well, if that's how you feel, then why the hell did you?"

"Good question. Maybe because I thought you were my *friend*. My *best* friend. Isn't that what best friends are meant to do? Listen to each other, help each other out with problems, basically be there for each other?"

Cat looks at me for a moment, as if she's weighing something up in her mind. "Yeah, well, if you thought about other people half as much as you think about yourself, they might *want* to listen to you. And if you opened your eyes and looked around for two seconds, you might realize you've actually got more important things to worry about than your own relationship!"

We're practically shouting now, and I try to lower my voice. I don't want Mum to hear all this. "I know that! Don't you think I know that?"

"I don't know *what* you know," Cat says. "We don't seem to talk properly anymore. Has it crossed your mind that *you* might be the one who's not been much of a best friend lately? You cancel arrangements, you don't ring when you say you will. All you care about is yourself and your new boyfriend. If you've had enough of me, that's fine because, to be honest, I've had enough of you too!"

The shock of her words instantly deflates my anger and my eyes start to sting. Is it true? Have I been *that* bad? I try to stop her as she grabs her jacket. "Cat, this is ridiculous."

"No, you're the one who's ridiculous. And you're boring. When you're not going on about Dylan, you're staying in reading books or planning lessons with your new friends. To be perfectly honest, I'm bored of you, and I'm bored of your petty problems."

"Cat, it's not petty. I need your advice." I'm openly crying now. "It's Dylan. He wants to sleep with me and I don't know what to do."

We catch each other's eyes in the silence. Cat sucks in her cheeks. "Well, you want to know what I think?"

"What?" I hold my breath.

"I think you should sort out your own problems. Screw him if you want. And screw you too."

Then she grabs the door handle and throws the door open so hard it hits the wall. For a second I think it's going to come off its hinges.

"Cat!" I call across the landing.

"Forget it, Ash. I've had enough."

Mum's in the hall as Cat reaches the bottom of the stairs.

"Thanks for the offer, Mrs. Walker, but I can't stay for dinner after all."

Mum doesn't say anything. She just watches from the hall as Cat calmly opens the front door and leaves.

I run back into my room and look out the window. Surely she's not just going to go like that? We've had loads of arguments over the years, me and Cat. I know she can fly off the handle at times, and I can be just as bad, but we've never argued like this before. It's always been over something stupid, like she's broken my straightener or I won't share my chips with her. But this is different. I can't even work out how it started. Why is she so angry with me?

Salty tears stream into my mouth and I wipe my nose on my sleeve as I watch her walk to the end of the road and around the corner, out of sight. She doesn't even look back.

A couple of minutes later, there's a soft knock on

the door. It's Mum. She doesn't say anything, just sits down on the bed next to me and puts her arms around me. I don't want to talk about it, and she doesn't ask. It's as if she understands me. For once. She holds me in her arms while I cry.

"Do you want to eat, love?" Mum kisses me on my forehead.

I shrug.

"I'll keep it warm for you. You just let me know if you want it, or if you need anything else, all right?"

I nod. Who is this woman? And where has my mum gone?

She leaves the room, closing the door gently behind her, and I spend the rest of the evening lying on my bed staring at the maroon flowers entwined together on my walls. What's happening to my life? Everything seems to be going wrong, and I can't seem to work out how to make it right.

And I still don't know what I'm going to do about Friday.

9

"Brilliant, this, isn't it?" Robyn shouts, beer sploshing out of her glass while she semi-dances, semi-sways over to me. At least someone's having fun. This is the first time I've been in Dylan's house and we've barely exchanged two sentences yet.

"Be with you in a minute," he said, dashing upstairs the second he let us in. "I left Mum and Dad's bedroom door open and I just heard a noise up there. Better check it out."

The next time I saw him, he was dragging some lad with puke all over his T-shirt into an armchair before disappearing again.

I look around the room. It's quite big. The house has two stories with three bedrooms upstairs and one big room on the first floor. There's a fireplace with a mantel above it filled with pictures of Dylan at various stages of childhood, some with his parents (presumably) smiling proudly beside him.

The room is divided by an archway. In the back half, a group of lads are sitting at the table, opening cans of beer and raiding the fridge. I spot Luke and call him over.

"Hey, girls," he says, grinning. "Where's Cat?"

"Oh, hi, Luke, nice to see you too. I'm fine, thank you!" I snap before I can stop myself. I'm not sure why — either it's because I don't like the fact that I have no idea where Cat is, or maybe it's because I'm stressed about what might or might not be happening tonight. "Sorry," I add quickly.

Luke puts an arm around my shoulders. "Come on, mate. It's a party. Let your hair down. Where's your boyfriend anyway?"

"Good question."

This whole evening was supposed to be about Dylan and me, and I've hardly seen him. I shuffle away from Luke before I can snap at him again. I'm probably best just going home. I grab my bag and start to walk away — although half of me is praying that someone will stop me before I get to the door. The evening might be a washout, but I haven't got any better plans.

"You can't go!" A panic-stricken Robyn grabs my arm. "I don't know anyone except you."

"You know Luke."

She blushes again. It's a disaster waiting to happen. Surely everyone knows Luke's only got eyes for Cat? Or maybe not. I catch him looking at Robyn. Maybe she's just what he needs to break the Cat habit.

"Hardly," Robyn says, interrupting my thoughts. "And anyway, I want to hang out with you. *Please.*"

I give in, relieved, and she drags me back for a dance.

Luke joins us on the dance floor: the three-foot-square space between the sofas in the front part of the room. He passes me a can of lager.

Robyn and I are soon doing a girl-band-style dance routine when Dylan sidles up behind me.

"You look gorgeous," he whispers.

"There you are!" I reply as I turn around to kiss him.

He leans forward and whispers in my ear. "Why don't we go upstairs for a bit?"

A lightning streak goes through my body. Fear? Excitement? This is it. We're actually going to do it. Am I ready? Do I want to?

He takes my hand, and I follow him up the stairs.

As we stand in his bedroom in the silence, I can hear grunting noises coming from the room next door. Dylan and I look at each other and laugh. Then he lies down on the bed and straightens the duvet next to him.

I sit down by his side. "Look, I haven't . . ."

"Don't worry." He shuts me up by kissing me, and I start to relax. Before long he's got my top off and is fiddling with my bra. It's undone in a second.

"You've clearly done this before," I say.

He laughs and I feel uncomfortable, exposed. I grab my blouse and hold it up against me.

"Have you?" I ask.

"What?"

"Done it before?"

"Well, yeah, but not with anyone as gorgeous as you." He kisses my shoulder.

"How many?"

"How many times or how many girls?"

This is getting worse. "How many girls?"

Dylan looks down and is quiet for a moment. "Four, OK? No, sorry, five. Five, that's it."

"Five?" I repeat quietly.

"I *am* two years older than you. Look, I really like you. I don't just do it with anyone. I've got to really fancy them. And I fancy you like mad."

I don't reply and he moves away. "We don't have to do this if you don't want to," he says. "I'm not in the habit of forcing myself on girls."

"I do want to," I say. At least I think I do. No, I'm sure. I move closer to him.

Dylan smiles. "Good. So do I," he says softly and leans over me. He kisses me really gently and slowly strokes my body. I feel myself relaxing again.

We've soon got our clothes off, and I don't look at him; I'm too embarrassed about my nakedness. And, yeah, OK, a bit nervous about what's about to happen—but I don't want him to see that. So instead, I pull him closer and kiss him a bit harder.

After a while, he moves away a little and looks at me. I know what he's asking, and I give him a quick nod.

Slowly, he pulls himself up and gets on top of me. Within moments, he's inside me. It feels good. At first. Then he pushes himself further into me and it hurts a little. He stops for a second and looks up. "You OK?"

I nod again. Then I shut my eyes and reach out to kiss him and we carry on. It's definitely hurting now. Not so much that I want him to stop. Not just yet. For a second, I think of that stupid quiz program that Dad loves — *Mastermind* — and that thing the guy says, "I've started so I'll finish." I kind of feel like that, and the thought nearly makes me laugh.

Dylan doesn't notice. He's holding himself up on one hand and has the other one on my shoulder. It looks as though he's doing press-ups. I glance at his face. He isn't looking at me; he seems in a world of his own now. He's got his head stretched up and his eyes closed, straining and grunting and pushing harder and faster all the time. My legs are starting to hurt from being so wide apart, and I'm beginning to feel sore inside. OK, I think I'm done now. I hope he'll finish soon.

A couple of minutes later he suddenly jerks and lets out a loud groan, then flops back down on top of me. He's heavy on my body. I wriggle a bit and he moves himself over to lie beside me.

"You were brilliant," he murmurs and kisses me on the cheek. What does he mean? I haven't done much. Just been there. I don't answer, and when I next look over, his eyes are closed.

A few minutes later he opens his eyes and grins at me.

I smile back a bit woodenly. Then a thought bursts into my head.

"No!" I'm upright.

"What? What is it?" Dylan sits up too.

"Condoms! We didn't use a condom."

"Aren't you on the pill?"

"Of course I'm not on the pill! I've never done it

before! Why would I be on the pill?" *How could we have been so stupid?* "What if I'm pregnant now?" I ask, my voice coming out in a squeak.

He touches my arm. "I'm sure you're not pregnant."

I pull my arm away. "What makes you so sure?" I snap. I know I'm being unreasonable but I can't help myself.

"I don't know. I just—"

"What about AIDS?" I say quietly. "Or chlamydia or something?"

He laughs. "I haven't got AIDS! Or chlamydia."

"You think it's funny, do you?"

"Ash, I didn't . . ." His voice trails away. "I'm sorry. What d'you want me to say?"

"I don't know. Nothing."

We sit in silence for a bit. Our clothes lie on the floor, twisted and inside out. My stomach twists with them. I don't know what to say to him. I want him to hold me, but I'm not going to ask. And he's not likely to want to now.

As the darkness of the room closes silently around me, I can hear the music downstairs; it feels like another world.

Dylan reaches out to touch my arm. "Do you want to get up?" he asks.

I don't answer.

"Come on, Ash, don't be like that. Please. You're making me feel awful." He leans over to kiss me and I turn my face away. "What have I done?"

I shake my head. What *has* he done? What has he

taken away from me? What have I given him? I don't want to be horrible—I just can't look at him.

"Look, d'you want some time on your own?" he asks gently.

I nod. *Of course I don't.*

"OK, if you're sure . . ." He gets out of bed and starts putting on his clothes. "See you in a bit?" he asks from the doorway.

"I'll be down soon," I reply, and he closes the door behind him.

As the darkness continues to build around me, emptying me, I keep telling myself I'm not going to cry. After a while, I get dressed and go to find the bathroom. Staring at myself in the mirror, I wash my face. What I've done—does it show?

Dylan is at the bottom of the stairs when I come down; he puts his arms around me straightaway.

"I'm sorry," I say.

"No, *I'm* sorry. Are you OK?"

I nod and let him hold me for a bit. Then he takes my hand and we go back to join the party.

Robyn spots me and drags me away. "I've just been snogging Luke on the dance floor!" she says excitedly. "Where've you been?"

"I've been with Dylan. So where's Luke now?"

"Over there, talking to Cat." Cat! Oh, no. Robyn is *so* going to get hurt. Why does it feel like my fault?

"Gimme a sec," I say.

I walk over to Cat and Luke. I haven't seen her or heard from her since our argument. "Cat?" I say nervously.

She looks at me briefly, then deliberately turns her back and carries on talking to Luke. It feels like an actual slap across my face.

"Fine!" I say and swing away from her, almost bumping into Robyn, who'd followed me over. I'm suddenly tired—of all of it. "I'm going home," I say to Robyn. As soon as the words are out, I realize how much I mean them. I desperately want to be tucked up, safe and warm, in my bed.

I leave Robyn and go to find Dylan. He's getting a beer out of the fridge.

"I've got to go," I tell him.

"Babe, really? Is it something I've done?" he asks. "You did want to—you know—didn't you? Please tell me you did."

"I did, honestly. It's fine, you've done nothing wrong." I force myself to smile. "It's me. I'm just tired and I need to go home."

"Really?"

"I'll see you soon, OK? Ring me tomorrow?"

"You sure you have to go?"

"Yeah, I'm knackered." We both laugh at this, and his face relaxes, relieved.

He comes to the door. "Speak to you tomorrow, then," he says, leaning over to give me a kiss. I start to walk away.

At the gate, I turn and look back at the house. Dylan's

inside, laughing with Luke. Is Dylan telling him what we did? No. He wouldn't. He's not like that.

I glance at the upstairs windows. The bedrooms are dark, the curtains drawn on the evening's brief secrets.

Dad is still up when I get in. "Your mum's in bed," he tells me.

"OK."

He turns to go into the living room but stops at the door. "Do you want a hot chocolate, love?"

My eyes fill with tears. He used to make me hot chocolate every night when I was little. I realize, yes, that is exactly what I want. "That'd be lovely, Dad, thanks."

He smiles. "I'll bring it up to you."

As I sit in bed in my pajamas, drinking hot chocolate, I look around my room. I gaze at the flowery wallpaper where, if you stare hard enough, it isn't flowers at all, but people and animals. There's an old witch-type woman's face and a monkey that turns into an elephant if you look at it from a different angle.

Then there's the familiar maroon carpet. It used to be shaggy, but it's worn almost bald in places now, with felt-tip stains in the corner from years ago that I've never managed to get rid of and a faded bit just by the bed where I was sick as a kid. Mum cleaned it up with bleach and accidentally dyed the carpet white. I was ill for a week. Mum and Dad took turns taking time off work to sit with me doing jigsaws and letting me tell them dreadful jokes. They always laughed, too. I can hardly imagine them laughing at anything now.

My bedroom. A collage of my life. It's so . . . safe.

Finishing off my hot chocolate, I switch the light out and turn to the wall. Almost without realizing it, I start to cry. Gently at first, the tears rolling from the corners of my eyes and falling across the bridge of my nose onto the pillow. I hold my stomach, bury my face in the quilt, and sob until I fall asleep.

10

I'm sitting on the side of my bed, half dressed and half asleep, when Mum appears at the door.

"Sweetheart, are you going to come down for breakfast?"

"I'm not hungry," I reply as I reach down to put my socks on.

I've pretty much lost my appetite this week, what with Mum and Dad, Cat and I still not speaking . . . and Dylan.

It's Tuesday and I haven't spoken to him since the party. He texted on Sunday, asking if I was OK and when he could see me again. I texted back that I had loads of homework and I'd let him know. He's tried to call, but I haven't answered my phone. I don't want to talk to him yet. He'll ask if I'm OK, and to be honest, I'm not sure I am. It's not just him — what we did — it's everything. If he asks me what's wrong, I might be in danger of spilling everything out, and then I'd be lost.

Better just to add him to the list of things I'm blocking out — even if it means I'm building so many walls around me I'm starting to feel stuck in a well.

Mum clears her throat.

I look up. "What, Mum?"

"It's just, your father and I — well, we'd like it if you would join us."

My stomach turns over. Her face is white. What the hell is going on? Half of me wants to know; the other half wants to run a mile with my hands over my ears. "OK, I'll be down in a minute," I say.

Mum's made semi-scrambled omelets, which we eat together in silence.

After about ten minutes of chewing and rustling and forks scraping on plates, I'm starting to relax. Maybe there's nothing going on; they just wanted my company.

Then Mum puts her knife and fork together, wipes her mouth, and looks like she's about to make a speech. Dad carries on eating, oblivious as usual, till she gives a little cough. He looks up, shovels one last bite into his mouth, and then takes his cue from her and pushes his plate away.

For a moment, I feel like I used to when I'd been talking during assembly and the headmaster's halfway through the notices and suddenly stops speaking. You daren't look up because you've been messing about and you know he's going to be looking right at you. Finally you chance it, and sometimes he is and sometimes he isn't. He never says anything, but you know he's clocked what you were doing and will remember. Those silent seconds of him staring at you are far more scary than

99

if he'd just shouted at you in front of the whole school. It's the uncertainty.

Mum gets up and takes the plates away.

"Thanks for breakfast, Mum." Is there still time to get away before anything awful happens? I start to leave the table.

"No." Mum whirls around at the sink, dropping a fork on the floor. She looks at Dad. "Oh, for God's sake, Gordon," she says, wearily running a hand through her hair. "I'm not doing this one on my own."

Dad holds his hand out to grab my arm. "Ashleigh, hang on a sec, love. We need to talk to you."

I sit back down. It's his voice that stops me more than anything. It sounds so grave. For a moment, I think perhaps someone has died.

Mum comes back to the table and sits with her head in her hands. Dad looks down at the table. I sit stock-still, barely breathing. An onlooker might have thought we were saying grace, except Mum doesn't look thankful for anything. I can't see her face, but her shoulders are shaking slightly.

"Mum?" Is she laughing? Surely not. An emptiness grabs at my stomach.

"Dad?"

He draws a sharp breath, looks out the window. When Mum eventually lifts her head up, her face is streaked with mascara. A skunk gone wrong.

I can't ignore this any longer. I can't block it out or pretend it's not really happening. This is real. Way too real.

"Mum? What's this about?" I ask through an empty throat, a tiny part of me still hoping I've got it all wrong. Maybe everything's OK with them. Maybe it's me — they know about the party, about Dylan. Or the shoplifting! Suddenly, all of those options feel better than the one I know inside is the real one. "Have I done something wrong?"

Mum's eyes fill again, shining blurrily at me. She shakes her head.

"It's us, love, it's not you," Dad says. "We don't want . . . we're not . . ." He looks at me, holds my eyes for a moment before speaking to the table. "We're getting a divorce."

And that's it. Four words, and the walls I've spent all these weeks building up tumble down so quickly it's as if they were never there.

Everything is quiet. Mum closes her mouth and looks as though she's holding her breath. Dad's eyes stay fixed on the table. There's no movement. I feel as if someone has clamped two massive hands over my ears and two more over my eyes, and my mind goes blank.

When I was about five, we went to the coast for a holiday. One evening, I went down to the beach with Dad. It was totally dark. No streetlights, no cars or roads or houses or anything. Only this great expanse of beach, and the black sky, and, in the distance, the sea. I remember standing there, holding my dad's hand and feeling very small and alone. If you listened carefully, all you could hear was the sea, rumbling in the distance. Nothing else. Just nature. Huge, bleak, dark, almost silent. It was like the beginning of the world. Or the end.

I can remember the sensation so clearly. First the silence, and the blackness, then gradually this slow rumbling in the distance. Something unfamiliar coming closer and closer. Scaring me.

I hadn't thought about that for years — till now.

I realize they're waiting for me to speak. What can I say? That I'm surprised? That would be a lie. Devastated? That would be too true. Should I beg them not to do it? Would it make any difference?

"Are you sure?" I hear myself ask in a shaky voice.

Mum makes a kind of choking sound and nods her head.

"I'm sorry, love," Dad says gently.

"Is there anything I can say that would make a difference?"

"We've tried everything," Dad says. "It's just not working. It's over."

My parents aren't working. My family is over. I can't make my brain compute the words, even though I think I should be able to. I mean, it's not as if this is the biggest surprise in the world. Life in this house has been pretty awful for a long time. But it's only now that

I realize there's a massive difference between endless arguments and actual divorce.

"When?" I ask. "I mean, are you doing it straightaway, having a trial separation, or what?"

Mum looks up. Fresh tears are streaking down her face. She wipes them away with her hand, smudging the mascara away so it crisscrosses around her cheek. A clown in a storm.

"Your father's moving out in a few weeks. Just as soon as he can get organized," she says, suddenly not sounding like my mum, but like—I don't know—just another person whose fight isn't with me.

"A few *weeks*? Dad?"

Dad lifts his head slightly. Still not enough to meet my eyes. He gives a small nod. "We can't do it anymore," Dad says. "Neither of us can do it anymore."

Mum bites her knuckles as a choking noise escapes.

"Where will you go?" I ask Dad.

"I'll stay in a studio apartment for a bit, till we get things sorted out."

"A *studio*?"

"Just for a little while."

I look at Mum. "This is definite?"

She shrugs, and then, almost imperceptibly, nods.

I turn to Dad. He looks beaten and worn out. "I think so," he adds.

I stare at them both. What have they done to each other? They're broken. I can see it. And yes, OK, a tiny bit of me knows they're probably doing the right thing—but there's a selfish part of me too, wondering if they've thought about me in all this. I know it's unfair, so I don't say anything, but I feel as if they're ripping up an agreement they had with each other and tearing me down the middle.

"I don't want you to get divorced," I say eventually.

Dad gets out of his chair and sits down next to me. He puts his arm around me as I sit stiff in my seat. "I know, love, I know. Neither of us wants it either, but we're out of options." He strokes my hair. Mum moves back to the sink.

When did my dad last touch me? It feels alien. I remember when he used to pick me up from Brownies. He'd wheel my bike while I walked along the walls on our street, holding his hand all the way. Then I'd jump down into his arms for a bear hug when we reached our house. Those hugs. Those safe arms.

"When will I see you?" I ask.

"That's up to you. I'll be there whenever you want me."

"Weekends and stuff?"

"Weekends, school holidays, whatever."

I nearly laugh. I'm only going to have two more school holidays—Christmas and Easter. Then what? University? Unlikely, given last summer's results. Work? What will I do, stack shelves in the grocery store for the rest of my life? My future suddenly has question marks everywhere. A panicky feeling is thudding in my chest and I need to get away.

I pull away from Dad and try to smile at him. "I need

to get to school." I leave the table and touch Mum's arm. "I'll see you later," I say.

In the doorway, I stop and turn back to them. Summoning up every bit of strength I've got, I force the tears out of my ears and out of my throat. "I still love you both," I say. "Whatever happens."

And then I get my stuff and leave the house.

I glance through the window as I close the gate. Dad's still sitting at the table, staring at nothing. Mum's washing up, her head down, hair fallen forward, almost in the sink.

I feel like an orphan.

I blow on my hands as I walk through the bitter streets. It doesn't help much, so I shove them in my pockets where I find an old cough drop that's unwrapped itself and oozed its smooth, liquid center into the lining of my coat. My pocket is now stuck together with semi-hardened, honey-flavored gunk. Perfect.

My mind is as cold as my hands when I get off the bus. Robyn's waiting at the bus stop, and we walk to school together in silence.

"You OK?" she asks after a bit.

"Uh-huh."

She looks at me with concern. I don't want concern; I want distraction. "Is it Dylan?"

"Is what Dylan?"

"It. You know. You look like death cooled down. Has something happened?"

"It's not Dylan."

"What, then?"

"Look, it's nothing, OK?" I snap. Cat wouldn't have badgered me like this. She'd have teased me or taken my mind off it with some mad plan.

We still haven't spoken.

I don't want to fall out with Robyn too. "I'm sorry." I force a smile. I need to change the subject. "Have you heard from Luke yet?"

"Oh, God." Robyn goes bright red. "I don't know what I was doing kissing him on Friday. I hardly know the guy!"

I think about Dylan and me and what *we* did on Friday. My own face starts to burn.

"I think he fancies Cat. I thought you and her were mates anyway," Robyn says.

"Yeah, correct. Were."

"Oh, sorry. Is that what's wrong?"

"Look, nothing's wrong, OK? Just leave it."

Robyn looks like I've stamped on her toe. She was only trying to be nice. "Look, I'm sorry. Really." I stop walking and turn to face her. "I'm having a bit of a hard time at the moment, and I wouldn't know where to start, or stop. I just want to try and forget about it for now. Is that OK?"

"Sure," she says with a smile. "But if you change your mind, then I'm here, right?"

"Right, deal." I feel ridiculously grateful. So much so that I almost think I could tell her everything on the spot and probably cry my eyes out the whole time. I suddenly realize Robyn's becoming the nearest thing I've got to a best friend.

Eventually, I smile back as much as I can with a numb face and mumble, "Thanks."

At the end of English, Robyn's waiting for me to get my stuff together. "I'll catch up with you," I say, taking my time.

Miss Murray's filling in the register at her desk and hasn't noticed I'm still there. I cough gently. She looks up and smiles straightaway. There's something about the way she smiles. It's not like my mum's big red secretary smile or Cat's scheming grin. It's like standing in a patch of sunlight. She does it every time, and right now my life is so dark, I need some of that sunshine.

I've been thinking about it during the lesson. How these lessons are the only place where I really feel I can let go of everything. I need more of that, so I've made a decision. I grimace at her. "I've been thinking about that group."

"The debating group?"

"Mmm."

Miss Murray puts her pen down. "And?"

"Well, I thought I might try it out. I could do with some distraction at the moment." I feel my voice crack as I speak. Oh, no. I can't start crying in front of Miss Murray.

"Is everything all right?" She runs a hand through her hair and focuses hard on my face. My eyes start to sting under her gaze.

"Yeah, fine." I look down. "I just, you know . . ." For a second, I want to tell her how awful everything is. I want to cry, and I want her to tell me it'll all be OK. She's the one who can *make* it OK.

Then I pull myself together and clear my throat. "I just thought I'd like to get involved. At least, I think I do. I mean, it's not all geeks, is it?"

Miss Murray laughs. "Yeah. You'll hate it."

I make a face.

"No, it isn't, but if you're worried, why don't you get someone else to join with you? Robyn, maybe? You made a good team in the death penalty debate."

I think for a second. She's right. Joining with Robyn is actually a really good idea. Robyn would love it. And, yeah, we *were* a pretty good team.

"OK, I'll do it," I say.

Miss Murray smiles again. "Well, that's great. We start next term. I'll give you more details when I've got them. You know the math teacher, Mr. Philips? He's running it with me."

"Great." I grin. Jesus. What are things coming to when a *teacher* is the only person who can make me smile?

"You're looking better," Robyn says as I catch up with her down the main drive. I tell her what I've just been talking about with Miss Murray.

"That's so cool!" Robyn enthuses.

"Really?" A debating club is *cool*? I try hard not to

think about the kind of words Cat might use to describe the idea. I'm not sure how many of them would be polite, but I know that "cool" would *definitely* not be one of them. Before Robyn can rethink her opinion, I carry on. "So Miss Murray asked if you might want to join too."

Robyn tilts her head to the side as she thinks. "Are you definitely joining?" she asks.

"I will if you will," I tell her.

She grins. "OK," she says. "You're on."

"That's great!" I'm about to say more when I spot Dylan, and his unexpected appearance snatches my words away.

He's waiting for me outside the gates, leaning against his car and fiddling with his phone. He hasn't noticed me, and a shot of nerves jams my throat. For a moment I feel like turning back and waiting till he's gone.

Then Robyn says, "Hey, there's Dylan," and he looks up. He grins, but it's different. Like when you smile for a camera because it's expected, as opposed to when you just can't help yourself and your whole face gives off a feeling of pleasure.

I smile back. *Say cheese.*

"See you tomorrow, then." Robyn takes this as her cue to exit, making me panic for a second. I don't want her to go. I'm suddenly nervous about being alone with Dylan; I don't know what to say to him. *Jesus, Ash, get it together. This boy was on top of your naked body last weekend. He's not exactly a stranger.*

"Yeah, see you," I say, trying to stay calm.

Dylan puts his arm around me, and I try to relax. He doesn't ask why I haven't answered his calls, and I don't offer any explanation. It feels like a barrier. So does the sex, the party, and what's happened with my parents. I suddenly realize we don't have anything to talk about.

"Good day at school?" he asks.

"Yeah, not bad."

"So what you been up to?"

How the hell am I supposed to answer that? *Oh, the usual, you know. Dad's leaving home, Mum's a wreck, and I've turned into a geek. How about you?*

I wish we could get back to how it was. I think I do anyway.

"Not a lot. What about you?" I say eventually.

"Same."

We *really* don't have anything to say to each other. I try to remember what we spent all our time talking about before. Before.

But I can't.

"You want a lift home?" he asks. "Or to maybe go for a walk or something?"

I pause for a moment. "I'd better get home, if that's OK?" It's weird. The thought of being at home is about the most painful thing I can imagine right now — apart from the thought of *not* being there.

"Want to go see a movie this evening?" Dylan asks casually as he drops me at the end of the street. Actually, the thought of getting engrossed in someone else's story is probably the best idea I've heard in days.

"Definitely!" I reply, and we smile genuinely at each other for the first time since the party.

And at least we don't have to talk at the cinema.

The first thing I notice when we get to the cinema is the fact that Dylan hasn't even tried to find out what's up with me. Is he totally oblivious to the change, or am I doing him a disservice and he just doesn't know how to go about asking? Maybe he thinks I'm not interested anymore.

Maybe I'm not.

The second thing I notice is Cat. Hanging on to Luke's arm. What the hell's that about? Cat can't stand Luke. She's been telling me that for years.

Half of me wants to run over and get the gossip, but of course I don't. She looks over in our direction, deliberately makes no eye contact, then whispers something in Luke's ear and they both laugh. She's gone and turned him against me too? After everything I've done for him.

Then Dylan spots them.

"Hey, look," he says, getting all excited. "Why don't we hook up with them, make it a foursome?"

"Actually, I'm kind of feeling a bit rubbish tonight. I don't know if I want to see a film after all."

He looks confused for a moment, and then his face brightens up. "You want to go back to my house, just watch telly . . . or something?" He puts his arm around me. "My parents won't be in till late."

"Yeah, fine." I don't know if his "or something" is

what I want either. What I do know is that I want to get out of there.

When we get in the car, he pulls me close to kiss me. It's the first real kiss we've had since the party.

"What's that for?" I smile uncertainly.

"Who says it's for anything?"

"Well, it must be for something. You've not done that for ages."

He pulls away. I shouldn't have said anything. "Yeah, well. I didn't know if you wanted to."

"It was nice."

"Come on." He starts the car. "Let's get back to my place."

Half an hour later, we're at his house, snogging on the sofa. *Corrie* is on the telly, and two barely touched cans of Stella are on the floor. Dylan is fiddling behind my back to get hold of my bra strap.

"Dylan . . ."

He carries on. A second later, it's undone. He groans as he moves his hand around from my back, but I pull myself away from him. "Stop. Wait."

He looks puzzled. "What's up?"

What *is* up? My first thought is to say I don't want to do it without a condom. My second thought is that I don't want to do it, full stop. I can't switch off from the unwanted pictures in my mind: Dad in some poky studio, Mum alone at home, leaning over the sink, holding on to it as though she'd crumple without it.

"Look, I'm not really in the mood," I begin. I've decided I'm going to tell him everything. I need to get it off my chest. Maybe I'll feel better about us if I do. Maybe things could feel more like they did a couple of weeks ago.

But he's moving away from me. "It's OK," he says. He sounds beaten. "I get it. D'you want me to take you home?"

"What? Why are you asking that?"

"Listen, I'm not the kind of guy who forces himself on girls who don't want it. I don't need to do that, you know." There's a hard edge in his voice. I haven't heard that before. To be honest, I don't blame him.

"I know you don't need to." My own voice has tightened.

"So, shall I take you home?"

What's the point in trying to explain? I'm tired. I haven't got the energy for this. I stand up. "Yeah," I say. "Maybe you'd better."

We drive home in silence.

I go through the next couple of days in a zombie-like state. I hardly even know what's going on around me. I'm shut off from all of it.

Friday morning, I skulk into English class. Miss Murray's frowning as I close the door behind me. We've each got ten-minute appointments to talk through a test she gave us last week. I know I've failed.

"Sit down, Ash."

113

I feel like turning around and walking straight out. I can't handle getting a major lecture on top of everything else, especially not from her. "Look, I know it wasn't very good. It's just—"

"Ash, what you've written is fine."

"Huh?"

"It's great. The Paper One question wasn't so strong; you need to refer to the texts a bit more. I suspect you didn't review last year's books terribly well."

I look at my feet.

"But the Paper Two section." She waves the paper at me. "Ash, it's excellent. You showed a very thorough grasp of *Wuthering Heights,* and you analyzed the poem brilliantly."

I stare at her. "You have got the right person, haven't you?"

She looks at the top of the page. "Well, as long as you're actually Ashleigh Walker and not an imposter."

"I wish I was. Wouldn't mind swapping my life for someone else's at the moment." I bite my lip the moment the words are out. Why did I say that?

Thing is, she makes me want to talk to her. Tell her everything. It's the way she looks at me, as if she's really listening, as if she cares about what I've got to say, her green eyes staring into mine as she folds a strand of hair behind her ear. It's as if she can see right inside my head. I can't remember anyone else ever looking at me like that.

"Do you want to talk about it, Ash?"

Yes, yes, I want to sit and talk with you all day.

114

I'm shocked at what I've just thought. Is that really what I want? I blush, as if I've accidentally said it out loud. "Nah. It's nothing," I reply quickly. "I was just messing about. I'm fine." All those years with Cat have left their mark. I am officially an expert at skirting around anything that might resemble a genuine feeling.

"Well, if you change your mind . . ."

"Yeah. Thanks."

"As long as you're sure. About your work, then. I've been looking back in the files and have noticed that your marks really don't seem to reflect your ability."

So it was just a well-disguised lecture after all.

"And I think you should come to the extra classes I'm running on Wednesdays."

"Extra classes!" I snort. "It already takes all my effort to get to the ones I've got."

"Yes, I'd wondered if there was a bit of an attendance problem."

Here we go.

"But that's not what this is about," she goes on. "My job is to get you through your A-levels, and, as far as English is concerned, you can do very well, but you've got a lot of catching up to do. You'll need to work pretty hard to get a good average after your grades last year. Look, just think about it."

What's she up to? Has Mr. Kenworthy left some notes behind suggesting she wind me up to get me back for everything I did to him? Extra work? I've only ever done that as a punishment. Detentions for bad behavior.

"I don't really think —"

"Anyone can change, you know," Miss Murray says, breaking in. "And it's nothing to be ashamed of if you want to pass your A-levels." She pauses. "How are you getting on with your applications?"

I look at her blankly.

"University applications."

I look away from her. "Not bothering."

"Ash, you must!" she says as though it really matters to her. "The deadline is this week. Just fill it in. Keep your options open."

"I don't even know what I'd study."

Miss Murray hands me my test and pauses while I look at the figure at the top: I didn't fail! In fact, I did rather well. Then she says, "I wouldn't have any doubts if I were you."

I stare at the test, then up at her. Her eyes seem to be telling me she knows something I don't. Directing me somewhere. It's like someone has come along while I was scrabbling about in a dark house trying to find my way around and shown me a door I hadn't seen. There's a chink of light underneath, and I want to know what's there. Anything's worth a try right now, even if it means turning into a complete nerd. And at least Cat isn't around to tease me about it.

"OK, I'll do it today," I hear myself saying.

Would *anything* she suggested sound like a good idea?

PART
2

11

It's the luggage that does it. Three big suitcases, a couple of bags, a few odds and ends. I don't know what I'd imagined, but it wasn't this. If anything, I suppose I'd pictured him going off with a duffel bag, maybe staying away a few days, then coming back saying they'd made a big mistake and were going to stick together after all.

If you looked around the rooms, you wouldn't think there was anything missing. But it's like one of those spot-the-difference cartoons in a puzzle book. The changes are so subtle, yet glaringly obvious once you've seen them. A photo missing here, a cup there. A heart a bit more broken than it was before.

From behind my bedroom door, I can hear Dad moving around the house.

I'm not going to watch him carry all his belongings away in bags and boxes.

I keep picking things up and putting them down, attempting to do my homework then realizing I've been staring at the same line for ten minutes and not taken in a word. I try tidying things away but find myself sitting on the floor, holding a sock and not knowing what I'm doing with it.

Then there's a knock on my door.

I stand in the middle of my room, biting my knuckles.

"Ash, love, it's Dad."

I can't answer. My throat hurts.

"Can I come in?" He waits a moment and then comes in anyway, sits on the bed. He holds his hand out to me, but lets it drop to his lap when I don't take it.

"Why don't you come and see me next Saturday?" he asks. "We'll do something nice together."

When's the last time we did anything nice together? Does he remember the happy times, like I do? Does he realize how long ago they were?

It'd be easier if I were a kid. Then he could pick me up on Saturdays and take me to the zoo and buy me an ice cream, spoil me rotten then drop me off at home for Mum to pick up the pieces. It's hard to imagine what we might do now. Sit and watch *Match of the Day* together? Read the weekend papers? Talk about . . . what? What *do* we talk about?

"Yeah, that'd be nice," I say.

"I'll ring you up about it, then. And see you next weekend."

"Yeah."

"Will you be OK?"

I nod. He stands up and kicks one foot against the other. Funny, I do that too. I suddenly—belatedly?—wonder how much we have in common.

"Look, I'd better, you know . . . I'll ring you."

I can't look up, and I don't trust myself to speak. If I stop and think about it, I still don't really understand why he's leaving, why they couldn't try again. Best not to stop and think about it.

"Are you going to give your old dad a hug, then?"

I lean into him and he holds me tight for a minute, kisses me gently on the forehead before shuffling over to the door. "It'll be all right, love."

I fold my arms tight around myself and nod.

Then he's gone.

I'm sitting on the window ledge where I used to wait for his car to come home, and now his car's crammed full of enough belongings to take him away from us.

He and Mum are talking in the hall, but I can't hear what they're saying. I don't want to.

Then Dad walks down the drive. He glances up at my window to wave. I instinctively jump back. I'm *not* going to wave him off. I'm not going to do that.

I watch the car drive to the end of the road, flash a turn signal, round the corner.

Gone. That's it. My dad's gone.

I stand in the window for a long time, watching while nothing happens in the street.

After a while, I can hear a muffled noise coming from downstairs.

Mum doesn't even notice me enter the kitchen. She's sitting at the table, head in her arms, body hunched and jolting with each sob as though she's retching.

Something inside me unblocks. I kneel down on the floor beside her and she stops for a moment, looks at me, her face contorted with grief. Without thinking, I slide my arms around her waist. Immediately, she wraps her arms around my head and we hold each other, rocking and sobbing, almost afraid to let go in case the other one is next to leave.

We sit like that for a long time as the house grows darker.

Monday morning, Mum's leaving for work as I come downstairs. Neither of us knows what to say, so we don't say anything. She looks awful. She hasn't bothered putting any makeup on, and her face is pale and thin. For the first time, I notice lines cutting down the edges of her cheeks.

As I eat breakfast on my own, I miss Dad's slurping and chewing.

"Don't be late for school!" Mum calls from the door, and for once I smile at the words. At the constancy of them.

And then my phone beeps.

It's a text from Dylan. The first contact we've had since last week. *Sorry not been in touch. Not sure how you feel. Thought you might text, but you haven't!!! Do you still want to go out with me???? x*

How am I meant to answer that? How can he just spring a question like that on me in a text? I can't deal with this right now. My dad's just walked out on us. Doesn't Dylan realize that's more important to me?

Well, no. Of course he doesn't, because I haven't told him. In fact, now that I think about it, I can hardly recall a proper conversation between us. A conversation about something that really matters. What exactly have we got in common? What's holding us together?

Maybe it's time to start facing facts. Dylan and me—we're not right. He's a nice guy; I'm a nice girl. We've had fun—but it just doesn't click. Doesn't work smoothly. Any of it. And it's about time I said so.

But do I really want to do it in a text?

I look at my phone. Sod it—he's asked the question. Without stopping to consider the irony of finally telling him my real feelings when it's about splitting up, I type my reply.

Am not sure, I write. Then I add, *I guess it's not really working. Maybe we should call it a day?* x

It's only after I've sent it that I realize how much I mean it. When my phone beeps again, I grab it quickly, surprising myself by how much I'm hoping his answer says he agrees.

I open the text.

Maybe you're right. We can still be friends though? x

I can't ignore the relief I feel, and I know for sure that this is what I want. I write my reply. *Of course. No hard feelings, I hope? Sorry it didn't work out. Take care.* x

A minute later, there's a reply.

123

OK. You too. See you around, love Dylan xx

I almost laugh. It's the first time either of us has ever used the word "love."

I stare at my phone. Can it really be that easy to split up with the boy I lost my virginity to less than a month ago? Can technology really be that advanced? Or is "advanced" the wrong word?

As my eyes glaze over and my mind numbs, I notice the most awful feeling creeping up inside me. I can't put my finger on it. I know it could have something to do with the fact that my dad's left home, my mum's falling apart, my best friend isn't speaking to me, and I've just broken up with my boyfriend, but I've still got a feeling it's something more than that.

It's only later, as I watch a woman with straggly hair and a screaming toddler get on the bus, that it hits me.

My period is late.

12

I find myself wandering past the English room as Miss Murray is coming out.

"Hi, Ash, are you all right?" she asks as she locks the door.

I don't know what possesses me to say what I say next. The words are out before I've even thought about them. "No. In fact, I'm pretty crap. Can I talk to you?"

She looks at her watch. I knew it. She never really meant it when she said she'd listen to me. She's just like all the other teachers, pretending she cares but really just counting the minutes till the bell rings and she doesn't have to think about us.

"Forget it." I turn away.

"I've got about half an hour till my next class—final one of the year." She smiles.

I'd forgotten it's nearly the end of term. Bloody Christmas soon.

"Why don't you come in?"

Then she's unlocking the door again. I follow her inside and my nerve takes a nosedive. What am I doing? A whole tumble of thoughts pile into my head. What if someone sees me and thinks I'm sucking up to the teachers? What if she laughs at me? What if I cry and can't stop? What if —

"Have a seat." Miss Murray sits down at her desk and pulls up another chair.

I sit down and put my bag on my knee. Hands in her lap, she leans forward, facing me. I look at my bag. Then I look at the walls — loads of books. Shelf after shelf of sets of hardback books: *Romeo and Juliet, To Kill a Mockingbird,* a brand new set of *Life of Pi.*

"Ash, how can I help?" Miss Murray touches me gently on my arm and I jump. You know that stupid joke where you say, "Have you ever seen a match burn twice?" You light a match: once. Then you blow it out and touch it on someone's arm: twice. It feels like that.

I stop looking around the room and meet her eyes. "I know this might sound really stupid to you, but I just feel like my life's falling apart."

"Go on," she says softly.

"My mum and dad have kind of . . . well, my dad's left home." I'm suddenly ashamed. Maybe she'll think there's something wrong with me that made my dad walk out. I don't want her to think that. OK, I admit it. I want her to like me. So what?

"Oh, Ash. I'm so sorry," she says. "How awful for you. No wonder you looked so down."

Yes! Exactly! Finally, *someone* recognizes that this is pretty rubbish for me, as well as for them. And of course, it's her. For the first time, I don't feel so selfish for feeling that this is something that's happening to *me* as well as to my parents.

I fiddle with the buckle on my bag while I carry on. "They argue loads, but that's normal, isn't it? I mean, he shouldn't just *leave*. I don't understand."

I glance up without moving my head.

She's still looking at me. "It's hard to say whether it's normal or not," she says. "Every marriage is different. But what I do know is that it can't be easy for you, being in the middle, feeling torn in half."

Yes! She understands me so well!

"It's a really horrible situation, for all of you."

I nod. "And my boyfriend and I have just split up. We weren't together for very long, and it was me who ended it, but . . . but . . ." I stop. My throat hurts.

Miss Murray leans forward in her chair. "But what, Ash? I mean, in itself this is all tough enough for you, but I think you're trying to tell me there's more?"

How does she do it? She just *gets* me. I take a deep breath. "I think I might be pregnant."

There's a long silence during which I stare at my feet. As soon as the words are out, I realize how terrified I am of them. I start to feel sick. The room is swaying from side to side, and that just seems to confirm it. Morning sickness. What the hell am I going to *do*?

"Oh, Ash. That's the last thing you need to be worrying about. You must feel like it's all too much."

I can't reply. My throat is too clogged up. I nod instead. That is exactly how I feel.

"It's OK. You can talk to me. Which do you want to tackle first? Your parents or your worries about being pregnant? You can tell me everything."

So I do just that. I tell her about my birthday, Dylan breaking up with his girlfriend, the arguments at home, falling out with Cat, Dylan's party, what happened afterward. I don't stop till I've spewed the whole lot out of me. Miss Murray listens to it all. She doesn't say much, but I don't want her to. I just want her to listen and to let me unload everything without judging me — and that's what she does.

How does she know exactly what I need?

She's handing me a box of tissues. While I blow my nose, she puts her hand on my arm again and looks at me really intently. It makes me want to climb inside her eyes and curl up. But it scares me too. I don't know why.

"Ash, you've got a hell of a lot going on here," she says gently. "You need to look after yourself. There are problems with all the people you're close to — your parents, your best friend, your boyfriend. It's hard enough having *one* of these things going so wrong — but all at once? Well, it's no wonder you feel like you can't cope. Anyone in your position would feel the same."

I listen to her, taking in every word. And it's weird. She doesn't say anything that makes any of it different. How could she? No one can change what's actually happening. But just the fact that someone is saying to me, "Yeah, Ash, your life is shit right now. I hear you" makes it *seem* different. She makes me feel . . . I dunno, kind of validated, if that makes sense.

"You can't do anything about your parents. And it's not your fault. You know that, don't you?"

I shrug.

"Ashleigh?"

"Yeah, whatever. I guess."

"Good. And it sounds like you've done the right thing with Dylan if you don't feel you have a future with him. And the pregnancy thing—well, that's just a matter of time. My guess would be that you're *not* pregnant, but if you're seriously worried, why not take a pregnancy test? With so much going on in your life, there's no point in wasting valuable time—and emotion—on a problem that may not even exist."

"I know, I know. I will. Just not yet. I guess I'm a bit too scared to face that just yet. It's been a week—and I'm usually quite regular. But I'm probably OK," I say, not believing it for a minute but not wanting to dwell on the idea of pregnancy too much.

"Going through stressful times can affect your cycle, you know," Miss Murray says.

"Yeah."

"The one thing you *can* do, though, is try to patch things up with Cat. She's probably missing you too, you know."

That thought hadn't even occurred to me. "You really think so?"

Miss Murray smiles. It feels like a rainbow on a miserable day. "I would put my lottery ticket on it," she says.

I laugh.

"Feeling a bit better?"

I nod. I am. I'm feeling a *lot* better.

I glance at my watch. Has half an hour passed already? "I'd better get going, hadn't I?"

"Unless you want to sit in on my next lesson." She smiles again.

I smile back. I blow my nose one last time, wipe my eyes, and get up. "Thank you so much."

"You can come and see me anytime, you know," she replies. "It's what I'm here for."

I'm thinking, *No, it's not. This is way beyond what you're here for.* But I don't say it. Instead, I shuffle awkwardly to the door. "Thanks," I repeat, feeling stupid that I can't think of anything different to say.

"You're more than welcome, Ash," she says seriously.

As I walk away, I hear her at her door. "Right, come on in, folks. Sorry to have kept you. Coats off, quiet down . . ."

She kept a whole class waiting because of me.

There's something in the back of my mind when I wake up. Just out of reach. Like when you get a bit of food stuck between your teeth, right at the back of your mouth.

Then I remember: Dad's left.

And I remember the same thing happened yesterday morning, too, and the one before that. I feel like someone's kicked me on a bruise. It's not like we used to have loads of quality time together. It's just, I don't know, there's something about the silence. The house echoes with too much emptiness.

Mum and I have been skirting around the subject. Not talking much at meals. I say "meals," but that's a bit grand for what's been going on around here. Toast and coffee, that's all I've seen her have.

She looks dreadful. Her hair's all thin and lanky. She hasn't gone to work since Monday; this is always a busy time, too, just before Christmas. She's spent the week mooching around in an old pair of sweatpants and a big, baggy top. Her eyes are as saggy as her sweater, with dark rings around them. When Mr. Wyman, her boss, phoned yesterday to ask for the Pritchard file, she wouldn't even get out of bed—just told me to tell him it was in the cabinet by the window, third drawer down, under "C."

"Pritchard? C?"

"Car thief," she replied and turned over.

I'm due at Dad's, so I go upstairs to say good-bye. She's up and sitting at her mirror putting makeup on. That's a good sign. I go over and kiss her cheek.

"Are you going to be OK?" I ask.

She smiles weakly at me in the mirror. "Of course, darling."

"You sure? I mean, I don't have to go. If you'd rather I didn't, I can always call him and tell him I —"

"Go." Mum turns around and takes hold of both of my hands. "I'm fine. I promise."

"OK. As long as you're sure."

Mum attempts another smile. "I am, darling. I'd be worse if I stopped you seeing your father."

"Let's do something nice later, shall we?"

"That'd be lovely," she says. "Just you and me?"

I kiss her hand. "We'll get a couple of DVDs, and loads of chocolate."

Her smile finally reaches her dark eyes. "I'll look forward to it. Now go, and have a lovely time."

"Love you," I say without thinking. "See you later — and you can pick the movie."

I can't believe the state of this place. My dad is living in a smelly little room with wallpaper peeling from the ceiling, a stove in the corner, and a bathroom in the corridor that he shares with four other flats.

He takes my hand. "Come on, love, let's get out of here."

"Definitely!" I shudder as he pulls the door closed. "Where are we going, then?"

"Well, where d'you want to go?"

"Um." Crikey. When did Dad and I last actually *do* something or *go* somewhere together? I can't even think.

We end up at McDonald's, where our joint skills at avoiding talking about what's really going on are instantly exposed, like a bright day showing up a dirty window. Sample conversation:

Dad: How's school, love?
Me: Fine.
Dad: Done anything interesting this week?
Me: Not really.
Dad: You going to have a Big Mac or McChicken?
Me: McChicken, I reckon. Meal deal. What about you?
Dad: Think I'll go for the Big Mac myself.

Elephant in the room, anyone?

As we finish up our food, I decide to try and talk about it.

"Dad . . ."

He looks at me, and for a second I wonder why his expression seems so familiar: dark eyes, pale skin, no hint that this is a face that ever knew how to smile. Then I realize where I've seen it before. On Mum.

"Is it . . . you know . . . are you—"

"Are we sure?" he breaks in, in a rare moment of actually understanding what I'm trying to say.

I nod. I feel ashamed even asking. And scared. Why ask a question when you don't want to hear the answer?

Dad reaches across the napkins and half-empty boxes and takes my hand. "I know that we didn't talk about all of this with you, and maybe that was our mistake," he says. "But, believe me, we talked to each other."

"Really?" I think back over the past weeks and months and, for the life of me, I just can't recall them having a conversation that didn't end in a screaming fight.

"Yes, really. We talked a lot. And you know something else?"

"What?"

"We went to see a counselor."

I can't help it—my jaw actually falls open.

"We went six times. We didn't want to involve you in it all. It didn't seem fair. We thought we might be able to work it out. But we can't, love. It's over."

I nod and try my hardest to force away the boulder in my throat so I can reply. It's not budging.

"Obviously, nothing in life is one hundred percent certain, but we're as sure as we can be. We wouldn't have even considered putting you through this if we weren't."

Dad squeezes my hand, and I squeeze his back. He looks so grateful for this one tiny offering that I feel as if I could melt into a pool of sadness and spill all over the floor.

Instead, I hear some grown-up-sounding words coming out of my mouth. "Dad, I understand. Thank you for talking about it."

And then, because I can't bear to see my dad looking like a broken man, and also because I realize that there's really not a lot more to say, I get up. "Thanks for lunch," I say.

As he stands up, I give him a hug. He grips me so hard it almost winds me. "I love you, sweetheart. We both do," he says croakily.

"I know, Dad. I love you too," I mumble.

"Come on. Let's go and mooch round some of your favorite shops."

We leave McDonald's and walk slowly down the street. I link my arm in his and find myself wondering if maybe it's all going to be OK. Not yet. But one day.

We wander through town for a bit. Dad buys me a couple of magazines in Smiths, and I help him pick a new tie in M&S, and then he walks me to the bus stop. He'd offered me a lift home, but I don't think Mum's ready to see his car roll up in the drive yet.

Just before the bus arrives, he opens his mouth to say something.

"What?" I ask.

"Well, I was going to tell you . . . I . . ." There's this really long pause.

I glance up the road. "Dad, the bus . . ."

He shakes his head. "It'll keep, love," he says. "Maybe next week?"

"It's Christmas next week!"

"I'll make you some dinner. Just you and me."

A mixture of panic and sadness grips me as I look at him: his tired, worn eyes and a couple of spots of gray in his hair. Have they sprung up in the past week, or have I just never noticed them before? "Yeah, OK," I say gently.

From the back of the bus, I watch him standing on the pavement—not waving, just standing, alone and upright. "Bye, Dad," I whisper. I turn back around, closing my eyes for a moment. Then I get my phone out and check out the latest *Cute Emergency* kitten video that Robyn's sent me. Good timing. I could totally do with something to make me smile right now.

"Hello?"

"Cat, it's me." I hold my breath while I wait for her to reply. She doesn't.

I have no idea how I'm going to fix this, but I know I've got to try. Ever since talking with Miss Murray, I've been seeing my argument with Cat a bit differently. I think she probably has every right to be pissed off with me. I'd gotten so caught up in my own problems, I stopped being a good friend to her.

"Cat, I'm . . . I'm sorry," I say. My voice is croaky.

Cat sighs dramatically.

"Please, let's make up. I was wrong and stupid and selfish and I'm sorry. Really. *Please* forgive me. I miss you. And you miss me too."

"Who says I do?"

"Please, Cat! I need to talk to you."

"Oh, God, what about this time? Don't tell me: Dylan."

"No, we've split up."

"Oh. Right. Lover boy dumps you and you come running back to me, then?"

"Cat, I'm . . . I think I might be pregnant." The words come out almost as a whisper, and I grip the phone while I wait for Cat to answer.

"Oh, bloody hell, Ash," she says eventually. "I'll be over in twenty minutes."

And she is. She turns up with a pregnancy testing kit, a hug, and a monster bar of Dairy Milk. "Well, I couldn't eat all that on my own," she says casually.

"I'm so sorry. I was a selfish, stupid idiot, and you were right to get fed up with me." I squeeze her tightly. "I've missed you so much!"

Cat peels my arms off her. "Yeah, I know," she says with a cheeky grin. "It must have been awful for you."

I nudge her in the ribs and she laughs. "I'm sorry, too," she says. "I was a stroppy cow. And yeah, OK, I've missed you as well."

And just like that, we're back to normal, and it's as if we never fell out.

"Right. How late are you?" she asks.

"About a week."

"A week? Bloody hell, Ash, I thought you were about two months gone by the way you sounded. A week's no biggie. I'm *always* a week late!"

"I know. But I'm not."

"OK. Have you done a pregnancy test yet?"

I shake my head. "Too scared. I can't face it. What if I am actually, you know . . ." I can't say the word again.

Cat hands me the pregnancy testing kit. "Look. Take the kit. And see if you can work up the courage to do it. If you still haven't started your period in another week or so, promise me you'll do it then?"

I nod. "I promise. Thank you." I shove the kit in a drawer.

"Good. OK." Cat lies back on my bed. "So, what's new with you then, apart from this?"

I take a breath. Where to start? "Well, my dad . . ." I begin.

Cat is upright. "Yes?"

"He's left home."

Cat stares at me. "No! Have they moved in together?"

"Huh? Moved out, you mean."

We lock eyes. Cat speaks slowly. "So, why has he gone?"

I shrug. "I guess they've just been making each other miserable for years. I think it was mutual. They're both pretty cut up about it, but both seem to think it's the right thing."

Cat gives me a funny look.

"What?" I demand.

She lets out a sigh. "OK, I'll tell you. But don't shoot the messenger, OK?"

My insides leap. "Tell me what?"

Cat bites her lip—the part that isn't covered in studs. "I think your dad might be having an affair," she says.

"What?" I nearly laugh. "Dad? An affair? No way!"

Then I think about the way he was trying to tell me something as I was leaving last weekend. Was that what he wanted to say? No! Surely not.

I stop smiling. "What makes you say that?" I ask quietly.

"I saw them."

"*Them*? Who? Where?"

Cat shrugs. "I don't know who she was. I saw them coming out of the deli by my mum's work at lunchtime a few weeks ago."

"What did she look like?"

"Kind of small. Light brown hair. Not exactly the type you imagine men leaving their wives for."

I wince.

"Sorry."

I think about the description. "Hang on a sec. Has she got a little round face, pointy chin, looks a bit like a mouse?"

"I didn't see them for long. But, yeah, I suppose so, probably."

I breathe a sigh of relief. "That's just Elaine!"

"Elaine?"

"Dad's accountant. She works with him."

"They had their arms round each other."

"Cat, seriously, it's just Elaine. It's fine. I'm positive, honestly. He'll have just been saying good-bye to her or something. They're good friends. They've worked together for years."

Cat lets out a breath. "Jesus, Ash, I've been terrified of telling you this." Then she laughs. "I have to admit, I never saw your dad as someone who'd do that. What a relief."

"Yeah. Jeez," I agree.

But then, out of nowhere, a memory comes into my mind. It was about two years ago. I'd gone to Dad's work after school. He was running late, and Elaine chatted to me while I waited for him. I didn't think anything of it at the time, but now I can't stop myself wondering—why was she there? It was way past the end of the day, and there was no one else around. Just her. And him. I mean, she was his accountant, and they did work together, so it made sense. But what if Cat was right? What if *that* is the real reason Dad and Mum are splitting up? What if everything else is just a cover? What if everything he's said to me is a lie?

Suddenly, I don't know what's real and what isn't, and I'm back to square one with all the crappy things in my life. Worse. Square *minus* one.

I swallow hard and make a decision. I'm not going to obsess about this. I'm not going to drag Cat through it all with me. I'm not going to be selfish. I'm going to be a proper friend.

I force a smile onto my face. "So," I say. "Tell me what's been going on in the life of Cat for the last few weeks."

Cat tells me about a guy she met at the skate park, and about her mum coming home drunk from her work event, and about the tattoo she's having done next week. She decided on a dragonfly in the end.

I listen to it all. And I'm grateful to have her back. More grateful than I can ever put into words.

But underneath, another part of my mind is busy elsewhere. It's picturing Mum the morning Dad left, sitting alone at the kitchen table in her dressing gown, hair unwashed and a cup of coffee in her hands.

Dad moving out so soon.

Did he leave to be with Elaine? Is that what he tried to tell me at the bus stop?

And the more I think about it, the more I talk myself into thinking the worst of my dad. Cat might be happy to be wrong, but I'm more and more convinced she was right. How could he do it?

I wish I hadn't seen him last weekend, or I wish I'd known so I could have given him a piece of my mind.

If he thinks I'm ever going to forgive him, he can forget it.

13

I hated Christmas Day when I was younger. Mum was always stressed and wound up and I never knew if it was my fault. Dad would spend the morning unshaved and grumpy with a hangover from the next-door neighbors' annual Christmas Eve party. Then Nan and Granddad would turn up, and we'd have the same conversations every year: How was I doing at school? Did I have a boyfriend? Wasn't my hair shorter than when they last saw me? Was I putting moisturizer on my elbows?

I didn't actually have anything against them; it was more the effect they had on the rest of us. Mum had never seen eye to eye with them. I think they'd wanted Dad to marry some dumpy little housewife. They couldn't get their heads around the idea of a woman having a husband, a daughter, *and* a job. "Heaven forbid!" That's what Nan always used to say. Suppose I told her I was thinking of doing something wild and crazy like getting my ears pierced—"Heaven forbid!"

One time, I was going out with this boy who played drums in a band. Phil Din, he called himself. He had a Mohawk, and piercings all over his face.

"Ash, your boyfriend's here," Mum called when he came to pick me up for an early escape.

"Heaven forbid!" Nan said, closing her eyes and

clasping her hand over her chest. "If I saw him coming toward me in the street, I'd hold tight onto my handbag and cross the road immediately."

I didn't know whether to laugh or get mad. Phil was the softest boy I'd ever met. He's certainly the only one who's ever stroked my hair gently while I puked vodka down someone's toilet.

Mum's parents both died when I was a baby. Then Nan and Granddad both died within a year of each other, and suddenly Christmas didn't feel like a big deal anymore. There was no Granddad falling asleep in an armchair, no charades, no arguments over whether we watch the Queen's Speech or not. No stressed Mum in the kitchen. Well, she'd be stressed, but it would just be her everyday stressed, not her Christmas Special stressed.

I never cried over my grandparents. At the time, I wondered if it made me heartless. When Dad told me Nan had died, I nearly laughed. I hated myself for that. What kind of a bitch did it make me? I didn't find it funny; it was just a nervous reaction, but it's still not what you want to do, is it? For ages after that, I was terrified of anyone telling me that someone had died. I used to go to this youth club, and one week Mum told me that Mandy Jacob's dad had died and that I was to tell her I was very sorry to hear the news. I was nearly sick before I went that night. What if I got halfway through saying it and burst out laughing? She'd never speak to me again.

In the end, I managed to mumble, "I'm sorry about your dad," in the middle of netball. She said, "Thanks" without looking at me, and then we got back to the game. It was such a relief. I wasn't so afraid of people dying after that.

I didn't laugh when Granddad went. I didn't cry either, but for a while I imagined I missed both of them. We'd usually only seen them a couple of times a year, so it wasn't very much to miss. I think it was the idea of not having any grandparents anymore that saddened me. I felt cut off from something, from the past.

The past few years, Christmas has been kind of OK. Bit of a low-key dinner, a few crackers and prezzies, and then I'd disappear to my room and text my friends while Mum and Dad watched the *Morecambe and Wise Christmas Special* for the millionth time. I never missed the old Christmas Day get-togethers.

Until this year.

Now I'd give anything to have them back.

When I come downstairs to see Mum on her own at the kitchen table — lank hair, saggy pajamas, flicking unenthusiastically through a magazine — I could easily cry. This isn't what Christmas morning should look like.

"Happy Christmas, Mum." I put a big smile on my face and kiss her on the cheek.

"Happy Christmas, love." She does the same back. If we don't say any of it out loud, maybe it's not so bad. I hand her a present.

"Oh, Ash, sweetheart, you shouldn't have."

I make a face. "It's Christmas, Mum. Of course I should have."

She carefully peels off the tape and pulls out the book. "*Heal Your Heart, Love Your Life.*" She turns it over to look at the back. "What's this, then?"

"Cat's mum used to go on about it," I say. "It's supposed to be brilliant. For women who are, you know, in your position and things."

She doesn't look up. A moment later, a tear drops onto her lap.

I bend down and look up at her face. "Mum, don't get upset. If you don't like it, I can always take it back. Don't cry."

She laughs and wipes her face. "It's lovely, darling. It's really thoughtful of you. Thank you." She kisses me on the cheek and gets up to blow her nose on a piece of paper towel.

She goes into the front room and comes back a moment later with a package. "This is for you."

"Oh, Mum."

She smiles as I rip the paper off. It's a pair of jeans. I pull them out and hold them up. They're actually really nice. "Mum, they're brilliant!"

"We had an intern at work last month," she says, hearing the shock in my voice. "She helped me."

I smile at her through a blur and throw my arms around her neck.

"Hey, watch it. You'll get me started again." She holds me tight for a second before bending down to pick up a piece of discarded wrapping paper. "Come on, let's get this mess cleared up."

We don't get dressed till midday. We just sit together

on the sofa in our dressing gowns, watching rubbish on the telly and eating toast.

Eventually I drag myself upstairs to put on some clothes. I'm supposed to be at Dad's at two.

Mum comes to the door to see me off.

"I wish I didn't have to go," I say. She has no idea how much I mean it.

"Don't be daft. You'll have a lovely time."

"What about you?"

"I'll be fine," she says. "I'm due down the road with David and Trish soon. They're doing the 'good neighbors' thing. They'll look after me, don't worry. Go on. I'll see you tonight."

The weird thing is, as I kiss her good-bye, I realize I'm looking forward to coming back home and spending the evening together.

"I'm not staying."

"What do you mean you're not staying?"

"I'll eat with you and that's it. Then I'm going home."

Dad moves aside to let me in.

"Any other guests?" I ask.

"Like who?"

"You tell me." I scowl into his eyes.

"Ashleigh, I don't know what this is all—"

"Like Elaine, for example?"

Dad turns away, puts on a pair of oven gloves. "Why would I invite Elaine?"

"I don't believe it! It's true, isn't it?"

He opens the tin can excuse for an oven in the corner of the room and bends down to check on the turkey. "Another few minutes," he mumbles.

"Dad! Are you just going to ignore me?"

He calmly closes the oven door and takes the gloves off. "I don't know what you're talking about."

"You and Mum."

"What about us?"

"Why did you really leave, Dad?"

He sits down on the bed. "Ash, your mum and I . . . things haven't been right for a long time."

"Well, it's no bloody wonder, is it?" I'm suddenly shouting. I don't care. I've held onto it—onto *all* of it, not just this—for too long, and it's coming out now with all the force of Niagara Falls.

"Don't swear please, Ashleigh. The walls are unbelievably thin in this place." He pats the bed beside him. "Why don't you sit down and tell me what this is all about?"

"Don't try coming over all reasonable. And don't lie to me."

"I won't lie to you."

I pause for a moment. The words catch in my throat. I can't get them out. I swallow hard. "You've been having an affair," I say. "Behind Mum's back. You've been seeing Elaine."

Dad nods slowly. "I see," he says. His voice has tightened. "That's what you think of me, is it?"

"I . . ." I stop, and suddenly—perhaps a tiny bit too late—wonder if I've got my facts right after all. Why was I so quick to jump on this idea and run with it? Did I need someone to blame? Was Dad the easiest target? Is he actually innocent after all?

Dad lifts my chin and turns me to face him. He looks me dead in the eyes.

"Ashleigh, in twenty-one years of marriage, I never once cheated on your mother," he says seriously. "Not with Elaine; not with anyone. You hear me?"

I nod.

"You believe me?"

I pause. Look in his eyes. See my dad there. My loyal, loving, trustworthy dad. I nod again. "I'm sorry," I say meekly.

"Ash, it's OK. But I swear to you it's true, OK?"

"OK."

"Good," he says. Then, for some reason, he looks awkward.

"Dad? What is it?"

He gets up and goes over to the window, all steamed up from the cooking and so grubby you can hardly see out of it. He wipes it with his sleeve and turns back to me. "It's precisely because I will never lie to you that I want to tell you this. I tried to tell you before but . . ."

I fold my arms and wait for him to go on.

"I swear to you, Elaine and I have only ever been friends . . ." he says again. I'm about to point out that he's already told me this, but before I get the chance, he quickly adds, ". . . but we have started seeing each other."

"Started? When?"

"We've had literally two dates."

"*Seriously?* That's a bit of a coincidence, isn't it?"

Dad shakes his head. "She invited me for dinner. Said I had to stop living off ready meals. It's just happened naturally. And it never, ever happened before. It never even crossed my mind."

I stare at him in disbelief. "And you expect me to believe that?"

Dad holds my eyes. "Yes, Ash," he says. "I do. Because it's the truth."

We stay like that for a moment. And in that moment, I realize that actually, yes, I do believe him. Almost. There's just one thing. "What about Cat?" I ask. "She saw you together. She said you had your arms round each other."

"What? When?"

"I dunno. A few weeks ago."

Dad rubs his chin, scratching at the stubble. Then he moves his hand away and laughs sadly. "Yes, I know," he says. "I know when she saw us. It was the day your mum and I had such an awful fight I knew our marriage was over. I was in pieces. Elaine dragged me out of the office for lunch. Afterward, she gave me a hug. I was crying in the street."

Dad's eyes fill with tears now, and before I can stop myself, I go to him and put my arms around him. His shoulders shake softly. "I'm sorry, Ash. I'm sorry," he mumbles into my neck.

"I'm sorry too, Dad. I shouldn't have thought you'd do something like that. I know you wouldn't."

Dad squeezes me closer before letting me go again and wiping a sleeve over his face.

"Just do one thing for me," I say.

"I'll do anything," Dad says. "What is it?"

"Tell Mum."

Dad breathes in sharply. "Ash, you have to understand, these things are quite complicated. It's not just a case of —"

"I can't keep this secret from her. It'll feel like I'm lying to her," I say. "You can't put me in that position."

There's a long pause. The only sound is a spitting noise from inside the oven. Then Dad nods. "You're right," he says. "It's not fair to either of you. She has to know."

"Right. Thank you."

Dad goes over to the oven and opens it. A waft of hot air comes out. "Turkey's done," he says. "You ready for dinner?"

"Totally. I'm starving!" I pull out one of the two plastic seats by the sad little flap that's opened out into a table. Dad joins me and picks up one of the crackers.

We pull the cracker and a mini yo-yo falls out onto the table. Feels appropriate, considering how up and down my life has become.

Dad puts a bright blue hat on his head, and I grab the other cracker and hold it out to him.

"Happy Christmas, Dad," I say.

Dad smiles at me. A smile that's full of sadness, but maybe also full of hope. "Happy Christmas, love," he replies.

14

"Have you done it yet?" Cat yells in my ear. We're in the Grapevine bar in town, celebrating New Year's Eve in the traditional English way—by getting drunk. The Grapevine is one of the few places that doesn't bother checking ID's. At least we'll all be legal next year anyway. The plan had been to come here for a dance, but it's so packed there's barely room to breathe, let alone move around in time with the music.

"Done what?" Robyn's behind me, handing me a glass of something bright orange with a cherry on top. "It's called a Happy New Year," she explains as I take the glass.

I clink glasses with both of them. "Cheers," I say.

"So. Done what?" Robyn persists.

Cat shakes her head and sighs at me. "Don't tell me Robyn doesn't even know about this?"

I feel my face heat up and take a swig of my cocktail to hide behind.

"What don't I know about?" Robyn asks.

Cat raises an eyebrow at me, and I shrug in reply.

"Ash thinks she might be pregnant—but she was too scared to take a test," Cat explains economically.

For a second, Robyn looks hurt.

"I'm sorry. I should have told you. I—I guess I was embarrassed. I didn't want to admit to what Dylan and I had done." I grimace. "Sorry."

Robyn shakes her head and smiles. "No, it's fine. Honestly," she says. "I mean, we've not been friends all that long, and it's really personal. I understand."

Cat swings an arm over her shoulder in a mock "sad violin music" performance. I nudge her arm and laugh.

"OK, now that we've got the gushy stuff out of the way . . . have you done the test yet?"

Robyn moves to stand closer to Cat and looks hard at me. "Yes," she says, siding with Cat. "Have you?"

I look down.

"Thought not," Cat says, reaching into her bag. She pulls out a paper bag with something inside it and holds it out to me.

"Cat!" I grab the bag from her. "What are you doing?"

"I knew you wouldn't have done it yet so I bought it on the way here. Think of it as a New Year's gift."

"How do you know I haven't started my period?"

"Have you?" Robyn asks.

I shake my head. I'm about three weeks late, if not more. Every day that's gone by I've been getting more and more convinced it's bad news. My stomach suddenly cramps out of fear. At least, I think that's what it is.

A moment later, the pair of them have knocked back their cocktails and placed themselves on either side of me. "Right, come on then," Cat orders, taking my arm. Robyn takes hold of the other one. I feel like I've been arrested and am about to be carted down to the station.

"Where are we going?" I ask.

Cat points ahead at the sign for the ladies' room. "We're going to get you an answer," she says.

The pair of them virtually shove me into the cubicle. I shut the door behind me. "Are you both planning to wait out there and listen to me pee on a stick?" I ask.

"Yup!" they reply in unison.

I guess there's nothing else for it, then.

I take the tester out of its wrapper and read the instructions on the box. My stomach cramps again. I must be even more terrified than I thought. I clutch my stomach. The pain has almost winded me. It's a dull, heavy stab, low down in my stomach.

A bit like period pain.

I look down and see something miraculous.

Blood.

Blood! I can't believe it! My period's started—I'm not pregnant!

"Aarrrrggghhhhh!" I scream.

"Ash, are you OK?" Robyn asks through the door.

I pull my bag open. I have never felt so happy to be rummaging around in my bag looking for a tampon before. Miss Murray was right. It must have been all the stress that made me so late.

I finish in the loo, shove the tester back in the box, and fling the door open. "I'm not pregnant!" I yell, grabbing both of them and jumping up and down. I dance around and around in a circle, pulling them both with me.

Cat's laughing as she pulls away. "You're sure?" she asks. "You did it properly?"

I hand her the kit. "I didn't need it," I reply. "I started my period! I'm free! Omigod, I'm so happy!"

Robyn grabs me and hugs me tight. "Yay! That's brilliant!"

"I know!" I grin at them both. "Right. Let's get the cocktails. It's my round!"

As we head back to the bar, I find myself wanting to run around the whole place screaming and hugging everyone, telling them I've got my life back.

As I knock back my second Happy New Year I realize that, actually, I'm not bothered about the people in the pub. The only person I really want to tell is Miss Murray.

I can't wait to see her. I'm glad we're back at school in a few days.

What? Did I *really* just think that?

Miss Murray's going through all the coursework we should have in our folders; more than half of mine's missing. How am I ever going to catch up? What was I doing all of last year?

I dawdle as we pack up, as usual. I wonder if she's noticed I'm always the last to leave. Or if she minds. "Catch up to you in a sec," I say to Robyn as I take my time organizing pens and books and rearranging my bag.

154

Then everyone else has gone.

"How was Christmas, Ash?" Miss Murray asks as I shuffle over to her desk.

"Kind of OK, I suppose."

"That sounds marginally better than it could have been." She smiles.

I can feel the heat of her eyes on me, and I nervously meet them. "How are you now?" she asks without taking her eyes away from mine. It makes my face burn. She's doing that thing she does, where she seems to reach right inside and see all the things you normally hide. Maybe she learned how to teach by studying *The Demon Headmaster*.

"I wanted to tell you . . . to say thanks. For last term. Talking and stuff." I can't get the words out. I feel like I'm back in those PE lessons trying to tell Miss Anderson why I can't go swimming. "I'm, I'm OK. I'm not worried anymore, about, you know . . ." I stammer, hoping she'll fill in the gaps and know what I'm talking about.

"You started your period?" she asks, just like that.

"Er, yeah."

She looks really pleased—as if it actually makes a difference to her. As if she cares. "Well, that's a relief, isn't it? I have to admit, I had wondered if everything was going to be all right."

She thought about me over the holidays?

"Nothing to stop you knuckling down to some good solid work now, is there?" she says as she fills in her grade book.

I point at the stack of homework we've just given in. "It's not very good, I'm afraid."

"No, I'm sure it isn't." She flicks through the papers. "But then, I'm not expecting much. Since you did so poorly last time." She winks, and my stomach does a little backflip. What the hell's that about? I mean. Seriously. A *teacher*? A *woman*?

I pull myself together. "I suppose I've no excuses anymore, have I?" I say.

"Oh, I'm sure you'll think of something." Then she smiles and closes her book. "By the way. You remember the debating group I told you about? We've got our first meeting next Monday. Are you coming?"

"I don't know. Maybe." Right now I'm not sure which urge is stronger: to be anywhere she is or to get as far away from her as I can till I've worked out why she has such a weird effect on me.

"You'll enjoy it."

Thing is, I *know* I will—if she's there. "OK. See you then," my mouth says before my brain has a chance to tell the rest of me to run like hell.

It's raining and dark by the time I get home. I'm climbing the stairs when I hear it—a huge crash downstairs. Oh, my God! I'm on my own and the house is being broken into. I'm stuck halfway up the stairs, twisting from side to side, feet stuck to the floor, trying to work out what to do. People talk about their knees knocking when they're scared, but I never realized that they actually do.

After another loud smash, I know I've got to do something. I pull my phone out of my bag. My first instinct is to text Cat, but what can she do? If she was here, she'd probably walk right up to the burglar and tell him to piss off, but over the phone? Not quite so easily done.

Robyn? She'd be lovely and supportive, but, again, there's not much she can do from the other end of a phone.

I could ring Dad and ask him to come over. He would—but I don't think Mum would want him in the house. Mum, then? No, she'll be on her way home from work by now, and she never answers when she's driving.

I take my shoes off, crouch low, and tiptoe down the stairs.

I'm a few feet away from the bottom of the stairs when I hear another crash. It sounds like someone's smashing all our windows in.

What do I do? Should I call the police?

Hunched over, almost in a ball, three steps from the bottom of the stairs, I'm paralyzed. It's like the time I was on my own in the house with a spider in my bedroom. I stood looking at it with a glass in one hand and a card in the other. All I had to do was put the glass over it, slip the card underneath, take it to the window, and chuck. But it took half an hour of sweaty eyeball-to-eyeball contact before I could get up the nerve to move.

I just can't seem to make a decision. Do I sneak out of the house, phone the police, confront the burglars on my own? I feel as if I'm in an action film where I have to make a run for it and need my partner to cover me—only I've got no partner.

I catch myself for a second. This is ridiculous. All I have to do is either get to the door and run out of it or make a phone call. Come on!

I've just about talked myself out of my panic and decided to call the police when I hear another crash. The only difference this time is that it's accompanied by a loud, long, piercing scream.

For a second, I literally feel my hairs stand up, like a massive domino-run all over my body. Then, very gradually, the feeling subsides as the sudden realization of what's going on knocks each one down.

Firstly: *It's Mum!*

Then: *That means it's not a burglar.*

Which leads to: *It's not an ax-wielding madman either.*

Until the last one, which stubbornly remains standing: *Why is she smashing the house up?*

As I enter the kitchen, I notice that the shelf where we keep all the old bits of chipped crockery is empty.

Mum's outside the back door in the garden. I can make her out quite clearly, even though it's dark. She hasn't seen me.

Her hair is plastered to her face from the rain, and her makeup's streaked. Is it raindrops or tears? I think it's probably both. She's soaked through: no coat on, just a long black skirt and a thick black sweater. She looks like a kitten that's been rescued from a river—a tiny, fragile creature with its fur all soaked and stuck down.

Her next scream interrupts my thoughts. "Aaaaarr-rgggghhh-you-bloody-buggering-shit-heap-of-a-bloody-BASTARD!"

My instinct is to duck as the nearly-new-but-slightly-soiled plate is hurled violently against the wall that stands between us.

I guess Dad's told her about Elaine, then.

Her face clouds over with confusion for a moment when I burst out into the garden, as if she doesn't recognize me. For a second, I see into the future: she's old and gray, she has dementia and can't remember my name. The thought pretty much breaks my heart in two.

"A-Ashleigh," she stammers, looking down at the cracked mug in her hand. It's the one with a picture of a balloon on it that used to change color when it was warm, one of my favorites, even though it doesn't change color anymore.

"Mum." I move toward her.

Fresh streaks are coursing down her face. "It's OK, Mum," I say softly as I approach her, ease my way over, reach out for the cup.

By now her expression has dissolved from determined maniac back into the face of the utterly miserable mother I realize I totally love. I gently prise the mug from her hand with a sense of achievement.

Once I've put it down safely out of her reach, I look back at her. Her shoulders are hunched over, her head drooping so far down it looks as if she'll fall forward and topple over in a minute. Without thinking, I put my arms around her. Almost as soon as I do, she puts her head on my shoulder. Her arms hang loosely by her sides, and her whole body starts to shake.

"He's got another . . . he's got . . . he's got . . . he . . . I can't . . . tell you. It's not . . . fair . . . on you," she sobs.

"Look, let's go inside, shall we?" I steer her back to the door.

Once we're in the house, I lower her onto a chair then put the kettle on. She's stopped crying and is now staring into space, clutching a soggy envelope.

I reach out for the envelope. "Can I?"

She hesitates for a moment. Then holds it out.

Dear Julia,

    There's no easy way to tell you this. I've started seeing somebody. It's Elaine from the office. I swear to you it has only just started.

    I'm sorry if the news is hurtful to you. I didn't want you to hear it from anyone else. We are both free to do what we like now, but I understand that it is very soon, and I know that this might be hard for you.

    We thought it might be practical for me to stay with her for a while and see how it goes. The studio isn't sensible for any of us.

    I hope you are all right. I don't want to hurt you. I think we both need to move on with our lives, and I hope you will also find someone.

    I wish you all the very best, always,
    Gordon

"I always knew she was after him," Mum whispers.

"I want to help you, Mum," I say, feeling useless.

She smiles weakly. "How can you?"

"Whatever I can do, I want to do it." I take hold of both her hands. They're cold. I rub them between mine and blow on them.

"Come on." Still holding her hand, I lead her toward the stairs. "I'm going to run you a bath."

I leave Mum to soak up the steam and lavender while I make us both a drink. After her bath, we sit up in her bed together, drinking hot chocolate.

"Remember that song you made up for me?" I say. "I'd ask for it over and over again."

She puts her drink down and looks at me. Then she starts singing, in a croaky voice, hoarse from crying. *"Little Ashleigh, pudding pie, has a twinkle in her eye."*

She puts her arm around me and I join in, surprised to find how much comfort the words still bring me. *"And her giggles, all the while, make her mummy laugh and smile."*

We grin at each other as we sing. By the time we get to *"As long as I have Ashleigh-pie, there'll never be a cause to cry,"* we're hugging each other and giggling like kids.

I don't notice the change, but at some point I realize her giggling has turned to huge, wounded sobs.

I hold her tight, rocking her gently till she wears herself out and falls asleep in my arms.

161

15

What on earth am I doing in a math classroom on a Monday evening with seven geeky students and a math teacher? Robyn is with me, which is something at least. But *she* isn't: Miss Murray.

Why does that make me feel so disappointed?

We're trying to agree on a topic for the first debate. Mr. Philips keeps coming up with tired old subjects like vivisection and euthanasia. Why are teachers *so* boring? *Most* teachers.

The door bursts open.

"Sorry I'm late," Miss Murray says breathlessly to the room as she slips into the seat next to Mr. Philips. Her coat's falling off her shoulder as she pushes her hair back and rubs her face with her hands. And suddenly, it all looks different. Now that she's here, I'm happy that I am too. I just don't know what it is about her — when she's in the room, it's as if someone's turned the lights and the heating on.

Robyn nudges me. "Oh, good. We can get started now," she says in a low voice.

I smile at her and feel my whole body relax.

"You all right?" Mr. Philips says quietly to Miss

Murray. We're meant to be working in pairs. I pretend to be working, but I'm straining my ears for Miss Murray's response.

"Unforeseen domestic emergency, I'm afraid," she whispers back to Mr. Philips.

What's that about? They sound cozy. Are she and Mr. Philips an item? I glance at him once the group discussion gets going. He's got really intense green eyes that clash with his red hair, and crinkly lines at the corners of them that make him look like he's always smiling. He's quite good-looking in an odd sort of way. She's not going out with him, is she? I don't want her to be.

After ten minutes, we all have to feed our ideas back to the group. A guy called Danny who I don't know suggests we discuss why the music charts are dominated by such talentless crap. Surely he'll get told off for that? But he doesn't.

"It's a good idea, Danny," Miss Murray says, nodding at him. "But let's look at it in more detail. Break it down. We need to think about examples of the 'talentless crap' that is in the charts. And examples of the good tunes. Reasons for both. Then decide if we have enough to build a debate around. What d'you think?"

What do we think? *I* think I have never heard a teacher use the word "crap" before. And I've never thought about how to analyze an argument before. I've only ever thrown myself into them—and maybe started figuring out how I got there once I'm stuck way too far in. I think she's like a switch that turns an old grainy black-and-white film into vibrant color. I think she wakes me up. I think I want to come up with a good idea because I'm hungry for her praise and for her to look at me and talk to me as if I've said something intelligent.

I think she does something to me that I don't understand—and for now, it's one thing I *don't* want to analyze.

It's dark when I get to the bus stop. I'm sure it's been winter forever. Robyn had to leave early because her mum was taking her to a dentist appointment. Everyone else has disappeared in one direction or another, and I'm on my own waiting for the bus. I get a flicker of nerves as I look down the street. It's raining hard, and there are big puddles at the curbs with the odd car anonymously slipping down the road and spraying the pavement in its wake like a water-skier.

Then this car slows down as it comes toward me. A black Fiat 500. My chest is thumping, and I pray that it's not a curb crawler with a thing for teenage girls. I shove my hands in my pockets, making as mean and unwelcoming a face as I can, but the driver slows right down. The car pulls over just past the bus stop. What am I going to do now? I glance around for my best escape route when the driver honks. I pretend I haven't noticed and start to walk briskly in the opposite direction.

"Ash!" a familiar voice calls from behind me. I spin around and feel like the biggest idiot in the world. It's Miss Murray!

"Where are you going?" she asks, leaning out of her window as I come toward her.

"Just home."

She smiles. "Where's home?"

"Oh, right. It's, er, Willow Drive, in the Manor estate. D'you know it?"

"Not the road, but I know the area. It's on my way home." She leans over to unlock the passenger door. "Get in. I'll drop you off."

"Are you sure?"

"It's pouring and you're getting drenched. Of course I'm sure. Come on, we can talk about the meeting. And about your schoolwork." She puts on a stern face as I get in the car.

"Ah, now I understand," I say with a smile as I put my seat belt on. "You just want to have a go at me for my last essay while I can't escape."

"Damn. You've cottoned on to my tactics at last," she says, slapping the steering wheel in fake frustration.

A comfortable silence follows, and then a moment later she says, "No, it's good to have the company on the way back. I hate driving in silence, and my radio's broken."

We've stopped at a traffic light, and she glances across at me. "Anyway, it's nice to have a chance to catch up with you, see how you're getting on."

"Right," I say, getting tongue-tied again. I'm replaying what she said about having company. Does she mean *my* company, or would anyone do? Am I special in any way? I mean—she pretty much makes everyone she talks to feel special, but would she give *any* student a lift home?

She gives me another quick glance, then laughs.

"What?" I ask guiltily.

"You look deep in thought."

I'm grateful for the dark, and for her eyes on the road so she can't see my face heat up. Is she psychic? Did she hear my thoughts?

OK, so she makes me feel special *and* paranoid.

"So what do you think of the group, then?" she goes on, telepathically knowing I need to change the subject.

"It's great, actually. I enjoyed thinking about why some things are more fun to argue about than others."

Miss Murray laughs. "So you're glad I twisted your arm into getting involved?"

"Yeah, I'm glad you talked me into it." Jesus. For a second, I hear myself and I'm relieved Cat can't hear me raving about an after-school club.

"Good. It's a nice group. I thought everyone had great ideas."

"Me too. I liked Aidan and Sal's one about dogs versus cats."

"Yeah, that was funny, wasn't it? Especially the way they did it, with Aidan as a cat and Sal as a dog. Very individual. And clever too, because on the surface it was about which one is cuter, but underneath, it was all about how we see ourselves and each other. That's probably a contender, actually."

And there she goes again. All we're doing is discussing a debate about pets, and yet she gets my mind making twelve million leaps. Aidan and Sal had basically said that dogs just want to love and cats just want to be served, and that we're all like one or the other.

I look at Miss Murray as she drives. Which one is she? Right now, I feel like the dog. I just want to be around her and make her smile.

The thought makes me edgy. I don't get why I'm thinking about her like this. It's not normal. Not normal for me anyway. I mean, I've never really thought about *anyone* like this. I think back to my boyfriends. I was really into Dylan to begin with, and, yeah, I checked my phone every five minutes to see if he'd texted, but it wasn't like this. I didn't want time to stand still whenever we were together so the moment would last longer. I didn't spend every minute thinking about what I could do that might make him smile.

Shouldn't I have felt like this about my boyfriends rather than about Miss Murray?

"Your suggestions were great too," she says. "I loved the one about the Internet being evil. I thought your ideas were bang on."

"Really?"

"Yes, really. Especially what you said about social networks and iPhones—how people are always looking for something more than they've got, looking to be somewhere other than where they are. It was clever. I liked it." Miss Murray laughs. "You remind me of myself sometimes in the way you think."

I want to wrap up what she's said and take it home with me. It feels like a gift. And I want to say something clever and witty so she'll keep on liking what I say — but I can't think of anything. We don't speak for a minute, and I have a brief panic. I don't want the journey to end in silence. I don't want it to end at all, actually. Each time we come to a set of lights, I will them to be red.

I decide to take a risk. "So, what was your unforeseen domestic emergency?" My voice trembles a bit.

She winces. "Didn't know you'd heard that. Well, I'd like to tell you that my washing machine exploded, but unfortunately it wasn't quite as simple as that." Then she looks across and half-frowns, half-grins. She doesn't say anything else.

"Is it something to do with Mr. Philips?"

"What would Mr. Philips have to do with it?" Her grin deepens, but she looks puzzled. I usually love it when she smiles, especially when it's me who's made her smile. It's like getting an A+ *and* a gold star on your work. Only this time I feel stupid. I wish I could take the words back. She says, "You don't think Mr. Philips and I are—"

"No, course not," I leap in. "I just meant . . ." What can I say? That *was* what I meant. My voice trails away. I'm an idiot and she's laughing at me; she thinks I'm a stupid kid who doesn't know anything.

She stops laughing. "I'm sorry," she says. "It's just that I didn't think you would imagine I'd be with someone like Mr. Philips. I thought you'd have known . . ." Her voice trails off.

"Known what?" I ask with more urgency than I can account for. We're nearly at the Manor estate, and my time is running out.

She turns into the estate and pauses before replying. I'm panicky and excited, and I'm sure she'll hear my heart over the engine.

Then she opens her mouth to speak. I hold my breath; letting it out would pierce the moment. I just want to stay sitting in her car with her, like this. I steal a quick look at her. As soon as she faces me again, I know I'll look away, embarrassed, caught out.

Her hair is tucked behind her ears, a few stray strands lazily brushing her cheek. I suddenly have the strongest sensation of wanting to reach out and curl them in place behind her ear. Oh, my God! What the hell am I thinking? What's happening to me?

My face burns. But I carry on looking at her. She's got laughter lines, like Mr. Philips. They make her look sophisticated. She's probably only five or six years older than me, but I suddenly feel boring and young. I don't want her to see me as a kid.

She turns to me and I instantly look away, just as I knew I would.

"Sorry, Ash," she says. "I didn't mean to laugh. It's only that . . . Mr. Philips isn't exactly my type, that's all. He's a nice man, a very nice man—just not for me."

I want to ask her something more, but I'm not sure I can find the right words.

"Now, where's this Willow Road?" she asks. The moment has passed. I give her directions and we drive in silence.

"Thanks for the lift." I fiddle with my seat belt as she pulls up at my house.

"It's fine, Ash. Any time. It was nice to have your company."

"Yeah, you too," I mumble.

"And Ash," she says, briefly putting her hand on my arm as I open the door, "I'm glad you joined the group. It's good to have you there."

My arm's burning and so is my face. I'm desperate to get away, and I want to stay all evening. As getting away is the only option, I step out of the car. "Thanks again," I say, and I stand in the road for a while as she drives off.

The street's quiet. Something about it feels different; something's shifted, but I don't quite know what. Or maybe I do, but I'm not ready to admit it just yet.

Looking up at the sky, I think about the way things change: faint blue day to this dense, jet-black night, marriage to divorce, certainty to uncertainty. Maybe *I'm* not everything I thought I was. The thought gives me a prickly sensation at the back of my neck, like an itch, only one that doesn't go away when you scratch it. It's like watching a horror film when you know something scary's coming up but you don't know what.

Perhaps nothing is as simple as it looks. Perhaps everything has another layer, a hidden room that only reveals itself when you accidentally stumble across the secret door.

Or perhaps I'm talking bollocks and it's time to go to bed.

16

"Another cup of tea, Ashleigh?" Elaine hovers over a tray of delicate white china teacups. I reply with a shrug. She looks nervously at Dad, who looks nervously at me.

"What?" Am I meant to be happy about this? Bizarrely, I'm only here for Mum. She said we should show them we're not bothered.

To be honest, I don't hold it against Dad. It's actually been quite nice at home not having arguments going on every day. And Elaine's not all that bad, I suppose. It's just weird. At least she's not a blond bimbo half his age. She looks stern when she listens to me, as she frowns and screws up her eyes.

"The cake's delicious," I say, smiling at Elaine through gritted teeth. Mum also said to be polite.

She beams at Dad, who gives me a grateful smile.

"I'll give you the recipe if you like," she says, cutting me another piece.

"Ash making a cake?" Dad says with a laugh. "That'll be the day."

"She's a talented young lady, Gordon." Elaine pats his knee and leaves her hand there. She gives me a quick wink—or is it a nervous twitch? "I'm sure she could do anything she wanted."

I'm looking at Dad's knee. Too much too soon, Elaine. I'm his daughter. He only split up with my Mum two months ago. *Move your hand.*

Dad shifts a bit in his seat and she eventually takes her hand away.

"Wouldn't mind another piece myself," Dad says. He holds out his plate and they smile as their eyes meet. Did he and Mum ever look at each other like that?

Next second, the front door opens, breaking their gaze, thank God.

"Jason, darling!" Elaine jumps up and flies to the door.

"Hi, Mum." A boy about my age squeezes past her, throwing a gray raincoat over the sofa.

"You're just in time to meet Ashleigh." She takes him by the hand.

"Hi, Ashleigh," he says without looking at me.

"Hi," I say. "It's Ash."

"Ash, this is Jason, Elaine's son," Dad chips in.

"Hi. It's Jayce," he says with half a grimace—or is it half a smile?

"Hi, Jayce," I say.

"Right, then." Jayce heads toward the stairs.

"Where are you going?" Elaine snaps.

"To my room. Why?"

"You've not forgotten we're going out for dinner?"

Jayce heaves a heavy sigh. "I'll be down in a minute. I'm just making a phone call."

"He's probably had a difficult day at work," Elaine says once he's out of earshot. "He's such a good lad." Then she and Dad exchange little conspiratorial smiles.

It's going to be a long evening.

I stare down at a huge white plate with a small circle of meat in the middle and tiny slivers of vegetables balanced beautifully across it. A line of sauce has been delicately drizzled around the edge of the plate. Fine dining. Polite clinks echo around the restaurant as well-dressed family groups and trendy young couples talk in waiting-room whispers across glass tables. Maybe I shouldn't have worn my jeans.

"How's school going, love?" Dad cuts into a minuscule piece of fish.

"Oh, you know. The usual."

He nods, as though he has the first clue what "the usual" is. When do we ever talk about school?

"What are you studying, Ashleigh?" Elaine asks with a smile. She's got a bit of spinach between her front teeth, but I don't want to tell her.

"English, law, and sociology."

"Oh, Jason did sociology!" she exclaims with delight, looking from one to the other of us as if this is a double date and she's just figured out that Jayce and I are soul mates. "Didn't you, Jason?"

"Yep." He demolishes most of his main course in one mouthful.

"What do you do now?" I ask.

"Work at Smiths."

I look at him for a beat before I burst out laughing. A second later, he starts too. Pretty soon the pair of us are hysterical, Jayce covering his mouth so he doesn't spit his food out onto his plate, and me covering my eyes so I can't see the looks of disapproval I know we're getting from Dad and Elaine.

"He's trainee manager, aren't you, Jason?" Elaine's saying somewhere in the distance. That just makes us laugh harder.

Eventually we calm down. Dad's face is bright red, and Elaine has pursed her lips.

"I'm sorry," I say. "But you can see the funny side, can't you?"

They look blankly at each other.

"It's just"—Jayce wipes his mouth—"just that after all those years of slaving away, and you being so proud of me doing all those 'interesting' A-levels—"

"Jason did psychology and theater studies as well, you know," Elaine interrupts. "And nearly got As in them both."

"Which means I actually got Bs," Jayce says to me. "And Ds in general studies and sociology. And, after all that, what am I doing? I'm just working in a shop."

"You are not *just* working in a shop," his mum counters. "You are training to be a manager."

"OK, Mum. Whatever."

"And you know very well you could have gone to

university," she adds. Then, looking at me, she says, "He had a place at Nottingham, you know."

Jayce glares at her.

"It wasn't me who told you to turn it down," she tells him.

"Defer." Jayce reddens slightly.

"Defer, then," she says, dabbing at her lips with a napkin. "But till when? Are you planning to go this year? You'll lose your place altogether if you don't. And then what? What on earth is holding you back?"

"I don't know." Jayce puts his knife and fork together. His face has colored even more deeply. "Can we drop it now, please?"

I glance at Dad. I've not got the giggles anymore.

"I'm going to university, I hope," I say, trying to direct the attention away from Jayce.

"What do you want to study?" he asks quickly, gratitude in his eyes.

"English, if I get the grades."

"Where have you applied?"

"Leeds is my top choice. Then Birmingham."

"Nice one. Well, good luck."

"I'll need it," I say with a smile. "The way things are going at the moment, I might be coming to you for a job stocking shelves come September."

Jayce laughs briefly, but then glances at his mum and stops.

Dad quickly picks up his menu. "Right, who's for dessert?" He smiles broadly around the table, and we study the choices with the eagerness of last-minute crammers before an exam.

You up? Got something I wanna run by you. I'm sitting up in bed early the next morning, texting Cat. I'm wide awake from an idea that I've just had.

My phone pings two seconds later. *Whassup?*

I text back my idea.

BRILLIANT! Do it!

Fab, thanks. Coffee later? I ask.

Yup. Back to bed for me now. Let me know how it goes xx

I put my phone away and creep into Mum's bedroom. She's still asleep. I'm standing just inside the door, like when I was little and had nightmares. I've got my laptop under my arm.

Mum opens an eye. "What's wrong?"

"Are you asleep?"

She looks at her clock and groans. "It's half past eight."

"I know."

"It's Sunday."

"I couldn't sleep." I perch on the side of her bed, holding my laptop next to me.

"What is it, Ash?"

"There's something I want you to do."

"Now?"

"I don't know what you'll make of it, but I think you should give it a try."

She rubs her eyes and sits up. "What is it?"

I put the laptop on the bed and open it up. "Take a look at these adverts."

"What are you buying?"

"I'm not buying anything."

"Selling?"

"Not selling."

I type in the web address for the site. "It's this . . ."

"You want to go fishing?"

"It's not about fishing."

"It's called *Fish in the Sea*. If it's not about fishing, what . . ." Mum's voice trails off as the penny drops.

I pull at my pajama sleeves. "I just don't think you should be on your own."

"I'm not on my own. I've got you."

"Mum, you know what I mean." I think about Dad and Elaine last night, and my resolve strengthens. "You deserve to have someone. A partner."

Mum sits up. "Oh, Ash, I don't know. It's only been a couple of months."

"Yeah, a couple of months of misery. Come on, Mum. What is there to lose?"

"I just don't think I'm ready."

"How will you know if you don't look?"

Mum straightens out the quilt in front of her. I perch on the bed and grab both her hands. "If you're not ready, I won't push it, but let's just have a look together."

Mum gives me a quick, tight smile. "All right, then," she says, shaking her head in resignation. "But I'm not doing anything without a cup of tea first."

Twenty minutes later we're sitting on her bed with a pot of tea for her, a steaming strong coffee for me, a plate of toast between us, and a screen full of descriptions of various men seeking love. Each has a one-line heading above his profile. That's all you get to see without signing up to the site.

"OK, let's just go through them one by one." I scroll down to the first one.

Professional male, GSOH, seeks attractive female for friendship, possibly more.

"What's GSOH?" Mum asks me.

"Good sense of humor. God, Mum, *everyone* knows that! Only you've got to have a really bad sense of humor to write it. So forget that one."

"What about this one?"

I look where she's pointing.

Young male, seeks an older female for fun times.

"Mum!"

She smiles. "I thought you didn't want me to be alone!"

"I know, but . . ."

"OK, this one, then."

Honest, open, medium-built male, good job. Seeks honest, straightforward, laid-back, slim female 25–35.

I stare at Mum.

"What?" She folds her arms.

"It's absolutely perfect. Except . . ."

"Yes?" She holds her stomach in.

"Well, you're not straightforward, you're not laid-back, you're kind of slim-*ish*, I suppose . . ."

"Anything else?"

"And you're forty-two!"

Mum lets her breath out and closes the laptop. "You're right. Why on earth am I doing this? I told you I'm not ready."

"Look, I didn't say you're not attractive. You're great. You're funny and smart and interesting and pretty—"

Mum sticks her tongue out at me.

"And you've got a brilliant SOH."

Her mouth starts to curl upward.

"What have you got to lose?"

"Oh, I don't know. How about my dignity, for starters?"

"Come on, Mum, let's do it. Strike while the iron's hot."

"Wait. That's it!" She opens the laptop again. Turning away from me, she taps a few keys.

"How's this?" she says a moment later and turns the screen to me.

Strike while the iron's hot! If you believe life begins at 40, then get in touch and let's see if it does.

"Brilliant! Especially for someone who isn't ready yet!"

Her smile wobbles. "Is this a good idea?"

"Yes!" And before she has time to argue, I'm signing her up to the website, showing her where to write her profile, and leaving her to get on with it.

17

A couple of weeks later, we're packing up at the end of English.

"Timed essay on Monday, don't forget!" Miss Murray shouts over the din. I'm trying to the be last to leave the classroom, as usual. Anything to gain a couple more minutes with her.

Robyn pauses by my side. "You coming?"

"See you in the morning," I say to her. "I just need to ask Miss Murray something."

Robyn heads off. Miss Murray looks up and smiles as I pause at her desk.

"I just wondered if you've got any advice," I say pathetically. *Really?* Can't I think of anything better?

"Advice?"

"I'm worried about the practice exams. I'm getting panic attacks and all that."

"You're going to be fine, Ash. I can feel it in my bones."

"What would your bones know about my feelings?" I ask, then stop breathing and look at my feet.

When I glance up, she's looking right at me. The

pounding in my ears almost blocks out her reply. "You'd be surprised."

I swallow hard. I can't speak, and we're locked in that game where you lose if you turn away or blink. It's too much for me, and I look down first.

"You're forgetting I was once in your position," Miss Murray's saying somewhere in the distance. "I know exactly what you're going through."

I can hardly bear the disappointment I feel. She didn't mean what I thought, then. But what *did* I think? What the hell do I *want* from her?

"I'll dig out some relaxation exercises for you if you like."

"Um, yeah, that'd be great, thanks."

"Anxiety is horrible. Go easy on yourself, OK?"

"Great, thanks. I'd, er, I'd better get going, then," I say ridiculously, holding my breath and not actually getting going at all while I wait for her to answer. She's started shuffling papers around on her desk. What's she thinking? What do I do now? Leave? Say something else? Keep standing here, looking into her eyes forever?

"Ash, I . . ." She breaks the painful thrill of the moment.

"What?"

She looks up. "Sorry, just trying to organize my mountain of marking." She points at the stack of papers on her desk and grimaces.

"Yeah, yes, of course. Sorry." I pick up my bag.

"No, don't be sorry. It's fine. I want to help. And I'll bring you the relaxation exercises for next lesson."

"Brilliant, thanks."

My mind's racing for something else I can say, something that can keep me here one minute longer—but I know I should go. Time with Miss Murray is always on a meter, always on the verge of running out. And I'm always wanting to catch those last moments before I have to go.

Does she know how I feel? Can she tell how much I want to—to what? What the hell *is* it that I want to do anyway? Touch her? Kiss her? What's the *matter* with me?

I drag myself to the door.

"Ash?"

"What?" I can't meet her eyes.

"Don't worry about the practice exams," she says with a smile. "You'll be fine. You're doing great—I'm proud of you."

And there it is. My crumb. The treasure that I can take away and store for later when I will turn it over and over, looking at it from every angle. My going-away gift that means I am able to leave.

"Thanks," I mumble as I shut the door and run to meet up with Cat in the yard. By the time we reach the bus stop, I've already replayed the conversation three times in my head.

The house is empty when I get in. Mum's got her first *Fish in the Sea* date. The deal is that I'm going to phone her at eight o'clock. If it's going well, she'll just let me know and get back to her meal. If not, I'm to pretend I'm having a personal crisis so she can make a quick getaway.

Eight o'clock on the dot, I call. Mum picks up instantly.

"Ash, tell me the house is burning down."

"What?"

"You've locked yourself out of the house, had to be rushed to the hospital — anything!"

"I take it he's not the man of your dreams, then?"

"I don't know about dreams, but he's boring me to sleep."

"OK, tell him I'm having a panic attack over my exams and you need to get home to calm me down. I'm a danger to myself in this state." That's the second time in one day I've used these exams in a panic-attack-related lie. It occurs to me that I probably *should* be a bit worried about them by now.

"Great. See you soon, then," Mum says.

"Good luck."

Half an hour later, I'm in my bedroom when I hear the front door open.

"I'm upstairs," I call. "You managed to get away before he bored you to death, then?"

Mum doesn't reply. Then I hear voices. I run to the top of the stairs. I try smiling politely while attempting to maintain the appearance of one who is mid–panic attack. Which I almost am now.

"Martin gave me a lift home," Mum says. *He insisted,* she mouths at me, her back to him.

"Hi, Martin." He doesn't look too bad — until I

get closer. He's wearing pointy cowboy boots — who wears actual pointy cowboy boots? — with slim jeans and a black leather jacket. Just wrong.

He wipes his palm down his jeans and reaches out to shake my hand.

Mum makes this please-help-me-get-rid-of-him face at me.

"Look," I say, holding my hand out and wobbling it. "I can't stop shaking. Mum, I don't know what to do," I say, forcing a wobble into my voice. "I really need you to help me."

"Oh, dear," Mum says woodenly. "I'm ever so sorry about this, Martin."

He smiles. He's got quite a nice smile, actually. "Not to worry."

Mum opens the door. "Thanks for a lovely evening," she calls down the drive as he fiddles with the gate.

"Yeah, she'd been trying to find something to help her sleep," I whisper.

Mum glares at me. For a second I think she's going to tell me off. Then she closes the front door and starts giggling. A moment later, I'm laughing too.

"Whose harebrained idea was this?" Mum gasps between guffaws.

"I think it was mine, but it might have been a bit yours too."

As we head for the kitchen and Mum puts the kettle on, we're clutching each other and roaring like maniacs. And for the first time in weeks, the laughter doesn't turn to tears.

18

I don't know if it was Miss Murray's words or what, but something clicked for me after my conversation with her, and I suddenly got to work. In fact, for the couple of weeks since then, it's been pretty much practice English exams for me and nothing else. I've barely seen Robyn or Cat, except for the odd evening when they've come over to study with me. In Robyn's case, we actually got loads of work done during those times. When Cat's been over, well, the word "study" is more like a euphemism for complete, all-out gossip-fest.

For the most part, I've been working on my own. Hard. And even kind of enjoying it.

And then, before I know it, the practice exams are finished. Over and done with, and I'm on the verge of getting my results!

We're having an extra session for Miss Murray to give us our English results and some feedback on how we did. I should have come in for tutor period earlier, but I didn't see the point in hanging around with nothing to do all afternoon.

Only thing is, she's not here. And, for that matter, nor is anyone else from my class. What's going on? To be honest, I don't care if none of the others get here. But where's Miss Murray?

Five to four. I peer through the window. Her desk has three piles of essay papers on it and a few open books around them. Empty Coke bottles are scattered on the tables around the room. Her bag has been left open on the floor by her chair.

I text Robyn. *Am at English. Where are you?*

I try the door. Locked. Something twists in my stomach — but why? It's not even four o'clock yet. Miss Murray's probably in the staff room; she'll be down in a minute.

Five past four. Ten past. Background noises — cars leaving, kids shouting, teachers hurrying home — they all die down as school empties for the day. What if something's happened to her? What the hell am I going to do? I can't go and see the headmaster; she hates me. I can't go home; how could I leave here without knowing if Miss Murray's OK?

My phone pings with a reply from Robyn. *Arrgghh! Forgot to tell you. No English this afternoon. Miss Murray sick or something. Sorrrrrrrrry!!!!*

I've just read the text when I hear someone behind me. I swing around just in time to see the surprise on Miss Murray's face.

"Ash! Oh, my God, I completely . . . I sent a message to your tutors, but you must have missed it. Ash, I'm sorry."

I've never seen her so flustered, not even when she came in late to the debating club that time.

"It's fine," I say, putting my phone away. Robyn must have gotten it wrong. Anyway, as long as Miss Murray's here now, it doesn't matter; I'm in no rush to get away. In fact, I'm happy that everyone else was around to get the message. It's just us.

My heart flips over at the thought of us spending time on our own. And, yeah, I could agonize about it and ask myself what the hell is going on—but I don't seem to want to bother anymore. All that matters is how I feel when I'm around her.

She looks at her watch. "We'll have to reschedule, I'm afraid."

She must see the disappointment on my face as she continues, "Something came up. I had to leave early this afternoon. I've just nipped back to collect my things."

"I don't mind having the lesson now if you want." I try to sound casual.

She's unlocking the door as she answers. "They'll be closing the place up in half an hour. We don't want to get trapped in here all weekend, do we?"

I can't imagine anything better than being stranded on my own with Miss Murray for two whole days.

"No, I suppose not," I say.

She's gone inside, and I don't know if I'm supposed to follow or go away. I hover at the door while she starts to clear her desk. She's bustling around, shoving piles of papers together and bundling them into her bag.

"D'you want me to go?" I ask hesitantly.

"Um, it's just . . ." She looks at me and pauses. I try to act like I don't mind what she says. I've got a casual smile fixed onto my face, which probably looks ridiculous. The silence is broken only by the sound of rain splattering unevenly against the window.

A second later, a knock on the door makes me jump like a thief with a guilty conscience. It's the janitors. "Can we get in?" one of them asks, pointing at her floor cleaner.

Miss Murray starts shoving papers into her bag again. "Two seconds," she says.

I shuffle my feet, and she looks at me again. "Look, I tell you what," she says. "Seeing as you've come in, why don't we nip round the corner to Starbucks and have a quick talk about your paper over a cuppa?" She looks across at the door. "I feel bad about letting you down when you've made the effort."

I try to keep my smile casual as I reply nonchalantly, "Fine, yeah, whatever."

Starbucks is nearly empty when we arrive. Who wants to hang out in a coffee shop just around the corner from school on a Friday afternoon? We get drinks and then I plonk myself down on a seat; Miss Murray squeezes in opposite.

I try to think of something to say, but my mind is empty. That's a lie. My mind is full. It's full of thoughts about her. Where was she earlier? What is it that was more important than us? Than me?

Miss Murray breaks the silence. "So, let's talk about your paper, then."

"Was it awful?"

She frowns. "I'll try and break it to you gently. . . . You got an A."

"An *A*?" I splutter. "I've *never* gotten an A."

"Well, you have now."

I stir my hot chocolate. "It's you who did that, you know," I mumble.

"No, Ash. It's you who did it. And you can do it again."

"But I did it for you," I say quietly.

She doesn't say anything, and I wish I could take the words back. When I look up, I can't read her expression. "What?" I ask.

"Thank you," she says. And just for a moment, I think I see her for who she is. Instead of the amazing mentor who teaches me and teases me and knows what I'm thinking better than I know myself, I just see another person. "Right, come on. Let's have a look at what you did right and wrong."

She opens the paper and leads me through my answers. All I can see are tick marks and "YES" and "WELL DONE!" written in red pen everywhere. I mean, there are a few critical comments here and there too, but not many. And there's the grade at the top of the front page. Like she said: A.

"You did brilliantly," she says, passing me the paper. "Just like I knew you would."

"I can't believe it," I say.

"Well, I can. And you should too."

"Thanks," I say. I take a swig of my hot chocolate and try to think about what to say next. I want to keep her interested. Want to keep her here. She's nearly finished her drink, and I don't want her to go.

I'm finding it harder and harder to keep my thoughts inside. Does she know how I feel about her? Do *I* know how I feel? What does it make me? And is she the same?

"Can I ask you a personal question?" I ask before I manage to stop myself.

"I can't promise I'll answer."

Can I really ask her? And now that I've got the chance, what *exactly* do I want to know? Eventually I chicken out and say, "Do you like teaching at St. John's?"

She looks surprised. Then, staring straight at me, she says, "Is that really what you wanted to ask me?"

I hold her eyes and hold my nerve. "What did you *think* I wanted to ask you?"

She laughs. "They must have put something in this hot chocolate, as I almost feel inclined to answer you honestly, and we can't have that, can we?"

"Can't we?"

She laughs again. "Come on, Ash, we're going round in circles."

"Tell you what, then. Why don't you answer the question you thought I was going to ask, and I'll see if I can guess what the question is?"

"All right, then. Yes."

"Yes, what?"

"Yes. That's the answer."

I laugh. "Oh, well, that narrows it down a bit."

"What, you want more than that?"

"It might help."

"All right." She stops smiling and gives me one of those direct looks that make me go still inside and forget anything I'm saying or thinking. "Yes, I am." Then she tilts her head to one side. "And, to be honest," she continues, "I think you are too."

I'm about to speak when she adds, "But maybe you don't know it yet."

My head is swimming with thoughts that I daren't say out loud. "Brilliant?" I ask in the end. "Talented? Overworked?"

She laughs.

"Highly irritating?"

"Now you're getting closer." Then she glances at her watch and suddenly gets up. "Ash, I've got to go," she says seriously, and before I know it, she's halfway to the door. I follow her like an obedient puppy. "I didn't realize how late it was getting," she says.

"We could always stay a bit longer." The words are out before I can stop them.

She pauses at the door and turns to me, her eyes dark.

"I mean, just to talk," I falter. Suddenly I've lost my footing. One small slip and I'm in unfamiliar territory. "We could have another drink or something . . ."

"Ash, I'm your teacher."

"Well, yeah, technically. Temporarily. But, hey, you're only a few years older than me. You could even be my big sister or—"

"It's not that simple." She heads out of the café, and I follow her into the street.

"No. 'Course not," I say as we walk. I'm desperately trying to keep some lightness in my voice, but I know she can see through it. She gets past all my defenses. She can read me like a book. She has been able to from the moment she first walked into our classroom.

"And it's not just about doing what you want," she's saying. "There are other people to consider. Another person. Do you understand what I'm saying?"

"I think so," I reply as we reach her car. "But you're right," I suddenly blurt out. "I think I am too."

"You're what?"

"I know what the question is."

"I really have to go, Ashleigh." She's holding her keys and facing me, and I'm standing in the rain, stupidly shuffling from one foot to the other. I don't know how to say good-bye to her. She glances at her watch again. "You'd better get going," she says. "Won't your mum be worried?"

My mum? Why should she be worried? She doesn't know that I spend every moment thinking about the next time I'm going to see you, or that the high point of my day is when you walk past me in the corridor on your way to the staff room at break. She doesn't know how disappointed I feel if I don't see you, or if I see you and you don't smile at me. She doesn't know how

I couldn't concentrate on what you were saying the other day when we sat together at your desk because all I could think about was how close you were — so close, at one point, that your leg touched mine. I didn't move a muscle in case it broke the contact, and when you moved your leg, I couldn't concentrate then either because I was too busy wondering if you'd moved on purpose.

She doesn't know that sometimes I look at your mouth when you're talking and I imagine kissing you. That I want to do it so much I'm scared in case one day I forget myself and just do it anyway. She doesn't know that I have never, not once, not even silently, admitted any of these thoughts before, even in my head.

"My mum'll be fine," I say eventually.

I'm the only one who's worried.

Miss Murray's looking at me so hard I wonder if she heard me thinking. Then she says, "Don't look so anxious. Come here." She takes hold of me and hugs me. She feels sorry for me. She thinks I'm a stupid, messed-up kid who needs comforting, and she's giving me a friendly hug, a motherly hug, letting me know it's all going to be OK.

I guess the hug probably lasts five seconds — if that — but it feels like forever, and I don't know how to let go. I can hear her breath in my ear, and I can't breathe out. I'm just breathing in and in, and any minute now I know I'm going to burst. She's holding me so gently, as though I might break, and I wonder if maybe I will.

Then she says, "I need to get going," and I step back as though she's scalded me.

"Sorry," I stammer.

"There's nothing to be sorry about," she says with a smile, but it's not like her usual smile, and I know she's retreated to some place where I'm not allowed to follow. It's part of the rules to the games we play. The rules she wrote and I haven't even read. "Have a good weekend, Ashleigh."

"Yeah, you too."

And then she's gone, and I'm standing in a side street in the rain, wondering where the hell to go from here.

19

My mother puts the microphone back in its holder and takes a small bow as applause ripples around Feathers. It's their monthly singer/songwriter night. It's basically karaoke, but they changed the name a couple of years ago when someone told the manager that no one does karaoke anymore. Whoever gave them that information was clearly wrong, as it's their busiest night every month.

I'm squashed in a corner with Tony, Fish in the Sea number two, who's clapping his hands together above his head as though she's served an ace in the final at Wimbledon. I'm not sure how I ended up being a gooseberry like this; she said it would be "safer" that way. He's all right, actually. Quite promising. He's a little bit taller than her, thin and wiry. Nice smile. They spoke loads on the phone before tonight. When he turned up, he brought a card—for me!

"What's this for?" I asked, ripping open the envelope. It was a good-luck card.

"Your A-levels," he said, winking at Mum. "Your mother says you get a bit anxious."

I stifled a laugh. It was quite sweet of him, really.

"She's ever so good, isn't she?" he says now, jumping up a little in his seat, his eyes following her as she picks her way around the tables back to us.

"Yeah." I sip my drink. "She's all right."

He touches her back briefly as she slips into the seat between us. "You were brilliant." He passes her lager and lime across the table. "To your mum," he says, lifting his glass. "Simon Cowell, I hope you're watching."

Mum laughs and smiles at him.

"Cheers, Tony." I clink his glass.

A little while ago, it might have been a bit weird seeing Mum with another man. Right now, I don't care about anything, except the fact that Miss Murray hugged me. It's all I've thought about for two weeks. We've not really spoken since. I've been too shy to think of excuses to hang around after lessons, and, more often than not, she's left in a bit of a hurry lately.

While Mum and Tony chat and laugh, I slip into one of my favorite fantasies. I've done something brilliant, written a book and won an award or something. Miss Murray's in the audience, and I thank all the people who have helped, then I pause and look at her. She's staring at me, her eyes shining as I dedicate the award to her, telling everyone that everything I did was for her, and everything I am is because of her. People look around and nudge one another and point and whisper, but I don't care, because I know that I love her, and that she loves me too.

"Another drink, Ash?" Tony's standing up and tapping his empty pint glass.

"Or shall we go, love?" Mum breaks in. "You look tired."

I'm about to suggest leaving when I spot a vaguely familiar face. "Jayce!" I call. Mum and Tony turn to see two smart young men in suits heading our way. I fumble over the introductions. What do you say? *Mum, this is your husband's girlfriend's son. Jayce, this is your new dad's wife and her boyfriend?* In the end I chicken out and let them all work it out for themselves—which leaves me wondering who his friend is.

"And this is Adam. From work," Jayce mutters. Then he adds quickly, "Let me get a round."

"Good timing, lads," Tony says. "Just a Coke for me, please. Designated driver."

"I'll help." I follow, leaving Adam with Mum and Tony.

"She's not got a bad voice, your mum," Jayce says as we make our way back across the pub with the drinks. The others are deep in conversation about their favorite musicals. "God, he's such an old fart," Jayce says as he nudges me and points at Adam.

"Why don't we do a turn together?" Mum says, her cheeks pink as she downs her drink and Jayce passes her a fresh one. Adam looks at Jayce.

"Nothing to do with me, mate; you're on your own here," Jayce tells him with a grin.

"What would we sing?" Adam asks Mum.

"Anything."

197

Adam passes the book of songs to Mum. "You choose."

"I know what we'll do." Mum smiles shyly at Tony, then passes the book to Adam.

"Ooh, yes. Robbie Williams and Nicole Kidman. I love that song."

Mum looks shocked. "You mean Frank and Nancy Sinatra!"

Adam shrugs. "I guess it's a generation thing." Then he knocks back half of his pint, drags his sleeve across his mouth, and takes his jacket off. He loosens his tie and bends down to take Mum's hand. "Right, come on then. Let's do it."

They make their way to the front of the pub, whispering to each other as a round of applause breaks out. The bar owner, Mr. Green, is taking a bow after his monthly rendition of "My Way."

Minutes later, the three of us are transfixed as Mum and Adam give an amazing performance of "Something Stupid." It's as if they've been rehearsing it for weeks. There's a roar of applause and calls for an encore when they've finished. They bow for ages, grinning at each other.

"Are you sure you two have never met before?" Jayce asks suspiciously as they squeeze back into their seats, eyes shining.

"Do you think they liked us?" asks Mum.

Tony puts his hand on hers. "They thought you were absolutely wonderful."

Mum leaves her hand for a couple of seconds, then

moves it and gives me a quick glance. I take a swig of my drink.

Jayce is looking sideways at Adam. "All this time, you had a hidden talent and I never knew."

"So, how long have you two known each other?" Mum asks Jayce.

"We met through work," he answers quickly.

"I order books and he bosses me about," Adam adds with a grin.

"You'd better watch what you get up to, then," Tony says. "Don't want to go upsetting the boss."

"Absolutely." Jayce drains his glass and waves it at Adam. "I keep telling him that."

Adam takes the glass and stands up. "Right, I'd better get the drinks then, hadn't I?" He points at Mum's glass. "What're you having, Ms. Sinatra?"

Outside the pub, we all hug each other as though we're lifelong buddies.

"Really nice to see you again, Ash," Jayce says.

"Yeah, you too," I slur, suddenly realizing I've had about five too many. And then, before I know it, Tony's driving us home, Mum humming gently, me in the back.

"Nice lads," he's saying to no one in particular, and it's midnight and I'm another day closer to seeing Miss Murray again.

20

My hands are shaking as I lift up my notes. We're in the gym, which is a bit of a joke as there are only about thirty people here altogether—ten from the debating group and then whatever friends we've each managed to drag along. I didn't tell any of mine about it, other than Robyn, obviously. I catch her eye and she gives me a big grin and a thumbs-up.

How on earth did we end up with *this* as a topic?

My heart is beating so hard it feels as if it's jamming up my throat. I squeeze my words around it. "We've heard many arguments on both sides of the question of gay rights around the world. Things are better than they were—in some countries. In others, things are pretty much as bad as they've ever been. So I just have one question . . ."

I catch Miss Murray's eye for a split second, my cheeks burning. She smiles, and I instantly look away.

"If it was you being told you couldn't marry the person you love, you being told you couldn't adopt a child, you who had to hide what you are for fear of imprisonment—would you still think it was OK? Gay people are just the same as everyone else in the world. Don't they"—I can't help it; I emphasize the *they*—"deserve the same rights as everyone else? Last time I looked, this is the twenty-first century, and it's about time the world stopped passing judgment on people because of who they happen to love. Love doesn't discriminate, and nor should the law. Not in this country. Not in this world. Not in this lifetime."

I take a tiny bow before sitting down and tidying my notes. It gives me a chance to look down and hide my burning face.

There's a moment of silence before my team starts to clap. I look up. Miss Murray is staring at me, an unreadable look on her face. Then she claps too. Most of the room is clapping. Some are on their feet. Robyn's cheering and whistling and clapping harder than anyone. A couple of girls at the back are giggling behind their hands. I don't care.

We win the vote by a landslide.

I should have left with Robyn and the rest of the team. They've gone to the pub for a drink to celebrate our win. I made up some excuse about having to call my mum first and said I'd meet them there. I feel really embarrassed lying to Robyn, but I can't help it. I can't leave yet.

I suppose that makes me a full-fledged nerd. I'm skipping a pint to help stack chairs and tables in a school gym.

I plonk some chairs down next to Miss Murray. Everyone else has gone except Mr. Philips.

Miss Murray smiles. "You were brilliant," she says.

"Thanks." I smile back. Embarrassed. I notice she's looking pale and tired. Not her usual self. "Are you OK?" I ask.

She turns away and picks up a couple more chairs. "I've been better."

I want to ask her what's wrong but can't seem to think of the words.

"OK if I leave you with this?" Mr. Philips is putting his jacket on. "Last train in five minutes!"

"Has everyone else gone?" she asks him.

"Yep. Just us in here."

"I don't mind helping finish off," I say.

"Thanks, Ashleigh," he says on his way out the door. "Good speech, by the way."

And then he's gone, and we're on our own.

I daren't look at her. I concentrate on piling up chairs as though it's the most engrossing thing I've ever done. She's carrying a stack toward me, and I don't trust myself to speak.

"Sorry if I'm not very talkative," Miss Murray says finally as she puts the chairs down and leans against them.

Before I manage to stop myself, I say, "It's not me, is it?"

Her face curls into a frown. "You? Why would it be you?"

"I don't know. I just thought . . ." My voice trails off.

How the hell can I say what I feel when her eyes are focused on me like they are now? I just want to lose myself in her. I think I am.

"I'm just going through a bad patch at home," she says lightly. Then she looks away and adds, "My partner has left me."

It's the most honest thing she's ever said to me, and the best, and the worst.

"Oh, I'm sorry." Am I? How can I be sorry that there's no "other person" anymore? For a ridiculous moment, I wonder if it's because she has feelings for me too. "When?"

"Over the weekend. It's been coming for a while." Her voice cracks a little, and she rubs her eyes with her fist.

"How could anyone leave you?" I whisper. "You're so — brilliant."

She grimaces. "You don't know me."

"I know some things." I take a tiny step toward her. "I know you're really smart, and you think about stuff, and you're caring."

"See, I told you, you clearly don't know me at all. I'm not really any of those things," she says bitterly, turning away from me to balance another chair on her pile. "I'm selfish, it turns out, and thoughtless and insensitive."

I look at her from behind as she talks. Wisps of hair lie carelessly on the back of her neck, and the desire to touch her shoots through me from my stomach to my throat. I edge closer to her.

"You're the best person I've ever known," I say, my voice shaking with nerves and longing. I want to kiss her neck. I don't know if I can stop myself.

Then she turns around and her face is centimeters away from mine. "Ash, I don't think—"

I stare at her mouth as she starts to speak. But she doesn't finish her sentence, and she's looking at me too. Suddenly, everything outside this room doesn't matter, doesn't exist. The only thing that means anything is what's happening now, here, between us.

I'm going to kiss her.

I am. I'm going to do it. I can almost feel her lips, soft against mine. The longing is so intense it's like a physical pain, pain like I've never known—the pain of needing someone so much.

I lean forward. Close my eyes. I'm—

"Ash, we . . . this isn't what I . . . you need to . . ." She stops midsentence, runs a hand through her hair, turns away from me.

My eyes snap open. "There's no one around." I smile, nervously, stupidly. "It's OK."

"No, Ashleigh, it's not OK." She turns around and looks at me, and I stop smiling when I see her face. "It is—definitely—not—OK."

She crosses the hall to pick up her coat. "You need to go home. Your mum will be wondering where you are."

"It's fine. She won't mind. She's cool."

"I need to finish my grading," she says, heading for the door.

I can't let her go. Can't let this moment end. It might

be the only one we get. I follow her to the door. "You said you liked me, you enjoy talking to me," I say weakly, my arms hanging limply by my sides, my face on fire.

"I do like you," Miss Murray says. "Of course I do, just not—"

"You made me feel special."

"Ash, you *are* special. You don't need me to tell you that. You just need to believe it yourself."

"Special to you."

Miss Murray lets out a breath. "OK, maybe you are special, in a way. I guess I see a bit of myself in you. And, yes, OK, perhaps that means I feel a closer bond than I should. A teacher's not supposed to have favorites—but yes, all right then, I admit it, I guess you're one of my favorite students." She tries for a smile. "Is that good enough?"

I step back. I feel like I'm falling, like she's punched me in the stomach. "A favorite student," I repeat. "That's all I am?"

Miss Murray stares at me. "Ash, what did you *think*?"

"I . . . I thought . . ." What *did* I think? My thoughts and my words drain away.

Miss Murray is leaning on the door. "Ash, come on. It's time to go." Her hand is so tight on the handle, her knuckles are pale. She's looking at the floor.

"Miss Murray."

"What?" She doesn't move.

I stare at her face, but she doesn't return the look. "I love you."

The air in the room has frozen, every atom suspended. Then her tense body slackens. Her hand loosens its grip on the door, and she turns her head slowly toward me. She meets my gaze for a moment. Her eyes have dark rings under them. Her forehead is creased with worry. Her cheeks are pale. I want to make it all OK. I want to make her happy. I desperately want to touch her face.

"I know," she says quietly.

Then she opens the door and waits for me to leave.

"See you on Monday?" I call as she locks the hall and heads toward her classroom, but she can't have heard me as she doesn't reply.

PART
3

21

"So, if you could open your books to page . . . where did you say you were up to? Right, yes, page one-three-three. Now, someone tell me what you've learned about this poem. You, yes, you, what's your name?"

I stare at the substitute teacher like a zombie. What the hell is going on? Miss Murray hasn't missed a single lesson since she started here.

I make a quick escape, pleading a desperate need for the loo. I soon find myself wandering aimlessly down the corridors.

"Shouldn't you be in class, Ashleigh?" I turn around and see the headmaster, Mrs. Banks, coming toward me.

"I was looking for you," I bluff, convincing no one. She folds her arms and stares at me. "It's about Miss Murray," I add quickly.

"Ah, yes, I was going to come and see you about her."

My heart flips over. "Me?"

"Don't worry, you aren't in trouble. I mean your whole class. In fact, I'll come back with you now and I can tell you all together."

"Tell us what?" I try to keep up as she marches down the corridor.

"You'll just have to wait, Ashleigh. I'm not in the habit of repeating myself."

She's found the only way of getting me back into that awful lesson.

So we hear the news together. Me, who spends every waking minute thinking about Miss Murray, and the rest of the class, who probably just see her absence as a good excuse to ditch.

"I know this is not an easy time for you." Mrs. Banks looks around at us. I fidget with my pen, trying to look as unconcerned as everyone else. Robyn and I exchange a quick look and a half-shrug.

"Your A-levels are nearly upon you . . ."

As if we need reminding.

"So I know it's not the best time for this to happen." She pauses, clicking her pen. I want to snatch the thing from her. Then she says, "I'm afraid Miss Murray has left us."

Left us? What do you mean? How can she leave us? How can she leave me? A dull pain creeps into my stomach while I try to maintain a bored, blank expression.

"Her contract was due to run to the end of this term, but sadly, for personal reasons, Miss Murray has had to leave early. She has done an excellent job, and we are very grateful to her. Mrs. Hollins here will teach you for the remainder of the term. Now, any questions?"

Can I trust myself to speak? Thankfully, Luke saves

me the job. "Why couldn't she stay for the whole year, miss?"

"As I've said, personal reasons. In other words, nothing to do with you. Or me, in fact."

"You mean you don't know, miss?"

Mrs. Banks flushes. "Any more questions?" she asks briskly. Luke's right. She clearly doesn't know.

Personal reasons. Is it me? Is it what happened, the things I said? Am I so completely awful to be around that she had to leave? Or is it something else, not me at all? How can I find out?

Mrs. Banks flashes her smarmy smile around the room. "Now, let's save our thoughts for studying, shall we? You'll need every bit of mental energy you can muster over the coming weeks." And she's out the door before anyone else has time to speak.

At the end of the day, I go over to Robyn's with her. I'm still in a daze. Robyn comes into her bedroom, where I'm sitting on the floor with my books around me, and hands me a plateful of Jaffa Cakes. Comfort eating.

"Thanks."

She sits on her bed. I glance over at her, assuming she'll be immersed in the book that to me is just a blur. But she's staring into space.

"I can't believe she's gone," she says without looking at me. "Do you know what I mean?" Then she looks at me so intensely that for a moment I'm confused.

Is Robyn in love with Miss Murray as well? Does she know how I feel?

"I think so," I reply hesitantly.

"I've never had a teacher like her," she says. "No one else ever seemed to really care about us like she did."

"You're talking as though she's dead or something."

"I just don't see her as the kind of person who would abandon us like that. She was too committed. Don't you think?"

The tears are falling from the bottom of my nose and my chin; I don't bother to wipe them away. "I'm sorry, I'm sorry."

Robyn slides down onto the floor and puts her arm around my shaking shoulders. "Hey, it's OK. You don't need to apologize for crying."

Her impossible efforts to understand make me feel even worse, and she holds me tighter and strokes my arm.

"It's OK, it's OK," she half whispers. I stop for a moment and look at her. She wipes a tear from my cheek with her palm and smooths my hair back. I suddenly realize how close she is and how tightly we're holding each other. For a second, she returns my look. Then, before stopping to think, my eyes are closed and I'm leaning toward her. Am I imagining she's Miss Murray? I don't know. I don't know anything anymore. I tighten my arms around her and brush her lips for a second, for a fraction of a second—

Suddenly she's pulling away from me, scrambling

out of my arms as though she's just discovered a beetle inside her sweater.

I put my hand to my face as though I've been slapped. I actually think I have been.

"What the hell do you think you're doing?" Robyn is shrieking at me from halfway across the room.

I start to get up. She takes a step backward and slips on one of my books. I move forward to try and stop her falling.

"Don't come near me," she spits, awkwardly regaining her balance.

"Robyn, I—"

"What do you think I am? What are *you?*"

"What d'you mean, what am I? You know what I am. I'm your friend."

"*Friend?* Is that what you do with your friends?"

"Look, I don't know what I was thinking. I thought you wanted . . ."

"Wanted what?"

"I didn't mean to do anything. I was just confused."

"*You're* confused. What do you think I am? I thought we were friends. I didn't know you had ulterior motives."

What can I say? *Hey, don't worry, it's not you I fancy, it's Miss Murray?* I keep my mouth shut.

"I think you should leave," Robyn says quietly.

"Oh, for heaven's sake, Robyn, can't we talk about—"

"There's nothing to talk about. I just think it'd be better if you went."

"I don't need this," I say quietly.

"No, nor do I." She's standing near the door, her arms are folded, and she's staring at me like I'm a stranger.

Neither of us says anything while I pack up my things. The silence shames me. "Robyn, I'm sorry, I didn't want to make you—"

"Look, it's nothing personal. I'm just not . . . like that."

"Nor am I. Well, I mean, not about you. I just don't know what I—"

"Ash," she says, opening her door even as she speaks, "I'm sorry, but I really don't want to talk about it. I'll see you at school, right?"

"Right. OK."

She gives me a quick, tight smile as she closes her door, and I walk home in a daze.

When I was in primary school, I joined the chess club. It was in one of those awful caravan-type rooms they used to put classes in when they didn't have enough proper classrooms. They were called "terrapins," and they were meant to be there for a term or two; they're probably still there now. It was on Thursdays after school, and I only went because I wanted to be with my "boyfriend," Jamie Middleton. We used to go around the back and practice kissing each other on the lips and wonder if we were doing it right.

I never improved at chess. I was too busy kissing Jamie Middleton. But one thing I remember about the game is that you always have to look at the pieces around you and think about five steps ahead if you're to stand any chance of winning. I remember my head spinning from trying to work out all the possible moves in one go. Sometimes I'd look at the board and realize I was being completely slaughtered. I hardly had any decent pieces left, and the game was closing in on me.

Yeah, I remember that feeling well. Checkmate.

22

"Pens down, please."

I hand in my law paper. Two years' work swapped for five flimsy sides of A4 paper.

Cat lights up a cigarette when we're barely out of the building. "That was a load of crap, wasn't it?"

"It was awful."

"Only three more, thankfully. Can't wait to get away from this dump. I bet you can't either."

"What d'you mean?"

Cat blushes for what I think must be the first time in her entire life and mumbles, "Well, you know. Get away from all the . . . people."

"Huh?"

"I just thought . . . Look, never mind. It's all garbage anyway."

"What's all garbage?" Heat rises in my face, spreading quickly to my ears.

"You know, what people are saying."

My voice comes out like it's being squeezed through a pipe. "What are they saying?"

Cat carries on walking without answering, taking

her jacket off as we get out into the street. The sun's shining right into my eyes. I grab her arm and make her stop. "What are they saying, Cat?"

Cat looks down at her feet. "Look, I know it's rubbish, and even if it isn't, it doesn't matter. You've got me, right?"

"Yes, right." I hold my breath.

Cat pauses while a group of girls passes us. I don't know if it's paranoia, but they start laughing a few feet away. They're talking about me; I just know they are.

"You and Miss Murray."

I hold my breath. My stomach is a vacuum; my ears feel like they're on fire.

"They're saying you're having an affair."

"*What?*"

"That she seduced you, and that's why she got the sack last month."

"She didn't get the—"

"Look, I'm not saying that's what happened. I'm just telling you the gossip, like you asked. I didn't start it. I don't even believe it."

"Sorry."

"And anyway, it's rubbish. Isn't it?"

"Of course it's rubbish! Who the hell is spreading this stuff?"

"Just people, you know. Mainly people who don't even know you."

"Oh, great." I roll my eyes. "That makes me feel a whole lot better."

Cat grins. "Come on. What does it matter what

people are saying about you? We just need to show them you don't give a damn."

"We?"

"Of course, we. That's what mates are for, and I'm your mate, aren't I?"

"Yeah." I smile at her. "Thank goodness."

"Right, come on, you daft bint," she says, walking away. "Exam's over. Let's celebrate."

"Cat, it was only the first one. I don't finish for another two weeks."

"Even more reason," she yells over her shoulder. "Don't want to waste time worrying. Come on, let's go for a drink."

"Cat, you are impossible." I hold my hands out in a giving-in kind of way.

I'm smiling as we turn the corner, but I stop as I see who's ahead of us. It's Robyn, with Luke. As soon as she sees me, Robyn suddenly throws her arms around Luke and whispers in his ear. He looks at her wide-eyed for a second, then stops, turns, puts his arms around her, and kisses her. Not like a peck on the cheek—he really goes for it, right there in the middle of the pavement, so we can't even get past them without stepping onto the road.

"'Scuse me." Cat barges past, knocking into Luke on the way.

"Cat, I . . ." Luke breaks off and tries to follow her, but Robyn doesn't look pleased and he stops.

Robyn looks embarrassed for a second, as if she knows she's been a right cow. Then she links an arm

218

into Luke's and glances at me as if to say, *Look, see. This is what I want. A man, right? Get the message?*

"You're both pathetic," I say as I push through the middle of them, breaking Robyn's precious contact with Luke's arm.

"Why?" Luke looks utterly confused. "What have we done?"

"Ask *her*," I tell him without turning back.

Cat can march pretty fast when she's in a bad mood, so I'm panting by the time I catch up with her.

"Arse."

"Me? What have I done wrong?"

"Not you, stupid." She gives half a smile. "Him. God, he just doesn't get it."

"I hate to say this, but I don't think I do either."

"All that. Snogging that mate of yours just to make me jealous. As if," she snorts.

"Oh, right, yeah. Well she's not exactly . . . We . . ." My voice trails off. How do I explain this one? I settle for "We're not such good mates anymore" and leave it at that.

"He's hardly talked to me since we went to the cinema that time. I think he thought we were going out with each other till I put him right—told him we were just mates and that was it."

"So you've never fancied Luke, not even a tiny little bit?"

"Look, he was better than nothing at a time when there wasn't exactly anyone else to hang out with." She looks at me meaningfully, and I redden. "Well, he's

219

slightly better than that. He can be a laugh, I suppose, and it's quite flattering to have someone at your heels telling you you're wonderful and doing anything you want in the hope that you'll give them a bit of what *they* want too."

"So you did it?"

"What?"

"Slept together?"

Cat bursts out laughing. "What are you on about? What would I be doing sleeping with Luke? It'd be like having sex with my brother."

"I just thought . . ."

"You know, you can be pretty thick at times." Cat punches me on my arm.

"Ow."

"And a wimp. Come on, the pub's waiting." And she's halfway down the street before I've had time to digest any of our conversation.

Cat takes me to a pub I've never been in before; I've never even noticed it. The Nag's Head. It's kind of cozy: L-shaped and tiny. There are only about eight tables, and all but two are empty. Two businessmen are talking at one, and a girl with choppy blond hair and a tiny gold stud in her nose is reading a book at another. She looks up from her drink as I squeeze onto a wooden bench seat in the corner of the L.

For some reason, I think about Miss Murray. Well, I think about her pretty much all the time, but something about the girl *makes* me think of her. It's her eyes, I think.

It's been nearly a month now and not a single word. Sometimes I think I'm going to burst with how much need there is inside me. Waking up every morning wondering if it will be the day I hear from her. Not knowing how to fill the hour between waking and the postman arriving. Other than checking e-mails and Facebook constantly on the off chance she contacts me online.

A small part of me knows it's not going to happen, but the rest of me doesn't want to admit it.

It's as though she's been rubbed out. I don't even know if she's still around or if she's moved away or what. I almost want to talk to Cat about her, but I wouldn't trust myself not to betray my feelings if I actually said her name out loud. And I can't do it. I daren't. Not even with Cat.

Sometimes I imagine bumping into her in town, and I try to think of all the things I'd say. But I can't, because I don't believe it'll happen. I think there's more chance of me spotting a UFO than ever seeing Miss Murray again.

How do you get used to living with a hole inside you?

Cat's staring at me intently. She fiddles with one of the pint glasses she just brought over. "Ash, you know that stuff, before?"

"What stuff?"

"You know. The conversation. About Miss Murray and stuff."

221

I reach for my drink. "Mmm-hmm."

"So, can I ask you something?"

"Cat, I've told you — there was nothing going on."

"No, I know that. I believe you."

I look at her. "OK. So what is it, then?"

Cat shifts in her seat. "Are you . . ." She pauses. Clears her throat.

"Am I what?"

"Nothing. Doesn't matter."

"No, what? What were you going to say?"

"Look, I don't want to ask in case I'm way out of line. You might be offended."

"I won't." Won't I? What's going on?

"How d'you know when you don't even know the question?"

"Look, I promise. Whatever you say, I won't be offended." My voice shakes. Why am I so scared?

"Sod it. OK. Ash, are you a lesbian?" she says. And it's out there. Just like that.

She stares at me; I stare back. Now what? I suddenly remember the time I sneaked out when I was grounded for coming home from a party with a huge love bite on my neck.

I'd gone over to Cat's, and her mum came home early. I dived into Cat's closet just as her mum came into the room. They talked for a bit and then I heard someone come toward the closet. Next second, the door opened and Cat's mum was peering down at me, crouched among a pile of sneakers with my head inside a long denim shirt. Neither of us said anything.

Believe me, there is *nothing* you can say when you get caught sitting in someone's closet. Nothing.

She never ratted on me, but she did send me home. The humiliation of feeling like such an idiot was punishment enough, and I think she knew that.

I had nowhere to turn — just like now.

"Um . . ." I say, cringing at the word "lesbian." I think I might be, but how do I know? Do my feelings over the past few months add up to enough to use a word like that?

The thing is, though, Cat's question makes me admit the truth to myself. I want to be with someone, and, yeah, if I'm honest, I've become fairly sure I want it to be a girl, but how can I start labeling myself if I haven't done anything about it yet? Wouldn't that be like calling yourself a pilot when you've never even been in a plane?

"It depends what you mean by the word," I say eventually, and Cat bursts out laughing.

"It's pretty obvious, Ash. Do you fancy boys or girls?"

"I don't fancy anyone," I answer, too quickly.

"OK, but if you did, would it be a boy or a girl?" she asks, slowly and carefully. I'm backed into a corner. I'm crouched among the shoes and shirts. I know the answer; it just feels like too much of a commitment to say it out loud. Once I've put it out there, that's it. Finally, I say, "OK, maybe a girl, I think."

Cat grins. "Well, halle-bloody-lujah!"

"What?"

"I knew it!"

"How could *you* know when *I* didn't?"

Cat looks serious for once. "I don't know. I suppose I've always known. Even when you weren't, if that makes sense."

It doesn't, but I know exactly what she means.

Then a thought occurs to me. I hesitate for a second. Then, "Cat, are you . . ."

She laughs. "No, Ash, I'm not gay. It would make life a whole lot easier if I was, I can tell you."

"I wouldn't count on it."

"Yeah, well. Anyway, I'm not. But you are."

I look down at my glass, cheeks burning.

"And I couldn't hang around forever waiting for you to tell me of your own accord." Cat lifts her drink. "Here's to queers!"

"Cat!"

"Chill. No one's listening." Cat winks and knocks back half her pint.

I don't know what to say. I look around the pub. The girl with the blond hair looks up at Cat briefly and glances over at me. I'm about to smile, but she's back in her book before I get the chance, and I feel cheated and stupid, like when you see someone waving and you wave back and then realize they meant the person behind you.

I guzzle my drink, hiding my blushes behind the glass.

• • •

Four pints later, I remember I'm supposed to be studying. I'm supposed to be taking A-levels, supposed to care about my future.

Cat and I stumble out of the pub, clinging onto each other's arms as we make our way toward the bus stop. The road's quiet, the sun just disappearing behind the neighborhood on our right. There are a couple of clouds in the sky, birds tweeting. I realize it's nearly summer, and for a split second I get a feeling of — I don't know what, exactly — optimism.

We're almost at the bus stop when I hear it.

"Oooh. Dykes!"

What? I pull my hand away from Cat's arm, glancing quickly at her. A group of four lads are sitting on a bench at the bus stop, smoking and laughing.

A couple of them are messing about on their phones; the other two are holding cans of beer and looking our way. One's lanky and tall. The other, next to him, looks stocky and shorter, with a face full of acne.

"Losers," Cat says dismissively.

"Hey, love, g'iz a kiss." The lanky guy leans forward to crush his cigarette on the pavement as we approach. I stare straight ahead and try to ignore them. My stride is wooden.

"I'll sort you out. Won't be a lezzer once you've tried me." He nudges the boy next to him, and they both laugh.

I look at Cat. She's staring down the lanky guy. She looks so calm and cool. Why is my heart fluttering with fear?

"So," she says to him. *What's she doing?* "You reckon you're so good you can get a girl to switch sides, do you?"

The lanky guy stands up. "At your service," he leers with a small bow. "And it just so happens I might be holding tryouts for my team. Wanna audition?" Then he turns around and nudges one of the guys still sitting on the bench. "Hey, Gav, you can film it. 'Josh Mathews Turns Gay Girls Straight.' Might go viral. I could set up a business, make a fortune."

Should I say something? But what? What could I say? *Sorry, mate, you've got your facts wrong; she's not actually a lezzer, but I am?*

His friend — Gav — looks up for a second. "Josh, chill out, mate. Don't be a jerk," he says, then goes back to whatever he was doing on his phone.

Just then, the number fifty-three bus rounds the corner. Our bus home. Josh glances at it as it approaches, then shrugs. "Too bad, girls," he says. "Next time, maybe. Unless you wanna do it on the bus."

His mates get up as the bus pulls into the stop. Cat gives Josh one last sneer. "Nah, it's OK, we'll get the next one," she says. "We prefer the sixty-nine."

Josh glances at her for a second, then bursts out laughing. "Touché, ladies, touché." Then he gets on the bus, and his friends follow.

We're left alone at the bus stop. I'm shaking.

Cat looks at me. "You shouldn't let that idiot get to you," she says, nudging my arm.

"I know," I say. The thing is, to her, he *was* just an

idiot, a stupid lad who'd had a few drinks and thought he could have a laugh intimidating a couple of girls and showing his mates what a big man he is. His mates who, to their credit, weren't actually interested in playing his childish game.

But I can't shake the incident off as easily as Cat can.

See, I've never really cared what people think of me — teachers, Mum and Dad, others at school. I've always said that no one could change me, that I'd never pretend to be something I'm not. And I always felt insulated by that certainty — or was it arrogance? I don't know. All I know is that I'm not so sure anymore. Maybe my whole life is going to be one big pretense from now on. I mean, what did I do just now? Stood silently by while Cat fought my corner. Kept my mouth shut.

Am I going to spend the rest of my life sneaking around, pretending to be something I'm not? Or am I going to be one of those who stand up and say what they are and somehow manage to brazen it out? I feel claustrophobic and trapped by a sudden awareness of my limited options.

It's all very well going around with two middle fingers stuck up at the world, but what happens when the world turns around and sticks them back up at you?

The world's a lot bigger than I am.

23

A few months ago, I was dreading this day, but I haven't got as much to leave behind now. Just a few years of my life. So what?

The old gardener's shed: What would we have done without it? It smells of stale smoke and old gossip. Cigarette butts all over the floor. Cat and I used to spend half our lives in here last year when I thought there was nothing more to school than skipping classes, messing about, and winding people up. It was worth hanging out with the smokers just to make sure you didn't get behind with the gossip.

There's no one here now, and the shed echoes with voices of the past.

The gym is still set out with row after row of desks. What a sight. Thank God I've finished. I shake my head and move on.

Inevitably, I end up walking toward *her* classroom.

I try the door and my heart does an irregular quick-step. It's not locked. What if she's here? Offer me anything in the world, and I'd swap it for that.

But of course she isn't.

It feels like a museum. Full of precious things but all old and mostly dead. It needs her to bring the place alive. The room feels as sad as me, with its worn books crammed onto every shelf, some with their spines missing, others jammed horizontally on top of each other, filling every spare bit of space.

I go over to my desk at the back and sit down. I feel under the tabletop for the hard chunks of chewing gum, molded smoothly into the underside of the desk. I could almost believe they were part of it if I hadn't contributed at least one or two of them myself.

The familiar graffiti scratched into the desk's surface:

Calum Jones is the finest boy in this school.

No he isn't, Andy Marsh is.

Looking over at her desk, now totally bare, I think of all the times I watched every move she made in our lessons.

Did she know what I was feeling as I watched her? I caught her eye once, and I was sure she held mine a little too long. Then she asked me to read a passage out loud. Did she do that on purpose?

I get up and walk over to the window. There's not much to see: a thin slice of a muddy green footpath and a medium-busy road in the rain. Not enough to distract a bored student, but I can't remember the last time I was bored in here.

"Ash."

I spin around. "Miss — Robyn."

"Miss Robyn? What is this, the Waltons?" Robyn smiles weakly at me from the door. "Can I come in?"

I turn away again. "It's a free country."

The door closes, and for a moment I don't know if she's come in or gone out. I'm not going to turn around and see. I carry on looking out the window, but aware of myself, standing stiffly, pretending to look and hoping Robyn's not—

"Ash," she repeats.

"What?" I don't look around this time.

She doesn't say anything. If she thinks I'm going to give in, she's got another thought coming. I'm not the one who threw her out of the house and then, for all I know, spread a load of rumors and lies around the whole school. But then I hear a sob, and I melt instantly.

"Robyn, what's wrong?" I turn around in time to see her slump into a chair and put her head in her hands. "What is it? What's happened? Is it Luke?"

She looks up and her face has a streak down each cheek, like those trails you sometimes get on the back porch in the morning but never any sign of the creature that left them. "Luke?"

"Well, what is it?"

"It's you, Ash."

"Me? What the hell have I done now? Or what am I *supposed* to have done?"

"It's what *I* did. Ash, I'm really sorry."

Tears run into her mouth as she talks. "I should never have treated you so badly. You were the best friend I've ever had."

"But we hardly—"

"I'd never really had a best friend. I've always been

the one on the outside of things. People like you and Cat never had any time for people like me."

"People like me and Cat?"

"You know what I mean, the ones that are always messing about and getting laughs, in the middle of the 'in' crowd."

"This is ridiculous. I've never been part of any 'in' crowd."

"And then, when you and Cat fell out and you and I started spending more time together, I suddenly felt like I was someone who mattered, like I belonged somewhere. And doing homework together and going to parties . . ."

"Party," I correct her. "Let's not let these rose-tinted specs get in the way too much." I allow myself a slight smile.

She returns my smile with a little laugh, then grabs a tissue from her pocket and snorts loudly into it. "I got it all out of proportion," she carries on, more calmly now as I sit down at the next desk. "But I was upset about Miss Murray leaving and everything. It threw me. I was confused. I'd even thought about doing the same thing at one point."

"*What?* With me?"

Robyn's neck has gone blotchy. "I've just never had a friendship that was like ours. Talking about books and planning debates together and stuff. I felt really close to you. I was overwhelmed."

"But those things you said to me. You made me feel like a leper."

"I know. I'm sorry, Ash. But when you—when it happened—I knew that wasn't what I wanted."

"But it wasn't what *I* wanted either. I told you."

"Perhaps not with me, but it *is* what you want with someone, isn't it?"

I look down at my hands. "What if it is?"

"Then it's absolutely *fine*! Ash, I'm so sorry. I was a bitch, and the last thing I wanted to do was lose you as a friend."

"What about the rumors?"

"What rumors?"

"Come on."

"Ash, what rumors?"

I feel almost ashamed as I say, "About Miss Murray." I can't bring myself to say the whole truth.

"Look, I haven't heard any rumors. But whatever they are, I promise you they've got nothing to do with me. Why would I spread rumors about the best teacher I've ever had?"

"About Miss Murray and me."

Robyn's eyes look like a dimmer switch being gradually turned up as she takes in what I'm saying. "Oh! Well, I haven't said anything, or heard anything. I don't know what you mean, and I don't even know if I *want* to know."

"There's nothing *to* know. That's what I'm telling you."

Robyn gets up and moves over to the window. "I was jealous," she says quietly to the windowpane. "I think most of the class probably was."

"Jealous? Of what?" I try to sound casual, but I can feel my heart rate increase.

"It was obvious you were her favorite."

"Rubbish." *More, more, tell me more!*

"Come on, Ash. You know you were special to her."

The pain that I've spent the last two months trying to stifle is wriggling around low down in my stomach. "What makes you say that?" I try to keep my voice calm.

"She'd always listen more intently when you were speaking, and take you more seriously than any of us. It's like you were her, what d'you call it, like her *protégée* or something."

"That's rubbish. She just thought I was a stupid kid. I was. I am."

"Ash, I'm only going to say this once. You weren't, you're not, and, for what it's worth, I don't believe for a minute she thought you were either. OK?"

Miss Murray's words come back to me from the last time I saw her. That I *was* special. That I reminded her of herself. "OK," I eventually manage through my tight throat.

We're looking at each other in the silence when Luke bursts in. "Oh, sorry. I was just . . . are you . . ."

"Give us five minutes," Robyn replies. "I'll meet you in the common room."

"Right, OK. Hi, Ash, y'all right?" And he's gone.

"You and Luke, then?"

"Yeah, well, I've always fancied him. You know that. Seems like he came to his senses at last." She smiles

233

shyly from under her eyelids. "I think it was that day I grabbed him and made him snog me that did it."

"Well, you look good together."

"Thanks, Ash. That means a lot to me." She glances at the door. "Look, I'd better go."

"Me too. Can't hang around in here all day." Although part of me wants to, just in case.

"Are you going to give us a hug, then?" Robyn asks.

"I don't know if I dare. You might think I'm trying to get off with you."

"Please." She looks so sad, as though she'll start crying again if I don't, so I do.

We stand there for ages, holding each other tight. Not in a funny way at all, just like really good mates.

"Right, see you, then," she says when we move apart. "You staying in here?"

"Yeah, just for a bit. See you, Robyn," I say, sounding much more final than I mean to. And she goes.

I don't stay long. "Bye," I whisper from the door, then look around to check no one's there to hear me talking to an empty classroom. "And thanks."

Then I close the door softly behind me and walk away.

24

I pause outside the door. "I don't think I can do it."

Cat stops beside me. "You'll be fine."

"Do I look OK?" I pull at the sleeves of my new coat as if I'm trying to hide inside it.

"You look great."

"Not too gay?"

"Ash, it's a gay club!"

"What if I see someone I know?"

"What if you do?"

"They might think I'm, you know . . ."

"Ash, you *are* 'you know.' And if they're in here, that means they probably are too!"

"*You're* not."

"Well, no. But I'm not exactly a raving homophobic ax-murderer either, am I? Come on. There's nothing to worry about."

I let her drag me through the door. I glance furtively around. It's about a third full. I can't see anyone I know. I turn to Cat. "It looks like any other bar."

She stares at me. "Well, whaddayaknow?" she says sarcastically. "The queers could almost pass for the same species as the straights. Get real, Ash! Come on, let's get a drink."

We make our way to the bar, snaking between the tables on the way.

Two older women are sitting together at one table. They've both got short hair. Is my hair too long? It's nearly down to my shoulders. Maybe I should have had it cut. Then I spot a younger couple, more my age. They've both got long hair, and they're both wearing makeup. They're smiling at each other and holding hands.

Cat follows my eye. "You'd never have guessed, would you?"

I shake my head.

A group of men are standing at the bar, drinking and chatting and laughing.

"Two bottles of Stella, please," Cat says to the guy behind the bar. He's gorgeous. Jet-black hair — perfectly parted — crisp white shirt, dark skin, deep brown eyes.

He smiles at Cat. "Coming right up, darling," he says.

One of the men at the bar nudges Cat. "Hands off, love, he's mine!"

"In your dreams, Nathan, in your dreams," the guy behind the bar says, winking as he passes the beers to Cat.

Cat pays for the drinks while I stand and stare. At all of it. At everyone. It's so . . . I can't describe it. I only feel it inside me. I haven't got the words yet, but I know I like it.

We head toward the dance floor on the other side

of the bar. It's busier around this side. About twenty people are dancing. Some in couples, pressed close, others in groups messing around and making each other laugh. There's an older woman dancing on her own, wearing a long, flowing skirt like a gypsy and a loose blouse. She's got her eyes closed and is gliding around, swinging her arms like we used to when we were little and played airplanes.

A tall, slender woman in skinny jeans and a low-cut white blouse is half dancing while she smiles at a red-haired woman next to her. They're staring into each other's eyes and gently moving from side to side. Then they kiss each other slowly, and the taller one slides a hand around the other one's waist. The redhead wraps her arms around the taller woman's neck. They're swaying as they kiss.

"What d'you reckon?" Cat asks.

I look at her without replying. I feel like I've come home.

"I thought you'd like it," she says, grinning.

"I don't know what to say." I grab her and hug her tight.

"Oi! Watch it." She pulls away. "Don't want people getting the wrong idea about *me*. Might spoil my chances with the boys."

I look around to see two men leaning against a pillar on the edge of the dance floor, their mouths pressed as tightly together as their bodies.

"Cat, I don't think you've got much of a chance with—"

"Joke, Ash!"

We knock back our beers, then Cat pulls me onto the dance floor. "C'mon, let's have a dance," she says as a new tune comes on with a deep dance beat.

We dance to about five tracks before I need a break and a drink. I get the next round and Cat and I stand, watching and drinking. The place is getting busier and busier.

I'm just finishing off a bottle when the unmistakable opening words to a new song come on.

"Gaga!" Cat shrieks and grabs me again. Loads of people get up from their tables, and we're swept along onto the dance floor.

The alcohol has loosened me up, and I'm spinning and jumping with the rest of them and grinning like an idiot at virtually anyone who catches my eye.

I close my eyes and sing every word of "Born This Way" at the top of my voice.

For a moment, I think I've fallen in love, but I don't know what with—just all this: the music, the dancing, all the gorgeous women on the dance floor, the hot, sticky air closing in around us, everyone in it together.

I don't stop dancing all night, except to fill up with beer. Cat and I are mucking about, twirling each other around like kids. At one point, Cat goes to the loo and I'm on my own. I don't care. I just keep dancing.

There's another woman dancing alone. She moves across the floor and inches toward me as a slow track comes on. She's centimeters away, smiling at me. I don't know what I'm meant to do, so I just carry on jigging about as though she was the usual foot or two away. Our bodies are almost touching, and we're both pretending they're not. At the end of the dance she gives me a quick smile before disappearing into the crowd.

I look around to see Cat laughing. Stumbling back toward her, I fall into two boys. "Oops, sorry." I look up at them. "Jayce!"

Jayce jumps away from Adam. "Ash! What are you doing here?"

I laugh. "What do you think? Same as you." Then I look at Adam's arm, still around Jayce's neck. "Or maybe not quite."

Jayce wriggles farther away from Adam, who suddenly hugs me. "I knew it!" He turns to Jayce and taps his forehead. "Told you, didn't I? My gaydar never lets me down."

I laugh. Did *everyone* know I was gay before I did?

Jayce grins. "Really? Ash, that's brilliant!"

"I wonder if our parents would agree."

Adam grimaces. "Oh, my God, it's perfect! You could be his beard."

"His *what*?"

"His beard—his pretend girlfriend," Adam explains. "That might get Elaine off our backs."

"Well, I'd like to help." I look Jayce up and down. "But he's not my type." They both laugh.

"Look, I'd better get back." I point in Cat's direction.

"Brilliant to see you, Ash." Jayce hugs me.

"Let's meet up soon."

As I head back to Cat, I think about the first time I met Jayce, his argument with his mum about deferring his university place and staying at home. He didn't want to leave Adam. It all makes sense now. But then, *everything* makes sense now.

A long while later, I look at my watch: twenty to two. How on earth did that happen? I'm not even tired, but I come off the floor for another refill, and I see someone familiar. I can't place her for a minute, but then it hits me — it's the blond-haired girl from the pub the other day!

She's standing on her own, hands in her jacket pockets as she leans against a pillar at the edge of the dance floor. She looks up as I pass, a hint of recognition in her eyes.

"Left your book at home, then?" I shout over the music. Oh, for heaven's sake, Ash. What a pathetic thing to say.

"It's a bit dark for reading," she replies, looking at me briefly before turning away. Oh, my God, her eyes are beautiful. They might be blue. They're big and wide and she's got long, thick eyelashes.

"D'you want a drink?" I ask without thinking, but she shakes her head.

"I can't. Sorry." She taps her watch. "I'm going to miss the night bus if I don't leave in a minute."

"Oh, right." I'm glad it's too dark for her to see my cheeks redden. "Sorry. See you, then." I turn to leave.

"Hang on." She's rummaging in her jeans, pulling out a scrap of paper. It's a Topshop receipt. She scribbles something on it and shoves it at me. For a second, I feel the heat of her hand on mine as she passes it to me, and I could almost close my fingers around hers. I look up at her and an electric tingle shoots up through my chest and into my mouth. Her mouth's slightly open. I want to kiss her. What the hell am I thinking? I don't even know her.

And then her hand's gone and she's moving away. "I'm Taylor, by the way. See you," she says, and I shove the paper into my pocket and go to find Cat.

As we leave the club to flag down a taxi, my voice is hoarse and my cheekbones ache from smiling.

25

The first thing to hit me is the crying. Everywhere. The school entrance hall is full of students, huddled in groups or in pairs, a few with parents. It seems as though at least half the people I can see are bawling their eyes out.

Annabelle Stewart, one of the smartest students in the school, is standing with her boyfriend. He's got his arms around her and her shoulders are shaking.

"Who's going to let me do medicine now?" she's sobbing.

"Look, you've still got three As and a B."

"That's useless! I needed four As," she says, gulping.

A boy in my law class who did about as much work as I did is talking into his mobile. I smile as I pass, but he doesn't smile back, just gives a halfhearted wave. "No, not one," he says into the phone. "I've said I want them regraded but I don't know if it'll make any difference . . . I know, I feel sick."

I'm like the hero in an action film, walking toward my fate, my doom. People falling by the wayside all around me. As I pass the staff room, I take a quick look through the glass door. It's full of students. On their phones, talking to teachers. Some grinning. Some panicking. A few of them crying. I wish Cat was here. I begged her on the phone this morning, but she wouldn't come. Said she knew she'd failed everything and didn't want to give Mrs. Banks the satisfaction. Robyn's coming this afternoon. We said we'd meet up later, either to celebrate or commiserate.

I head toward the scrum at the far end of the corridor. It's like last call at Feathers on karaoke night. Eventually I push and wriggle my way to the front of the crowd and start looking down the list. I see Cat's results before mine. History: X. That means she didn't turn up. General studies: X. Law and geography: both E, the lowest grade that could technically count as a pass. Maybe she'll be pleased.

I spot Robyn's results too. She's got a B in English. She'll be well pleased with that.

Then I see my name: Ashleigh Walker.

Law: D. Could have been worse. Sociology: E. It's a pass, at least. General studies: C. How the hell I managed that, I don't know. Then I rub my eyes, glance around for a second to check that this is real, and look again at the last one.

English: A.

I keep staring at it. I'm scared to believe it in case I get home and there's a letter saying they've made a mistake.

I scribble my results down on a scrap of paper and push my way through the crowd. I walk back down the corridor in a daze. Who can I talk to about it? I need to make sure it's right. I want to laugh and jump up and down. It's only now I realize how much I wanted it.

The only person I want to see is Miss Murray. I know I've not thought about her as much lately, but, being here and seeing those results, she's the only person I want to share this moment with.

I don't notice anyone around me as I walk down the corridor on my own. I need to get out of here.

But as I turn the corner, I look up — and suddenly the entrance hall is spinning around me.

When we were about thirteen, Cat and I used to go to the fair on Saturday afternoons in the summer, once we'd gotten bored with the poolrooms and the local arts center. It was just another place to hang out, thinking we looked grown up, chewing gum and wearing too much eyeliner. It was always the Tilt-A-Whirl, or the speedway if you wanted to look cool. That's where you sat on a motorbike, or if you were *really* cool you stood by the side of it while the ride simply went round and round. Basically it was a carousel, only with bikes instead of horses, and it went a tiny bit faster.

It was harder to be cool on the Tilt-A-Whirl, as they'd always choose our car to keep spinning. "Push us faster!" we'd shout.

"That's what me girlfriend said and now she's pregnant," the long-haired Tilt-A-Whirl guy would say and we'd laugh, although I never quite got it. And then he'd spin the ride and my head would be thrown back and my stomach would feel cold and empty and I couldn't help screaming and laughing. Then I'd step off the ride and the ground would be spinning. I couldn't walk in a straight line. If I stood in one spot and closed my eyes, I was at the center of the universe with the whole thing revolving around me. It was brilliant, for a second. Then I'd open my eyes and feel sick.

Now, I'm right back there, the floor rotating away from me. Because she's standing right in front of me.

I reach out for something to steady myself. The only thing I'd wanted, the only thing I'd thought about, every single moment of every day for weeks. And now she's just here, in the same room, chatting to a couple of students as though nothing has happened, as though she never left.

I stumble toward a chair, shuffling sideways like a crab so I don't need to turn away. I know she's going to look across in a moment and, when she does, she'll see me. And I'm sitting on a plastic orange chair in the middle of the entrance hall, on my own.

So I stand up again. Then she spots me. She glances my way for a split second and catches my eye, but she doesn't hold it long enough for me to do anything. What would I do anyway? Smile? *Oh, hi there, long time no see and all that.* I don't think so.

She carries on talking a bit longer, then breaks away.

She's coming toward me. What am I going to do? My legs are turning into liquid and my cheeks are on fire. My arms feel six feet long, hanging uselessly by my sides.

"Hello, Ash." She looks at me seriously, as though she's a police officer who's caught me red-handed burglarizing someone's house. It takes me a second to remember that I haven't done anything wrong. At least, I don't think I have.

I can't speak. I'm like one of those contestants on a daytime quiz show who can't answer a simple question. "It's always harder when you're in front of the camera," the host tells them when they don't know the capital of France. *Bollocks, you're just thick,* ten million people around the country are thinking. Well, now I know how it feels. I can't remember the appropriate reply to "Hello."

Miss Murray's rummaging in her bag. She pulls out an envelope with my name on it.

"Here. I was going to send it if I didn't see you."

I take it. It feels like a card.

"I wanted to say well done," she says while I stare at the envelope. I don't know whether to tear it open or save it forever.

I look up. "Thanks."

She smiles. "I always knew you could do it."

"Not without you, I couldn't."

"Annie, wonderful to see you," a familiar voice rumbles behind me. Mrs. bloody Banks.

"Hello there, Mary." Miss Murray returns Banks's wooden smile.

"I think congratulations are in order," the principal continues. "You did a fine job there. A fine job. One hundred percent pass rate. Well done."

"Thank you. That's very kind of you," Miss Murray says, "but, really, the credit must go to the students."

"Of course, of course. And well done to you too, Ashleigh," Mrs. Banks says, wiping a piece of invisible fluff from her skirt. "Anyway, mustn't keep you."

Miss Murray looks at her watch. "I'd better be going myself, actually."

"All the best, then," Mrs. Banks says and walks off as though I wasn't there.

"So, are you coming back?" I ask casually once Banks is out of earshot.

"I've got a new job." She looks away and runs her hand through her hair. "In London."

"London? That's about a million miles away."

She smiles. "I think it's a bit less than that, actually." Then she stops smiling. "You'll be fine, Ash."

"How do you know?"

"You can do anything you want, so make sure you do. Don't let anything stop you. Or anyone."

I nod. I don't reply. What can I say?

"You've got a great future ahead of you, I promise." She puts her bag on her shoulder. "I'll see you," she says.

"Will you?" I whisper.

She smiles weakly and turns to go.

She stops at the door, looks around the hall, and catches my eye. I stare at her as though I'm watching the action from the outside. She doesn't smile or anything. Just looks at me for a moment, then walks out the door. She's left me again. And I know she's gone for good this time.

26

A car horn startles me as I'm stumbling out of school, about to rip the envelope open.

"Ash."

It's Mum. What's she doing here? I shove the card into my bag.

"I couldn't wait," she says through the window. She's in Tony's car; he's at the wheel.

"Well?" she asks. I shrug. "Ash, how did you do?" Her voice is tight. A bit like the old Mum.

I hand her the slip of paper with my results.

"Oh," she says.

"Yeah. Rubbish," I reply.

"They're not *that* bad. You got a C in general studies—and an A in English! Ash, that's absolutely marvelous!"

I shrug again. "No one'll ever take me now. I only got one decent grade."

"The D and E are both passes," Tony says quietly.

Mum turns her tightness onto him. "Tony, I think I can handle this. Ash, get in."

I climb in the car and we head home.

"An A, an E, and a D, plus everyone knows general studies doesn't count," I say when we get in the house. Tony's dropped us off. Mum says she's taking the morning off to help me figure out what to do next. "I'll just have to get a job."

"What, working the register at Tesco?"

I look up at Mum. "Are you angry with me?"

She pauses for a moment, then speaks gently. "Of course I'm not angry," she says carefully. "I know you did your best, and it's not been an easy year for you."

"Mmm."

"And I know your father and I haven't exactly helped."

I feel a stab of guilt. That's exactly what I'd just thought, but it's not fair. "Mum, don't blame yourself," I tell her. "It's no one's fault but my own. I'm the one who's messed up."

Mum tries to smile at me. "And you're the one who's done really well in English too, and I'm proud of you. I'm *really* proud of you. That's why I want you to make something of yourself. I don't want you to be waiting tables or stocking shelves. You're a clever girl, Ash. I just want you to make the most of your life."

It sounds like a rehearsed speech. Not natural. In fact, now that I think about it, my conversations with Mum have all felt a bit strained again lately.

"OK, me too. But how?"

"Let's start by making your A grade worthwhile and get you in somewhere."

Four "no ways," two "we'll get back to yous," and three "phone back tomorrows" later, and I'm on the phone to one of the universities in Manchester. After my whirlwind online search, I can't even remember which one this is.

"This is the last one, right?" I say to Mum while I wait to be connected to the English department. "It's humiliating."

I get put through to the head of English. I've only spoken to secretaries so far.

"When can you come for an interview?" he drawls after a few questions about my results.

"Er, um . . ."

"Would tomorrow at twelve o'clock suit you?"

"Honestly?"

"Unless you've got something more important to do?" he says with a laugh.

"No! I mean, of course not! Tomorrow at twelve—just hang on."

Mum's nodding at me. "I'll take you," she whispers.

"Tomorrow, twelve o'clock is fine," I hear myself saying. "Great! Thank you." I scribble some instructions and put the phone down in a daze.

"What happened? What did he say?"

"He said they've still got a couple of spots, and that

he's interested in the A. He said they might be able to fit me in, but he wants to meet me before saying definitely."

"Ash, that's wonderful. They'll love you. Why wouldn't they?" Mum takes a step toward me, then leans forward and hugs me awkwardly. I hug her back briefly. What the hell's going on here? I thought we'd become close again. I want to ask her what's the matter, but something stops me. I'm not really sure what.

As soon as Mum's gone back to work, I grab my bag.

My hands are shaking as I open the envelope from Miss Murray. It is a card. It's got a picture of someone climbing a ladder. Right at the top of the ladder, there's a bunch of stars.

I open the card. She's written across both sides.

Dear Ash,

You did it! You got that A! I am so proud of you. Remember you thought at one point that you couldn't do it? I always knew you would.

Now you're moving into a whole new phase of your life, to a place where you will question everything you thought was true and immovable. Just remember, what you actually need isn't always what you think you need.

I won't forget you. Good luck with your dreams,
Annie M.

That's *it*? What the hell is that supposed to mean? I know she's trying to tell me something, but what? That

I wasn't really in love with her? That I didn't even know my own feelings? What? And now that she's gone for good, I know I'm never likely to get an answer.

I read her words again and again, getting more indignant each time. "I won't forget you"? Yeah, sure you won't.

Then I realize: I'm *indignant*, not heartbroken. It's changed. It's finally shifted. It doesn't get right inside me anymore. All those weeks of waiting, thinking about her all the time, believing she was everything I had ever wanted — it just became a habit. Like brushing your teeth. You don't do it because you desperately want to, it's just part of your morning routine. Wake up, brush teeth, get dressed, think about Miss Murray. And it changes so gradually that you don't even notice. Well, now I do. Yeah, maybe she's right. Maybe I *don't* need her anymore.

All that time I thought she was my future, I was wrong. She wasn't my future at all. She was the *door* to my future. But I'm through that door now, and ready to close it behind me.

I know exactly what I have to do.

"Hello?" A quiet voice answers after four rings.

"Hi, is this, um, Taylor?" I squeeze the words through the nerves clogging up my throat.

"Yeah, that's me."

"Oh, hi, it's, er, it's Ash."

Silence.

"From the other night. From the club."

"Oh, hi!"

Now what? "Well, you gave me your phone number, so I thought I'd ring."

Pause. Then she says, really softly, "Do you want to meet up?"

"I'd love to. How about this weekend?"

"Saturday?" she suggests.

"Saturday would be great!"

We arrange to meet at the town hall Saturday afternoon. After I put the phone down, I jump about in my room, alternately punching the air and biting my fist, cringing. Oh, my God, what will I wear? What will we do? Where do you *go* on a date with a girl?

I'm still thinking about it the next day as Mum and I drive to Manchester. I stare out the window, running over it all in my head while Mum listens to Radio Four. I can't remember exactly what Taylor looks like. I shut my eyes and try to picture her, but I can only see her hair. And her eyes. Big, blue eyes, they were. Or were they green? They were lovely anyway.

"This is it." Mum pulls me away from my daydreams as she parks, and a knot of nerves clutches at my stomach. "I'll get a cup of tea." She points to a sign for the cafeteria.

Twenty minutes later, I'm in a small, square office, sitting in front of a huge desk that takes up half the space. It's stacked about a foot high with papers. One wall is covered in postcards, another has a notice board plastered with memos and agendas for meetings. The other two walls have theater posters all over them.

The thin man with wild black hair and little round glasses sitting behind the desk leans back in his chair, clasping his hands behind his head. Mr. Anderson, he's called. Alan Anderson. He says I should call him Al, but that doesn't feel right.

"You had an extremely good reference from your teacher," he says once he's introduced himself and told me a bit about the course. "One of the most glowing I've ever seen, in fact."

"My — my teacher?" I stammer.

He smiles. "I gave her a call this morning." He leans forward and shuffles through some papers. "A Miss — what was it now — Murphy? Moore?"

I swallow. "Miss Murray," I say quietly.

He stabs the air with a finger. "That's it! Said you were a shining star and would be a credit to any course you were in. She says we'd be lucky to have you."

He spoke to her this morning? She said that about me? For a moment I'm so thrown I can't speak.

The man laughs. "That's a good thing, by the way. So, anyway, tell me a bit about yourself."

I take a breath. What can I tell him?

"Let's start with why you want to do this course."

OK, I can do this. I looked up the course details earlier, and I really liked what I saw. "Well, the fact that it's not all about writers who have been dead for hundreds of years appeals to me," I begin.

Mr. Anderson throws back his head and laughs. "I like it," he says. "I like your honesty."

"I—I mean, obviously Shakespeare and all of those are great," I carry on quickly, "but I'm more interested in modern literature. I enjoy reading poems and books and thinking about how they reflect what's going on in the world around me."

He's looking at me and nodding, and I decide to be brave and take another step.

"And I, um, I like the fact that you've got a module called Literature, Culture, and Identity," I say, blushing furiously in case he knows why I like the sound of it. "I—I'm interested in that kind of thing."

I stop talking and look down.

A moment later, Mr. Anderson is speaking again. "You're interesting," he says.

I glance up at him and smile. He smiles back. "I think you're the type of young person we would like in our course. And with your impressive reference as well . . ." He scratches his chin, then nods. "Ah, to hell with it. Let's do it. You're in. Now, have you got anything you'd like to ask me?"

I stare at him. "Er . . . are you offering me a place?"

"I certainly am." He laughs. "Is that your only question?"

My mind is suddenly *full* of questions, but I seem to have lost the power of speech. "Thank you so much, Mr. Anderson!" I manage in the end.

"Al," he says, correcting me. "And you're welcome." He shuffles some papers on his desk. "If you'd like to see my secretary on your way out, she'll give you all the necessary documentation. The book lists will be sent out in the next couple of weeks, and I recommend you get started as soon as possible. Once you arrive, there'll be plenty of other things to distract you from your studies for the first week or two." He smiles again and holds out his hand. I reach forward and shake it awkwardly. "See you in a month or so, then," he says.

"Yeah, great. Wow. Thank you." I stumble out of his office and pick up the paperwork, then make my way to the cafeteria.

"I did it," I say numbly. "They want me."

"Yes!" Mum punches the air, then grabs me and pulls me in for a hug. "That's amazing, Ash! And of course they do. Who wouldn't?" There's a hint of sadness lurking behind her eyes as she moves away. "I'll miss you," she says.

"You've got Tony."

Mum drops her arms and turns away.

"What's happened?"

She shakes her head.

"Mum?"

"Oh, Ash, I'm just not sure I'm really ready to get serious about someone."

"Serious? Does he want to?"

She nods. "He's talking about us moving in together. Not now, but, you know, sometime."

"Wow. That's a bit . . . soon?"

"Exactly." She picks at the cuffs of her jacket. "He's a

nice man. A lovely man. It's not him that's the problem. It's me. I just don't think I can do it. Not yet. I can't give out something that I haven't got."

"Oh, Mum." I want to hug her. I don't know what's stopping me.

"Ash," she says quietly. She's going to tell me off. What have I done?

"What?"

She pauses for ages. She's looking at me through narrow eyes, examining me.

"What?"

Then she smiles. "No, it's nothing. Just, well done, love."

I don't ask again. I daren't. It was that look. What was it? What isn't she saying? Why don't I want to ask?

I spend the whole journey home trying to remember when exactly it was that we stopped communicating again.

27

"Ash, mail for you."

A month ago, those words would have had my heart leaping out of bed before the rest of me. Jumping at the possibility that it might be a letter from *her*. Not anymore.

Especially after Saturday.

Two days ago, Taylor and I met up in town as planned. We mooched round the shops all afternoon, talking and talking the whole time. I don't even know what we talked about—but we didn't seem to stop once. We had a pizza in the park for lunch. That was the best bit, as we had to sit quite close together so we could share it without dropping pieces everywhere.

I was seeing Cat in the evening, so we had to part a bit sooner than I'd have liked. But I'd promised myself I wouldn't do what I did with Dylan and dump Cat the minute someone new was on the scene.

We parted with an awkward kiss on the cheek and a promise to meet up again today. We said we'd catch a matinee in town.

So I'm in my bedroom trying to decide what to wear when Mum calls again. "I've made you some toast."

I put off the clothing dilemma and head downstairs for some breakfast.

Mum's in the kitchen, standing by the sink as she washes her plate and dries her hands. She hands me a postcard showing a picture of a sunny bay with about a million hotels lining a scrap of sand that you could miss if you tripped. I flip the postcard over.

Hi Ash,

   This is where Luke and I have eloped to!!! I wish! He's getting on really well with my family, though. He and Dad keep going off for "man to man" talks. (That means it's serious.) We're in the third hotel from the end. Can you see the arrow? Having a brilliant trip, but we've not had much time on our own together, if you know what I mean (!!).

   Weather's fantastic. See you when we get back. Hope things are good with you.

   Love,
   Robyn xxxxx
   P.S. Really glad we made up.

I smile as I put the card down. I'm glad about those two. It was about time Luke gave up on Cat and went for someone who actually wanted his company. And I'm glad that Robyn sent me the card. Glad we're friends again.

Mum looks at her watch. "Damn, I'm late. Better go. Don't forget the plumber."

"What about him?"

"He's coming to fix the washing machine at two. Make sure you're in."

At two? I'm meeting Taylor at one o'clock.

"Mum, he can't! *I* can't! I'm not in."

"Oh, Ash, you promised."

"Did I?" *Did I?*

"Yesterday. We talked about it."

"I didn't know it was today!"

"I didn't realize you had plans." She looks at me quizzically.

"I haven't," I say quickly, hating the heat in my cheeks that I know is giving me away. "OK, I'll do it," I say, more to stop her asking questions than anything else.

"Right. Thank you." She grabs her bag. "See you later."

I'm sitting in my pajamas staring at Taylor's number on my phone and wishing I didn't have to cancel when it rings.

It's Cat, calling from work. Her mum's gotten her a summer job in a new whole-food shop in the precinct. A friend of hers runs it. "Fancy coming in for an herbal tea and a piece of gluten-free carrot cake?" she asks.

"Sounds delicious," I say sarcastically. "Anyway, I can't. I've got to stay in for the plumber."

"Bummer."

I laugh and we arrange to meet up tomorrow. Then I end the call and dial Taylor's number.

Hearing her voice makes my insides jitter.

"OK, never mind," she says quickly once I tell her what's happened. "Maybe some other time."

"Yeah, definitely," I reply.

"Bye, then," she says.

"Right. Bye." And the line goes dead. I stare at my phone. Shit. She probably thinks I made it up. *Oh, I've just remembered the plumber's coming.* That's the kind of thing I've been saying to teachers for the past seven years when what I really mean is, *Your lessons are boring and I've got better things to do with my time.* She thinks I'm not interested.

Unless she's the one who's not interested — maybe she wanted an excuse to get out of meeting up anyway.

Then I think about Saturday. All the hours, all the talking, all the laughing.

Sod it. I dial again.

She answers straightaway.

"Hi, it's me again."

"I know."

"Oh. Yeah. Of course. Look, if you still want to meet up, why don't you come over here?"

I hold my breath in the pause that drags on forever. Or maybe for two seconds. *Please say yes.*

"You're sure?" she asks softly. "I mean, if you don't want to, it's —"

"I'm sure!" I say. "I'm positive!"

"OK then."

I want to laugh. "Great. Great! Right, I'll see you in a bit. Come over at twelve-ish? We can have lunch or something."

"Sounds good."

I give her directions and we hang up. She'll be here in three hours!

How the hell am I going to fill them?

After spinning around in circles like a cartoon character with one foot nailed to the floor, I pull myself together. By the time I've gotten dressed (six changes of mind), brushed my teeth (twice), and tidied my bedroom (why? Who says we'll be spending any time in there?), there's only (only? It still feels like too long) half an hour to go. I spend it rearranging cushions in the front room, snatching looks out the window, checking myself in the mirror, and spreading the newspaper out on the kitchen table to look slightly messy but casual, in a bohemian sort of way, if a copy of the *Telegraph* can do that.

Quarter to twelve. Taylor's due in fifteen minutes. In a flash of inspiration, I remember she was reading a book when I first saw her, and I dash upstairs to my room to find a suitably impressive novel. All my A-level texts look too, well, A-levelly.

I quickly grab one of Mum's book-group novels — it's one that I tried to start three times and finally gave up on. I just hope Taylor hasn't read it and doesn't want to compare notes.

Five to twelve, I'm sitting in the front room trying to relax with the book in my hand, staring blankly at a random page.

The doorbell rings. This is it. I get up and let her in.

She smiles and I'm not sure whether to hug, kiss, shake her hand, or what. So I shuffle backward and let her into the house.

"D'you want a cup of tea?" I ask as she follows me into the kitchen.

"Yeah, great."

She stands close to me as the kettle starts to boil. My hands are shaking. I'll probably spill boiling water all over myself.

I have a better idea. Before stopping to think about it, I take her hand and lead her into the living room. "Or would you prefer . . ." I open the liquor cabinet, led by a combination of boldness and nerves—if that's possible. I pull out a bottle. "Wine?"

She laughs and holds out her hand. It's shaking as much as mine. "Might be just what's needed," she says.

I grab a couple of glasses and open the wine.

"Good thing I got the bus," Taylor says with a smile as I pour her a drink.

I want to tell her she's pretty when she smiles. I don't though. "Have you got a car?" I say instead.

"Yeah, it's just a knackered old Micra, but it gets me from A to B."

I like the idea of her having her own car.

I pass her a glass and our hands touch briefly. "D'you want to listen to some music?" I ask.

"Yeah, great."

"The best speakers are upstairs." I try to keep breathing normally while I wait for her to reply.

Taylor meets my eyes. "Cool," she says. Her cheeks have reddened a touch.

As we climb the stairs to my bedroom, my legs feel like lumps of clay.

I put my phone in the dock and pick a random playlist. I don't really care what we listen to. Taylor sits down on my bed, and I refill her glass and sit down next to her. Our hands touch briefly—accidentally?—as I pass her glass to her.

I watch her hands as she lifts the glass to her lips. Her fingers are slim. Not dainty. Firm and smooth. Her nails are perfect, not bitten down to the quick like mine. Plain, but strong. She's got a thin gold chain on her wrist.

"Will your mum notice it's gone?" She points at the bottle.

"Probably not. I can always replace it before she goes in there again."

Taylor takes a sip of her drink and moves back so she's leaning against the wall with her legs stretched out in front of her. I turn so I'm sitting cross-legged facing her.

"So, what have you been up to since I last saw you?" I ask.

Taylor laughs. "All of two days ago."

I smile. "Yeah. All of that long."

She smiles back. "Thinking about you," she says.

My heart leaps through my throat and out of my mouth and bounces on the ceiling.

"Yeah, me too," I mumble. "I mean, thinking about you. Not thinking about me."

Taylor laughs again. Then she looks at me and doesn't say anything. She holds my gaze for . . . a second? A minute? Ages anyway, but nowhere near long enough.

Then she holds out her wineglass.

"You want more?"

She shakes her head. "No, can you put it on the side for me?"

I take the glass, and this time there's no accidental brushing of fingers. This time it's definitely intentional. She touches the back of my hand, briefly closes her hand around mine, and then passes me her glass. I put it on the side, and mine too. I've only had a few glugs, but it's made me woozy already. Something has anyway.

"It's gone straight to my head," I say.

"Lie down, you'll feel better," she tells me. "Here. Use my legs as a pillow if you like."

I do what she says, and I'm floating just above the bed. I don't know if it's having half a glass of wine for my lunch, or if it's nerves and excitement. Or maybe it's her fingers stroking my hair, so gently I've got to hold my breath to feel them.

I feel as if I've been waiting for this moment my whole life. Now that it's here, part of me wants to run away from it, another part wants it all to happen now, and yet another part wants to make the anticipation last as long as possible—just stay in this place, lying here like this, with Taylor running her hands through my hair, cool tunes in the background, and something always about to take place but never quite happening.

"Are you nervous?" she asks.

"I don't know. Yeah, a bit. Are you?"

"A bit. What are you nervous about?"

"The same as you."

"D'you want me to stop?" She moves her hand away.

"No." I reach out and take hold of her hand. It feels smooth and lovely. I place it back on my head and leave mine just above hers, resting on her leg.

"Has this ever happened for you before?" she asks.

I grimace. "Is it obvious?"

"What?"

"That no. No, it hasn't. What about you?"

"No, me neither."

"Really?" I ask, surprised.

"Why? What did you think?"

"You just seem so . . . confident."

She laughs. "If you knew how I'm feeling inside at the moment, you wouldn't say that."

I sit up, suddenly scared. "Look, you sure you don't want some more wine, or something to eat or—"

"I think I know what I want." Taylor looks me in the eyes, and I feel myself dissolve. Then she leans forward, and before I have time to say or think another word, she's kissing me. And I'm kissing her too.

It starts almost in slow motion. Her lips, soft on mine, little light kisses, tiptoeing. Then she opens her mouth slightly, kissing me with more force. I keep thinking how perfectly our mouths fit together. Her lips are so gentle, her tongue drawing me in. I'm losing myself in her.

I stop and catch my breath. "Look, shall we . . . lie down?"

She doesn't answer, just lies down on the bed and reaches out for me.

"I'll take that as a 'yes' then, shall I?" I ask, smiling down at her and wondering how I can feel so comfortable with someone I've only met a couple of times. She doesn't feel like a stranger, though. She feels more familiar than anyone I've ever known.

She smiles back at me, pulls me down beside her. She's lying on her back, and I'm propped up on one elbow next to her.

I lean forward and close my eyes as our mouths meet again—and within moments the mood shifts gear. Before I know it, we're so wrapped up in each other, I can hardly tell what's me and what's her. I just know that nothing in my whole life has ever felt so right. Lips on lips. Hands reaching for skin. Tops thrown on the floor. Our bodies pressed together. So easy, so new, and so familiar all at the same time.

I break off to look at her.

"Don't stare, you're embarrassing me." She pulls me toward her, and I stop thinking about anything after that. All I care about is this moment, right now with her, and I don't want it to stop, ever.

And then a small noise downstairs changes everything.

28

I freeze in terror.

A key turning. The front door opening. My mum's voice.

"Ash!"

"Oh, my God!" I leap up from the bed and start looking for my top. It's lying in a heap on the floor with my bra screwed up inside it.

Cat and I once went to this posh gym with a Jacuzzi and sauna and everything. Her mum had been given some free passes. The Jacuzzi worked on a timer: three minutes on, three minutes off. While it was bubbling, you couldn't see anything under the water, and Cat decided we were going to play dares. I had to take my swimsuit off and put it back on again before the bubbles stopped. I got it off in about half a minute. Easy, I thought. But it got tangled up when I was trying to put it back on. I couldn't find where to put my legs. I kept putting them through the armholes.

"Come on, Ash, you've got about ten seconds,"

Cat said. My suit was still twisted a million ways. Eventually, I tugged it on and stretched it over my body just before the bubbles stopped and the water became see-through again.

"Jeez, that was close," I gasped, but Cat was laughing and pointing at me.

"It's inside out," she managed to say, heaving with laughter.

I had to wait for the bubbles and do it all again before I could get out.

I remember that panicky feeling—thinking, yikes, someone's going to get in when the bubbles stop and I'm going to be sitting here starkers with a crumpled, inside out bathing suit in my hand.

Only this is much, *much* worse. This is my mum, and I'm in my bedroom with another girl who's also got no top on and is, at this moment, sitting on my bed looking terrified.

Panicking, I try to unscramble my top, but I just seem to tangle it up even more.

"Quick, get your clothes on," I hiss and throw Taylor's sweater across to her.

I finally unscramble my bra, and I call down as I straighten my top. "Coming, Mum!"

Taylor looks at me and raises an eyebrow.

Mum's on her way up the stairs. "I left a folder at home that I need for this afternoon, so I thought I'd get it and grab a quick sandwich while I'm here," she calls.

Taylor pulls her sweater on seconds before Mum's face pokes around the door. "Hi, love," she says. "Oh, sorry, I didn't know you had company."

"This is Taylor, from . . . from . . ." What do I say? *From the gay club Cat took me to a couple of weeks ago?*

"Work," Taylor blurts out.

"Work? What work?" Mum looks blank.

"She works at the whole-food café," I say quickly, "where Cat works. There might be a job there for me."

"Oh, really? That's great. Nice to meet you, Taylor."

I'm sure Mum's giving us funny looks. She knows what's going on. Oh, no. Please, no.

"Do you girls want to have a bite to eat with me?"

I look at Taylor and she half shrugs, half nods. "Yeah, OK," I reply. I really just want to stay up here with Taylor, but I don't want Mum getting even more suspicious. Or spotting the bottle of wine on my bedside table.

"OK. You'd better come down now, then. I've got to be back in half an hour."

The second she's gone, Taylor breathes out an enormous sigh of relief. Then she leans forward and points at the seams on my top. It's inside out. I laugh and move toward her.

"Not now, we've got to go down," she says, getting up from the bed.

"Mmm, is that a promise?"

She kisses my ear. "Well, if you can wait half an hour . . ."

• • •

271

"So, what exactly do you do, Taylor?" Mum asks as we tuck into a pasta salad.

"I work in computers."

The room freezes. My mouth stops chomping.

"I thought you said she worked at a café, Ash?"

"Yeah, she does," I falter.

"I design websites, Mrs. Walker."

"Call me Julia," Mum says. "So you make websites? That's interesting."

"Yeah. I'm, er, I'm designing one for the café." She smiles at my mum. The girl's a genius.

"Really?" Mum stops eating and seems to actually notice Taylor for the first time. "Hey, maybe you could help me."

"Mum, what do you need a website for?"

"Not me personally. Work," she says. "Their website is clunky and dull. I've been saying for ages we need to update it." She speaks to Taylor, even though it was me who asked the question. She's hardly met my eyes since she walked in. I don't even want to *think* about whether she noticed anything in my bedroom.

"What kind of thing are you after, Mrs. —Julia?"

"Well, you know, nothing fancy. Just something clear and easy to use."

"I could come and have a look if you like," Taylor says.

"That would be great." Mum smiles. "Have you got a card or anything?"

Cool as anything, Taylor reaches into her back

pocket and pulls out a card. "Give me a call anytime and we can fix something up."

"Or I could just go to Cat's café and find you."

"She's not there anymore," I butt in quickly. "She's just about finished the site for them, haven't you?" I glare at Taylor.

She nods quickly. "Yeah," she says. "Better just to give me a call."

It's *so* obvious we're lying. Miraculously, Mum doesn't seem to notice.

She puts Taylor's card in her pocket. "Lovely," she says. "Thanks for this." Then she gets up to take her plate to the sink. "Right, I need to get back. Don't forget the plumber, Ash. Nice meeting you, Taylor."

"Yeah, you too, Julia."

I hold my breath till I hear the front door close. Till I can relax again.

"That was close," Taylor sighs. "I'm glad she didn't ask me where Cat's café is because I haven't got a clue."

I lean on my hands and look across the table at her. "I'd like to get to know you more," I say.

"Yeah, I'd like to get to know you more as well," she says shyly and smiles at me with her gorgeous eyes.

I slide around the bench over to her side. "Wasn't there something you promised me about half an hour ago?"

She turns her face close to me. "Now, what was that? Maybe you'll have to remind me . . ."

A moment later, her lips meet mine, and I pray the plumber will be late.

29

End of August. Beginning of the night. My eighteenth birthday. Half an hour till the others are here. Everyone's coming to our house for dinner. Everyone except Taylor, that is. She's working late, but she's going to meet us afterward. We've met up four times in the last two weeks and either texted or called at least ten times a day in between.

Mum pokes her head around the door. "All set?"

This is my chance. I've got to find out what's going on between us, why all our communication seems to have broken down. And more than that, I've decided, I need to tell her something. Whatever the risks.

"Mum?" I'm going to do it. I really am.

"Damn, I've just remembered, I didn't get any soda water. I'll just pop to the store. Can it wait?"

I nod.

I mustn't lose my nerve. I've got to tell her.

We used to go to this place in Wales every year at spring half term. A little B and B with a long back garden that led down to a stream. On the other side of the stream, there was a tree with a big thick branch that reached right across the water, and a rope hanging down from the branch.

There'd always be a crowd there on a Saturday evening: small groups of girls giggling and twirling their ponytails and chewing gum, skinny lads who'd climb the tree and swing across the stream on the rope. It wasn't very high or very wide, so it never looked all that difficult — from my side of the river anyway. You just had to grab the rope and swing across.

If it was hot, the lads would take off their shirts and clamber along the branch, some of them thumping their chests and letting out a Tarzan call, others nervously holding on to the tree, knees shaking. They'd shout "Geronimo!" as they grabbed the rope and swung across, and the girls would scream and clap their hands over their mouths and eyes until they heard the landing *splosh* on the other side of the stream.

Cat came with us once and, being Cat, she decided if it was good enough for a gang of skinny lads, it was good enough for us. So we went down there in our shorts and T-shirts and sneakers on a hot Saturday afternoon and climbed the tree. Glancing down at the swirling water below us, I realized that it looked a bit higher from up here.

Cat swung across straightaway, no problem. Then it was my turn. I held on to the branch with both hands, looking down. Frozen.

A group of hikers stopped to watch, and I kept

thinking, *Right, this is it. I'm going to jump. I'm going to do it now.* I let go of the branch, took hold of the rope, and felt my heart speed up. *I'm going to do it. Now!* And then I chickened out and grabbed the branch again.

Some of the hikers started to move away; a woman with red cheeks and white hair and a map in her hand smiled broadly at me. She looked right into my eyes, and then she said something I've never forgotten: "You can do it, you know. I'll hold my breath while you jump."

So I did. I took the rope in both hands and swung across. It was so easy I felt a bit stupid as I landed in the shallow water on the other side.

As I landed, I could hear the hikers cheering. I looked up. The woman with the white hair waved and clapped. "I knew you could do it," she said before she moved off.

And she'd been right. The worst part was the fear—looking down at the rushing water that seemed miles away. But once you were on that branch, there was no going back.

There's no going back now either. I need this said.

Cat arrives just as Mum's leaving. Then Jayce and Adam turn up, without Elaine and Dad.

"Mum's driving me mad, fussing and faffing around," Jayce says, coming in and taking his coat off as Adam joins Cat in the kitchen. "We thought we'd go out later, so we've come in Adam's car. You going to come out with us after the meal?"

"I was thinking of coming out before it, actually," I say nervously as we follow Adam into the kitchen.

"Huh?"

I tell them my plan, my hands shaking along with my voice.

Jayce grabs me and gives me a quick squeeze. "Oh, my God, Ash. You're so brave!"

"I wanted to tell her before everyone came round, but she's buggered off."

"Probably knows what's coming," Cat laughs.

I cover my face with my hands. *Oh, God, why am I doing this?*

Adam leans into Jayce's shoulder. "Why don't you do the same? Get your mum off your back once and for all?" He turns to me. "Only yesterday she told him about this girl she'd met at the butcher's. And Jayce is a vegetarian as well as everything else!"

Jayce doesn't say anything.

I look at him. "Why don't you?" I say softly. "Might make it easier for both of us if we do it together."

Jayce looks at Adam, then back at me. "D'you know what? Sod it. I've waited long enough," he says. "I'm sick of pretending. I'm tired of saying nothing when Mum goes on about marriage and grandchildren. I've had enough of telling lies. Ash, let's do it. You tell your mum; I'll tell mine."

"You're sure?"

"Not in the slightest, but I'm in."

"You mean you're out," Cat corrects him. It makes us all laugh.

"Then, yes, let's do it," I say.

"Here." He passes me a glass of wine. "This might help."

I raise my glass. "No going back?"

He clinks his glass against mine. "No going back."

Then the doorbell rings.

"Here we go," Jayce says as I get up to open the door for Dad and Elaine.

"Hello, darling," Elaine says brightly. She gives me a peck on the cheek, then wipes the spot with her thumb. "Where's the present, Gordon?"

Dad follows her into the house and hands me a heavy box wrapped in shiny paper with cartoon animals on it. "Happy birthday, love," he mumbles, stepping nervously into the living room.

"Mum'll be back in a minute."

"Right," he says casually, his eyes darting around the room. He's not been here since last year.

"Ooh, what you got there?" Cat is behind me.

"Hi there, Cat," Dad says. "How are you?"

"Fine, thanks, Mr. Walker," she says, a bit over-politely. I'm not sure she's ever been a hundred percent convinced he never did anything wrong.

Jayce comes over to join us.

Elaine rushes over to him and starts fiddling with his shirt. "I should have given this an iron," she says. "I told you not to rush off this morning."

278

Jayce shrugs her off. "Mum, lay off, will you? I'm not a kid."

Elaine turns back to me. "Why don't you open your present, Ashleigh, darling?"

I pull at the paper to reveal a massive dictionary and a collection of contemporary poetry.

"Your mum said the book is on your course book list," Dad says. "It was Elaine's idea, actually."

"They're brilliant. Thanks, both of you."

"Oh, it's nothing," Elaine says, beaming.

Dad hangs his and Elaine's coats up in the cloakroom as Luke and Robyn arrive.

"Happy birthday," Robyn sings, hugging me tightly and handing me a present. I rip it open—three fluffy notebooks and a fountain pen. They're not exactly my kind of thing, but it's such a thoughtful gift and they'll make me think of Robyn and smile when I use them.

"Thought they might come in handy. You know, for your studying and stuff. Or you could use them as diaries," she says.

I smile and give her a quick hug. "Thank you."

"All right, mate." Luke thrusts a bottle-shaped present into my hands.

"Cheers, Luke. Nice one."

Mum arrives with two bottles of soda water as I'm shutting the door. She pauses to take in the scene.

"Dad's in the kitchen," I whisper. "With Elaine. You OK with that?"

"Yep, fine. It's not like it's the first time I've seen them together." Then she slaps on the secretary smile she reserves especially for get-togethers with Dad and Elaine and heads for the kitchen.

"You ready for this?" Cat whispers.

"Not remotely. But I have to do it," I say, realizing my words are starting to slur a little. I've had two glasses of wine already. "What have I got to lose?"

Mum's talking to Dad and Elaine as I enter the kitchen. I notice Elaine's left hand is clenched tightly as she talks.

"Ashleigh." She gives me a hug I didn't ask for as I join them. "We were just saying—you've done yourself proud, getting into university. You'll be a graduate before Jayce even starts a course, by the looks of things."

"You all set for it, love?" Dad asks, looking awkward and out of place in a kitchen he owned for twenty years.

"I hope so."

Jayce stands next to me in the doorway.

"When am I going to do it?" I whisper. "I can't get Mum on her own."

I'm sure she suspects. She doesn't want to hear it. She's doing everything she can to avoid giving me the chance to tell her. Well, tough. She's going to have to listen. I'm not going to hide what I am just because she doesn't like it.

Jayce pulls me into the living room. "Why don't we just tell them all?"

Tell Dad?

"You'll have to tell him one day," Jayce says, reading my mind.

"Oh, God, whose stupid idea was this?"

"Yours," he says, laughing. "And it's a good one. We'll do it together. All of them in one go."

I take a deep breath. "OK."

He tosses a coin to see who goes first, and I lose as I knew I would.

"Good luck." Jayce hugs me and nudges me back toward the kitchen. "I'm right behind you."

I pour myself another glass of wine, knock it straight back, and pour another one for afterward. My heart's pounding so fast and so hard in my chest that it's snatching my breath away. I feel like I've just run a mile.

Everyone's in the kitchen.

OK, here we go.

30

"Um . . ." I say in a quiet voice. No one looks up. They're deep in conversation. Why am I doing this?

Jayce comes to my side and clears his throat. " 'Scuse me," he says, his voice wobbling.

Elaine looks up. "What's the matter, darling?"

This is it, then. Last chance to escape. I could sneak out, run off, make something up.

But I want to get to the other side of this. I want it done. Jayce looks at me.

"There's . . . um . . . there's something we want to tell you."

Elaine turns to me. Mum and Dad stop talking and look over at me too. I stare back at them, not seeing anyone.

"What is it, love?" Mum says quietly.

How long have I been standing in front of everyone, a full wineglass in my hand, my mouth opening and closing but nothing coming out?

I glance at Mum. I think about what she's been through this year — what we've been through together. How it felt, for a while, as if we'd become best friends, and then how it all seemed to change—how we somehow stopped being able to communicate with each other again. I look at Dad, smiling benignly at me from a million miles away.

Will this bring us closer or make that chasm impossible to cross forever?

Then I think about the white-haired woman with the map. No going back. I'm letting go of the branch, reaching for the rope.

"I, er, I just want to say thanks for the presents," I mumble.

Dad smiles.

Mum looks surprised. "Is that it?" she asks.

Just do it. Just say it. It's only fear.

"No," I whisper.

The kitchen is totally silent.

I'll hold my breath while you jump.

"There's something else, something I want you to know." *It doesn't matter if neither of them can look you in the face again,* I keep saying to myself. *You're going to university next month.*

Jayce nods at the glass of wine in my hand that was meant for afterward, and I take a slug of it. He smiles at me and takes hold of my hand while I carry on. "I don't know if you've guessed already, or if it's going to come as a shock"—I take another gulp of wine and wipe my mouth—"but I'm gay."

Silence.

"That's it. I'm gay."

Mum stares at me.

Dad looks at me, then at Jayce. "But I thought . . ."

"Leave it, Gordon." Elaine grabs his hand.

Mum covers her face with her hands. Oh, God. She's shaking her head. My legs start to give way.

Then this amazing thing happens. Mum moves her hands. She's smiling.

"At last!" she says. Then she holds her arms out toward me. I let go of Jayce's hand to go to her. I fall into her arms as she hugs me. Then she holds me away from her and looks into my eyes. "I've been waiting for you to tell me," she says.

"But—but these last few weeks . . ." I stammer.

"I know. I didn't know what to say. I didn't want to be the one to bring it up. I wanted it to happen when *you* were ready. And then it just seemed to get in the way."

"But you've been so—"

"I've been wanting you to tell me. I think I forgot how to talk about anything else. I'm sorry, Ash." She hugs me again. "You could have told me a long time ago, you know."

"I didn't even *know* a long time ago."

"Well, I did," she says and kisses me on the cheek. "And I'm proud of you, whatever you are."

It's official, then. *Everyone* knew I was gay before I did.

Or maybe not quite everyone.

I turn around just in time to see Dad leaving the kitchen. Elaine goes out after him. I follow them into the hall. Dad's putting on his coat.

"Dad . . ."

He doesn't reply.

"Dad, where are you going? Elaine, what's going on?"

Elaine turns to me. "He's got a bit of a stomachache coming on and thought he'd better leave you to it. Didn't want to ruin the meal."

"Dad." I go to touch his arm, and he pulls it away from me as though I'm infected.

"I'm sorry," he says. "I—I just don't want to talk about it, Ash."

"Dad, give me some respect. You could at least tell me the truth, not make up stupid lies about a stomachache."

"Respect?" he says, his voice gravelly. His eyes have moisture in the corners. "Lies? Really, Ashleigh?"

"Gordon." Elaine's voice is tight. "A lot of teenagers go through phases like this. It won't help if you make it into more than it—"

"It's not a phase."

Elaine stops and looks at me. "What, dear?"

"I said it's not a phase." Anger is starting to burn into my cheeks and around the sides of my neck. "I'm gay. It's what I am. You don't have to like it, but it's true, Dad, and ignoring me won't make it any different."

Dad looks into my face for a moment, his eyelids low over his dark eyes. "I'm sorry, Ash. I just need a bit of time. It's not just you, it's . . ." He holds his arms out as if to encompass the whole house in them. "It's all of it," he says. "I'm sorry. I just can't do it." Then he opens the door.

"Dad, you can't leave." I follow him out onto the drive. "Not like this." Tears are burning in the corners of my eyes. "I've coped with a lot from you and Mum over the last year. I didn't exactly like what happened. But you're my dad, aren't you? I didn't disown you when you left me."

"I didn't leave *you*, Ash."

I brush my sleeve across my eyes. "I didn't want you and Mum to split up, but it's what you needed to do." I look at Elaine. "And maybe it's for the best. Maybe you're happier now."

Dad drops his head. His arms hang limply by his sides.

"But I'm happier now too," I say. "So if you don't like it, then OK. But it's not going to change. And if you don't want me to be happy, well, tough. You're not going to stop me, and nor is anyone else." Then I run down the drive, away from them all. I sit on the wall by the front gate and cry into my hands.

I used to play hopscotch out here with Micky Evans from next door. Looking at the pavement, I can still picture the grid, scratched out with stones. I stare at the invisible squares on the pavement and wonder where all those years went.

Then someone's sitting next to me.

"Ash, I . . ." Dad's looking at the road in front of us. "I want you to be happy, of course I do." He shakes his head. "I just don't get it," he says softly. "I don't understand what we did wrong."

"Oh, for God's sake, Dad. You didn't do anything

wrong. It's me. And it's not wrong. Nothing has ever felt so *right*."

"But, why?" He looks so pained, so hurt. Why does everything always have to be so personal? Why does this have to be about him? "Dad, it's just me. It's just what I am, who I am. And it's who I want to be. Just accept it. Just accept me."

He looks at me for a long time. "Of course I accept you, love," he says. "I just don't understand it. I'm not saying it's wrong, but I can't say I like it either."

"Well, I suppose that'll have to do for the time being." I stand up as Elaine appears, her face pale. She looks like those water paints we used to have at school when someone had mixed too much white with the pink. Jayce is behind her.

"What is it?" Dad stands up. "What's happened?"

"Jason wants to talk to us," Elaine says flatly.

"What is it?" Dad repeats, looking at Jayce.

Jayce looks at me, and I try to smile encouragingly. I probably look demented. Elaine and Dad sit back down on the wall, holding hands. They look like a couple in a hospital waiting room, waiting for news of their desperately ill son. A pang of anger stabs at my chest. *We're not bloody dying. We're just gay. It's not the end of the world.*

"Mum, I want to tell you something too." Jayce is in front of them, and I get up to stand next to him.

"Look, it's not easy, this. And I don't know what you'll think. We made a kind of agreement, me and Ash." Dad and Elaine glance at me. Jayce's face is open and pleading; theirs are shut tight. "We were going to do it together," Jayce continues. "A joint thing. But now it seems a bit—"

"Oh, for goodness' sake, child, what is it?" Elaine bursts in, pulling her hand away from Dad and folding her arms.

Jayce takes a deep breath. He looks like a kid playing soldiers, filling his chest with air. *Be a man, son.* Then he lets his breath out again and looks up at the house.

I follow his eyes to my bedroom window. I remember standing on that windowsill with Micky Evans. We took turns to stand on the ledge with nothing on, facing the road. We used to time each other, see how long we could brave it out, flashing our growing bodies at the world. I lasted nearly five minutes once. But the truth that neither of us said out loud was that we wanted to stare at each other's bodies—see what the other half looked like.

Jayce nods as though he's made a pact with himself. "It's not just Ash who had something to tell you today. I have too. It's Adam. We . . . he, he's not just my friend, Mum. He's my . . . he's my . . ."

Elaine covers her face with her hands.

"We're lovers. We're in love."

Elaine's shoulders sag.

Dad stands up. "Is this some kind of a joke, son?" he asks, his eyes narrowed. "Because if it is, it's not funny."

"It's not a joke. It's true," Jayce replies, his voice

rising with the color in his cheeks. "It's always been true." He looks back at Elaine. "And if you're honest with yourself, Mum, you must have known."

"How must she have known?" Dad asks.

"When did you last see me with a girlfriend, Mum? Why do you think I didn't want to go away to university? You must have suspected."

"Of course she didn't suspect," Dad says limply. He turns to Elaine. "You didn't suspect anything, did you?"

"Gordon, can I handle this?" Elaine's voice bites into the air between them. She looks up at Jayce. "Yes, you're right. You're right. Happy now? I *did* suspect. I wondered a few years ago if you might be a . . . homosexual."

"Mum."

"It's the classic story, isn't it? I was cleaning your room, and I saw a magazine. But I didn't want to believe it. I suppose I thought it might pass if I didn't mention it. I didn't want to encourage you into it by telling you it was wrong."

"It's not wrong!" Jayce and I exclaim in unison, but Elaine ignores us. She must have been rehearsing this speech for years.

"We all like to break the rules at times. The first thing we want to do when we see a notice saying DO NOT ENTER is get in there, find out what's so great that someone wants to keep us away from it." She pauses to look at Jayce, as though she's just remembered he's there. "And I didn't want to do that to you. I didn't want to make you more likely to be like that . . ." She gets up and stands in front of him. Lifts his chin up with her finger and puts her other hand on his shoulder. "Maybe I should have tried *something*. I don't know."

Jayce shakes Elaine's hand away. "Mum, there's nothing you could have—"

"But you're my son, Jason, my only son, and I love you." She smiles a pinched smile at him. "Nothing will ever change that."

"Right."

"Do one thing for me, though."

"What?" Jayce's voice is raw.

"Just don't convince yourself it has to be forever. You could have any girl you wanted, you know, a handsome young man like you."

"Mum, I don't want any girl. I want Adam."

"I know, darling." Elaine puts her fingers up to his mouth. Then she turns to Dad, who's now sitting on the wall, staring at the sky. "Come on. Shall we go? Leave the youngsters to have some fun without us clogging up the space."

Dad gets up.

"Aren't you coming back inside, Dad?" I ask him.

"It might be best if we don't, all things considered. I'll ring you during the week," he says as he stands up. "Happy birthday, love."

I'm shuffling from foot to foot as Dad jangles his keys in his hand. *Hug me, Dad.* I stand in front of him awkwardly.

He looks at me for a split second. "Come here, sweet

pea," he says almost roughly. He hasn't called me that in years.

And then he folds me into his arms. I hold him as tightly as I can for a minute, and when he breaks away, my face is wet. His eyes are bright and he clears his throat. "It'll be all right, love. Just give me a bit of time," he says.

Jayce and I watch them get into Dad's car and drive away. "You OK?" He turns to me. My lips are trembling, and I swallow hard.

"Come on," I say. "Let's go back in."

"Go back in? It's a bit late for that now!"

I smile.

"That's better." Jayce tilts my chin up, just like his mum did with him. "Ready?"

I nod, and we go into the house.

Robyn sways over to me, spilling her wine a little on the way. "I'm so proud of you." She hugs me.

"Thanks, Robyn."

"Yeah, me too," Luke adds. He gives me a big hug, then suddenly pulls away. "I'm still allowed to do that, aren't I?" he asks awkwardly.

"Course you are, you big buffoon," I tell him. "I don't think it's infectious!"

Mum comes out of the kitchen. "Don't worry, darling," she says, smiling gently at me and lifting a strand of hair from my cheek. "Dad'll come round. You've done the right thing."

"Yeah."

Cat and Adam are behind Mum. They rush over to hug me and Jayce.

"This calls for a celebration," Adam says, his arm still around Jayce's shoulders. "Come on. Let's get this birthday meal eaten and go out clubbing."

"Can we come?" Robyn grabs Luke's arm.

Adam grins. "Course you can. Cat, are you joining us?"

"Try and stop me."

Adam looks at Mum. "Julia?"

"That's all right." Mum laughs. "I've got a date with George Clooney."

"Mum, are you sure?" I ask.

"Of course I am, darling. Come on, let's eat first. I've got a feeling you'll need to line your stomachs."

We eat dinner quickly, on a high from everything that's happened. On the way out, I hug Mum, holding her close. "Thank you," I whisper. "For dinner—and for everything."

Mum smiles and strokes my cheek. "There's nothing to thank me for. Now, get out there and have some fun; you deserve it." She pauses and smiles softly at me. "And say hi to Taylor for me," she adds.

I text Taylor on the way out, and she replies straightaway, saying she's finished work and she'll meet us at the club. As we go in, I look around for her and spot her at the bar. I get one of those back-flipping butterfly routines in my stomach as she looks up and sees me.

I wonder if maybe she'll come home with me tonight. If it'll last. If she'll visit me in Manchester. I wonder if my dad will ever get used to having a lesbian for a daughter. If my mum will ever fall in love again. If I'll ever get the chance to thank Miss Murray for showing me the door that led me here.

And I wonder how many times in one lifetime you get to start again as someone else.

Who knows? Who cares?

The music swirls around me. I look at my friends — dancing in a circle, laughing and falling over one another's feet — and I realize I'm ready to turn the page on all those questions — and on everything that's brought me to this point.

And as Taylor grabs my hand and pulls me close, I can't help having a sneaky feeling that the next chapter is going to be a good one.

ACKNOWLEDGMENTS

When I write acknowledgments, I usually have to think back over the past year. As I started writing this book fifteen years ago, a lot more people have been involved this time. Which means I barely know where to start. So I'm kind of going to duck out of even trying. But there are a few that I really must include.

The first is to Michael Schmidt and the Manchester Metropolitan University where this book's journey began with my Novel Writing MA. This course gave me invaluable tools and experiences. I still associate many of the scenes with those passionate workshop sessions — and the equally passionate discussions in the pub afterward over a few pints and multiple packets of crisps. For this, I am also grateful to my fellow MA students. Hey, Julie Brown, the "lesbian teen angst saga" is finally out there!

The second thank-you goes to my amazing agent, Catherine Clarke, who always knew this book would be published one day and whose loyalty, determination, hard work and friendship are among the things I am most grateful for.

The third thank-you goes to my publishers, Orion and Candlewick, for their decision to publish, support and champion this book. In particular, Amber Caravéo for her brilliant editing and Fiona Kennedy for her "Times have changed and we are ready to move with them" text, which I still treasure.

Before anyone asks—and I'm sure they will—this book is not about me. Yes, I came out; yes, there are a few anecdotes dotted throughout that were inspired by real events (at which point, a big shout out to Fiz Kyffin, who has not only been a wonderful friend for almost four decades, but without whom I would never have had the "she got a boyfriend, I got a hamster" story). But that's it. This is a work of fiction. The characters, events and story are all Ashleigh's.

One thing Ashleigh and I have in common is that we both had a brilliant English teacher. Jenny Richardson—as the hundreds of students she taught over her long career will testify—is an incredibly special person and amazing teacher. She made me stop being a "work-shy tearaway" and instead become someone who wanted to succeed, and she helped me to fall in love with literature. As well as anything else, this book is a salute to Jenny and teachers like her, who change the lives of their pupils—often without even knowing they have done so.

Finally I want to thank Laura Tonge, for more than I can fit on this page. Laura, you are the other half of everything, your love gives me the courage and the desire to get this book out there, and you make all of this possible, wonderful and perfect.

I know that many others have been involved in this journey to varying degrees. I have huge gratitude in my heart to friends, colleagues, fellow writers, family and many others who have cheered this book on for more than a decade. A massive, heartfelt thank-you to you all. I hope you enjoy the end result.